Then
ITHITME

Andrea von Stumm

To Dorry,
with deepest
affection &
gratitude!

Cluff & Sons

Andrea.

First published in Great Britain in 2016 by Cluff & Sons

Edited, designed and produced by Tandem Publishing http://tandem-publishing.yolasite.com/

ISBN: 978-1-5272-0050-0

10 9 8 7 6 5 4 3 2 1

A CIP catalogue record for this book is available from the British Library.

Printed and bound in Great Britain by CPI Group (UK) Ltd, Croydon CR0 4YY.

To my late, forever loved, forever missed father.

To the cherished SW family, thankfully mine.

To Anita, Magic Jake and Bülent, deep in my heart.

To Algy Cluff, Jan Moijto and 'Tony the Duck', of invaluable support.

Not least, to my friend Sam Carter. Were it not for his incisive editing and bemused patience, this book might have lingered at the bottom of some drawer.

AKRASIA: (/əˈkreɪzɪə/; Ionic Greek ἀκρασία.) Lacking command over oneself; the state of acting against one's better judgement.

'Drug addiction, like chronic alcoholism, is more often a symptom than a disease ... of the type that baffles analysis and defies cure. An odd disease of the volition to which mystics have attached the name of *acedia,* a condition of spiritual despondency and mental paralysis that leaves the sufferer lucid, yet impotent.'
Peter Quennell (*The Romantic Catastrophe*)

'There are children who are too old to be children. It stops being a problem when they get older. They grow into themselves – but before that happens, it's perpetually awkward.'
Joan Wickersham

'It is worse than a crime, Sire, it's a mistake.'
Antoine de la Meurthe to Napoleon upon learning of the Duke of Enghien's execution.

CONTENTS

1 The Telegram   1

2 The Motorcycle   6

3 Sunday Lunch   10

4 The Doll   18

5 Kenya   23

6 No Mosquitos   32

7 Graduation   35

8 - I The Cruise, Leonor   43

8 - II The Cruise , Ping Pong or Zoo?   50

9 Hector Vich, Unplugged   55

10 New York   60

11 Hector's Achilles' Heel   67

12 Being, the Beginning of Becoming   71

13 Triskaidekaphobia   75

14 Iris   76

15 Acedia, AmarK, Alarm   81

16 Houseboat Evening, Weird   89

17 Reshuffling of Cards   97

18 Formentor   100

19 Shebam! Pow! Blop! Whizz!   105

20 A Bird, a Cage   110

21 Criss-Crossing   113

22 Another Day After   118

23 The Kiss   121

24 Beauty Needs Beast   126

25 Seen That Movie Too…   131

26 A Talk in Central Park   138

27 Packing. Past Caring   143

28 Life & Short   145

29 Four Years, Five Pages   148

30 Contagion   153
31 Lover Didn't Do It   158
32 On the Plane   168
33 A Funeral, a Wedding   173
34 Whatever Happened to Babe Banes?   174
35 Vanushed   180
36 Future, a Foretaste   182
37 One Freak Funeral…   189
38 … And a Weird Wedding   195
39 Parenthesis – Acceleration   200
40 Lamu, Frederik and Benita   204
41 A Logical Mess   210
42 Deranged Young Men   215
43 Zen?   222
44 Who Would Have Thought That?   227
45 David & Goliath   232
46 Simplicity, a Pause & a Drink   236
47 Bitter Moon   238
48 Money, an Opiate?   241
49 Domino Effect   247
50 Some Godmother   250
51 The Impossible Takes Longer   254

PART ONE

1

THE TELEGRAM

It hit me shortly after the turn of the century.

That particular New Year's Eve remains, for billions of people, coloured with distinct memories. The fuss having been compounded by superstitions, Nostradamus, Mayan prophecies, millennium bug and all.

It's pretty monochrome to me. A blackout had turned the night into a curtain. I shall, however, never forget the tiny guest-house perched way above Gstaad where I had found refuge.

Gstaad is the winter headquarters of the boarding school where Cedric, Ricardo and I spent our youth. It is also where I had intended to celebrate the slide into the next millennium.

At noon, I strolled up and down the main street. After a while, something inside me shuddered.

It wasn't just the kitschy parade of wealth, familiar to me: mink-lined prams, siliconed babes of uncertain ages, purportedly neglected or else too-flashy cars. It certainly wasn't listening to seven different languages within as many minutes, equally familiar. No. It was something hard to define, then and now. Perhaps the sensation that a page turned should remain just so.

Ungraceful? Certainly not ungrateful. To have spent three years at Le Rosey in the seventies was a privilege. Not because of its reputation as 'the school of kings' and the most expensive in the world. Indeed, the Shah, some sheikhs, a Churchill or two figure on the list of alumni – alongside the offspring of David Niven, the odd Niarchos, Thyssen, Rothschild *et al.* As a schoolgirl back then, you weren't aware of any *Who's Who.* We were merely a mixed bunch, encompassing a dozen or more nationalities and religions with contrasting emotional backgrounds and perspectives. Such surroundings opened the mind. The words 'Only one race: the human race' were carved above the entrance. (The famously arrogant Spanish writer José-Luis de Vilallonga quipped, in his book *Gold Gotha*, that the one colour reigning supreme at Le Rosey was green: the dollar. He never set foot in the school.)

But back to December 31ˢᵗ, 1999.

So I saunter back and forth on the main street, recognising many faces, feeling lonely. Cédric and Ricardo wouldn't be there.

Scintillating and star-studded as the night promised to be, I wanted out, there and then. So I returned to my own peculiar car and drove at random an hour or so. As it was getting dark, and as my short-sightedness makes driving at night haphazard, I needed a place to stay. Not easy. I was completely off-track and short of petrol.

Just as the engine began coughing, I saw a discreet B&B sign. The chalet looked welcoming.

More charming still were the owners, an elderly British couple who might have stepped out of a Somerset Maugham story and who had, in fact, lived in India. The room I was shown into smelled of fresh wax. Thick curtains matching dark blue and crimson red cushions, a large bed with linen sheets: a jewel.

Introductions having been made and my being stranded plausibly explained, Evelyne, almost shyly, asked:

'Aleana, would you have supper with us?'

'I'd love to,' I hesitated to answer, 'but would hate to intrude...'

'Are you joking, darling girl? Have you forgotten what night *this* is?'

A flicker of concern crossed her serene face.

'I'm afraid we are rather old-fashioned. Do you have something like ... a dress?'

I caught my reflection in the cupboard mirror. From my appearance, jeans, an oversized sweater and boots, Evelyne had little way of knowing that one of my suitcases contained nothing but evening gowns and the sort of jewellery ill-suited to the surroundings. And, of course, my guitar.

'I think I can manage. When would you like me to come down?'

'No rush. Rob will bring a cocktail to keep you company while you bathe and change. Dinner will be around nine. All right?'

Some question! A drink in the bathroom while getting ready is one of my least objectionable habits. The only thing I missed was music. No sooner had the thought crossed my mind than Cole Porter's melodious voice ascended towards my unexpected quarters. Wow.

The same exclamation escaped both of them when I descended the stairs. I had chosen a turquoise sari matching my eyes and earrings – a present from Hector, long ago. My hair was still wet. Presumptuous or not, the mirror did not reveal my age, forty-two. Unless mirrors lie, of course.

The table was sumptuously laid and dinner, prepared with infinite care, exquisite.

I couldn't believe my luck. No glitter, nor glamour; just warmth and sincerity. We talked as total strangers sometimes do: laying bare sentiments and fears, revealing weaknesses and longings, nostalgia or hopes. We also laughed, from deep inside. Evelyne and Robert loved each other beyond belief. Not because 'she was a harlot and he a thief', to quote a poet whose name alas I cannot remember. No. They just did.

To elaborate on my feelings would be long and boring, so I'll skip it. As glasses were filled, the lights went out. Minutes before midnight.

'A power cut. The grid in the village must be overloaded,' sighed Rob.

'Isn't that wonderful!' exclaimed his ever-joyous wife, drawing open the curtains.

Outside, utter whiteness. The snow had turned opaque. Brushed by the flickering candles inside, it formed gracious garlands. No more music, of course. Twelve distant church tolls announced a new century. We hugged, somewhat demurely. They were Brits, after all. And I am me.

Evelyne then whispered something strange into my ear: 'Don't ever try to predict the past.'

We lingered by the fireplace and might have done so longer had I not asked why they had welcomed a perfectly unknown traveller and had they not answered that I reminded them of their daughter, married to 'the wrong man' and vanished ever since.

'She was almost as pretty as you are ... and we, possibly too self-involved.'

This sobered me up. Images hard to delete do.

Handed a candelabra, I went to bed.

At dawn, leaving a letter and earrings behind, I slipped out.

Never seen the kind couple again. As I said, pages turn...

The drive back was an odyssey. Under iridescent skies, the roads were skiddy, many drivers drunk but, thank Dog, an open petrol station in sight.

By the door of my Geneva loft lay a telegram. I tossed it on the sofa, assuming it would be a New Year greeting, not interested who from. Or, truth be told, afraid of whom it might not be from. A foamy bath and half a bottle of Sancerre later, I erased the messages from my answering machine without listening to them. Inside my CD console, a Cole Porter disc. Life. Coincidences. You know.

Time to write my satirical column for the *Herald Tribune*. From Geneva? *Oui!* It always annoys me when people think of Switzerland as a cultural desert full of cuckoo-clocks. (Which, by the way, were invented in Germany.) Or bang on about William Tell's apple. What about Calvin or Henri Dunant, the founder of the Red Cross? What about Carl Jung, architects such as Le Corbusier or mathematicians such as Euler, hmm? On a per-capita basis, Switzerland ranks no. 1 in terms of Nobel Prize laureates. Three times the rate of the US.

I finally opened the telegram.

ALEANA. RICARDO DECEASED. CAR CRASH. DRIVER HE OR CEDRIC? LATTER DISAPPEARED. WAS TOLD TO INFORM. ALSO TO ENTREAT YOU NOT COME. CONDOLENCES, SINCERE.

Sent from Positano, in Italy, it was unsigned.

As the words sunk in, I did not feel shell-shocked. Not even shocked. Numbed? No. It felt more like drowning. Some say that people deprived of oxygen see their past rewind in slow motion. They also claim it's a pleasant experience, as deaths go.

2

THE MOTORCYCLE

(October 1973)

Friday, around midnight. Two shapes furtively sneak across the courtyard, briefly ducking behind the old fountain. They proceed towards the staff parking lot. In spite of the full moon, one could be the other's shadow: same stature, same profile, same gait. One more hesitant than the other, however.

They reach the object of their desire: a pristine vintage 350cc BMW motorcycle... A jewel.

Which of the two cracks the lock? Which of the two mounts while the other pushes it towards the school gate? Soon the engine gently starts; then it roars ferociously.

Screams of excitement fill the autumn air as they slalom up and down the winding roads amongst vineyards. Freedom! To teenagers such as Cedric and Ricardo, freedom is synonymous with speed. After a short pause for a fag and a sip from a whisky-filled flask – both smuggled in and out of Le Rosey – they shoot down towards the lake. The Route du Lac, between Lausanne and Geneva, allows them to accelerate. It's pretty deserted at this hour.

Again they stop after a while. Flask now empty.

'What a meteor!' exclaims one.

'Driven by ego, not by principle, as your father...'

'Spare me his wisecracks, man,' grunts his accomplice.

Off they race again, elated and singing. Then: the dog strolling across the road. Then: the skidding, the slipping, the impact against a fence.

One of the boys lies motionless near the bike. The other struggles to his feet, limping. The former now opens his eyes but cannot move.

'Is the bike fucked?'

'Shouldn't think so, no. Lateral hit. You?'

'Get help. Just my leg...'

Cedric does not panic. Never does. His clothes are torn and blood-stained. Standing by the road, looking forlorn, he realises the chances of someone stopping are slim. This is Switzerland. Trouble is taboo.

After a while, however, a van with foreign number plates stops. The Belgian driver even agrees to help carry Ricardo into the back seat.

He drops them in the next village where, because it's the grape harvest, an *auberge* is still open. Before rushing off (who wants trouble, regardless of nationality?) the kind man sing-songs: '*Le bonheur de malheurs évités se compose!* Remember that, young men. You were lucky this once.'

Phone calls are made. The BMW's towing away organised, someone's cousin's brother being a mechanic.

Half an hour later Le Rosey's headmaster screeched to a halt in front of the door. Without a word, he lifted Ricardo into his car, leaving Cedric to his limping devices.

On the way back from the Nyon hospital, Mr Johan remained obstinately silent.

Cedric and he were now sitting across each other in the Director's office. At almost three o'clock in the morning.

'Can't offer you a brandy. A bit shaken, right? Not stirred. I know you,' he mumbled, with puzzling bonhomie given the circumstances.

Mr Johan, a Colonel from the Swiss Army in his late sixties who had led a rehabilitation centre for post-war delinquents, stood up, lit yet another Benson & Hedges and, towering from his imposing height over a hunched Cedric, asked him in a tone admitting no evasion:

'Who was driving Mr Langon's motorcycle?'

His head now high, Cedric answered:

'Me.'

'Of course,' coughed the chain-smoking headmaster.

He turned his back on one of his favourite pupils and gazed at the moonlit park beyond the bay window. Twenty years of severity, of refrained emotions, of heart-breaking partings. You witnessed the turning from potential to potency, from immaturity to adulthood, and then they were gone, and you soon relegated to a bland memory. The huge chestnuts lining the alley were a reminder of the passing of time and inexorable growth.

When he faced Cedric again, his patriarchal eyes were tinged with icy weariness.

'Look here. I see you pupils as family and this school as their home...'

'I know sir.'

'What got into you boys, stealing Mr Langon's cherished BMW? Don't you respect your German teacher?'

Cedric sighed, contrite.

'Sir, Ric and I have a very ... informal relationship with Georg – Mr Langon, I mean. He's so ... young. We talk about cars and bikes and stuff. He often says he wishes we could ride with him but of course, rules and regulations ... well. It being mid-term and he in Germany, we thought that he wouldn't mind. Perhaps, that is...'

'There *is* no perhaps,' snapped Mr Johan.

Knowing what the answer would be: 'Whose idea was it?'

'Mine.'

The headmaster slammed his desk.

'To settle into the role of the blame-taker bodes ill for your future! You're not brave or helping your friend, believe me. As you know, Ricardo's father calls you two Romulus and Remus. Being your history teacher, I dare hope you know the story.'

'Sort of, sir,' whispered Cedric. Truth being he had never taken the trouble to research the legend, myth, whatever.

'They're twins. King can't-remember-his-name's sons. Suckled by a she-wolf, raised by a shepherd. To cut a long story short, Remus is captured. Romulus rescues him – and kills their father, but that's beside the point. Point being that Romulus ends up stabbing his brother. Rivalry overpowering kinship. See?'

Cedric didn't. He was too exhausted to think. Mr Johan, bored by the sound of his own voice, switched off the lights.

'Be packed by Sunday. I regret. Others have been given less time for minor offences, as you know.'

'I do. Goodnight, sir.'

Happiness of avoided misfortunes is composed, the van-driver had said. A motto? Belgian sarcasm?! In any case, one sentence Cedric would never forget.

3

SUNDAY LUNCH

Interrupting negotiations with the Ciga Hotel group – incidentally, owned by Rosey alumnus the Aga Khan – Cedric's father chartered a plane from Venice. Mr Johan's call had alarmed him. Not because of the bike story, which he found rather puerile; he would pay for its repair, case closed. No: it was because his son had claimed to be responsible. A lie. Far more disturbing was the ascendency that teacher's son, was it Renaldo, Rodrigo, Roberto, whatever, exerted over his own. Not altogether bad. After all, Ced had become more extroverted, more confident, more … daring. Yes. But to the point of stealing and drink-driving?

Aware that the headmaster systematically refused invitations from parents, be they royalty or rogues, he found it easy to convince Mr Johan to join him for lunch – another cause for alarm? Or was it the suggestion they meet at the same *auberge* where the boys had been dropped off, as famous for its Sunday lunches as Johan for his appetite, that had done the trick? The man was also notorious for disliking fancy places. Hector Vich, not the sighing type, sighed.

Both men arrived at L'Auberge du Lac at one on the dot. Mr Vich in a Fiat 500 with tinted windows. An understatement of sorts.

They were led to a discreet corner table.

'Let's order,' snapped Mr Johan, in purest Colonel-fashion after a vigorous handshake.

Both men agreed with the menu. Wine was decanted in a hurry, the place's owner sensing that 'refreshments' were called for.

'We know whose initiative this ... outrage was, do we not?' asked the headmaster.

'We do.'

Pleasantries discarded, Mr Johan went on.

'What you might be unaware of, Mr Vich, is that I'm not always true to my reputation for impartiality. I have my weak spots... It's not only because Ricardo is Mr Moralli's son – one of our teachers as you know. Nor because I feel indebted to you.'

Hector Vich had once been offered a considerable sum for a percentage of the twenty-nine hectares Le Rosey was spread on and which he owned. He relinquished the offer, thus the also considerable profit. This Mr Johan had only learnt by coincidence.

'As you might know, teachers' offspring attend the school for free. A matter of principle.'

Hector Vich also knew that quite a few pupils whose parents, due to political or other grave circumstances, could no longer afford the tuition fees, were allowed to remain at Le Rosey. Another matter of principle.

The first course arrived. Thinly sliced duck with a rosemary and cranberry sauce caused a delectable interruption.

'Forgetting last Friday's incident, or is the word accident?' Hector Vich suavely resumed, 'what do you make of that, well, special friendship? From what I gather, it developed rather gradually over the last year, or is it two...?'

Mr Johan scrutinised his vis-à-vis carefully. Was Cedric's father, a hotel-chain tycoon reputed to be no fool, playing games? Was he as naïve and distracted as his asymmetrically buttoned shirt and vagueness suggested? Was he trying to defuse the situation? His son must have told him that he'd been expelled.

No. The man was authentically candid and Mr Johan, square and stiff as the Swiss are caricatured to be, liked eccentrics. In truth, he had liked Hector Vich since their very first meeting, years earlier.

Some acceptance interviews are more memorable than others. The forty-something father and his thirteen-year-old son had walked into his office, one with nonchalance, the other with a puppy demeanour. Most striking: their amber eyes, the effect enhanced by raven-black hair. The father's more copper-coloured; the son's more gold. What big cats dangled off their genealogical tree? (Johan chuckled at his own vision.)

The conversation had immediately taken an unexpected turn, Hector Vich embarking on a disjointed speech about Switzerland's military past and political peculiarities. He spoke about his country with bemused pride, the latter much to the Colonel's liking.

As if suddenly recalling the purpose of the meeting, he had retrieved a bulky folder from his briefcase (its handle having been chewed off by some animal, by the look of it).

'Cedric's academic record since – whenever. Would you care to peruse?'

Mr Johan leafed through it, already guessing its contents. First class grades, except in science, excellent recommendations from previous teachers, and numerous remarks about the boy's introverted character – when not engaged in sports, where he also seemed to excel. He looked at the thirteen-year-old. Well-built and dressed, with a frank facial expression, there was a striking … aloofness about him.

'What do you know about Le Rosey, Cedric?'

'Nice things,' he smiled shyly. 'About 150 boys from the

age of 8 and about 40 girls from the age of 12, I think. That it moves to the mountains in the winter trimester.' (Here he beamed.) 'That there is a French and an English section, meaning some prepare for SATs or A-levels, some for the Baccalaureate or the Swiss Maturité, er … and that the classes are small, so no one can sleep through them leaning on the radiator at the back … sir.'

The headmaster was pleased. Clear elocution, precise answer, a touch of cheekiness and – ever so important – reverence.

'Can you imagine adapting to the school? I am disinclined to have students come and go' (sidelong glance at Hector Vich).

'Oh yes! But I know it's very expensive' (coy glance at his father).

'I'll manage if you work hard and behave well,' he smiled, obviously very fond of his boy. 'With the director's permission, why don't you walk around?'

It was agreed that Cedric would start attending in September 1971 – preparing for the June 1975 baccalaureate.

'One last thing, Mr Vich. Where do you reside?'

'In the air. Airborne, if you prefer. I keep a junior suite in every hotel of the chain, meaning a dozen or so impersonal residences. Yes, I know, an unsettling lifestyle for an only child. But … my house near Geneva, where Ced grew up is, um, no longer at my disposal. Thing is that I'm highly allergic to animal fur.'

Johan repressed a laugh. What on earth had allergies to do with…

'My wife left me. Not for a ski-instructor or the vaudevillesque best friend. Dogs! Her notion was that dogs needed her more than Ced, by then six, perhaps seven? Anyway. First the kennels for stray dogs but then, snobbism prevailing over sentiment, greyhound-breeding. Couldn't take it anymore.'

'I see,' mumbled Johan. And so he would. His own ex lived for horses and not much else – other than the occasional jockey.

Such memories came back to Jerome Johan while sipping a smoky Gamaret Grand Cru with cassis notes. Vich excused himself: an urgent phone call.

Cedric had changed. Still aloof, still shy, but no longer a rough diamond. His personality had crystallised. Ricardo had influenced this evolution. For better? For worse? The motorbike story, though of no transcendental gravity, violated Le Rosey's code of honour.

Johan had no desire to expel Cedric. Expelling Ricardo, the real culprit? No way: Moralli's life would be shattered. A widower near retirement, he was also an old friend. Hmm. What was authority for, if not to bend a rule or two once in a while?

When Hector Vich returned to the table, various hotel deals later it seemed, Johan's mind was made up. But let the man fret, he thought.

A miscalculation. Vich wasn't fretting at all.

'Mr Moralli will be here in time for coffee,' he announced gleefully. 'Now. Where's this famous *zabaglione*?'

The headmaster was not amused. To convoke Ricardo's father would have been incumbent upon him and no one else.

'Forgive me,' Vich hastened to add. 'I did not mean to meddle but please, do understand my point of view. Having always wished to meet that gentleman, I sent my driver to pick him up. The train from Napoli is on time, would you believe it?'

Had the foamy dessert, heavily soaked with Marsala, not been presented at this very moment, Johan might have expressed his indignation in no uncertain terms.

Cedric's father ate slowly, absorbed in some sort of rêverie, possibly inspired by the faded posters hanging on the walls: depictions of the Matterhorn, the Château de Chillon near Montreux, old steam trains, Zermatt locals fitted with wooden skis and the like. Typical decorations in traditional *auberges* such as this, reminding one that Switzerland, a truly poor country only a century earlier, yes, had gone to great lengths to promote tourism.

'My son has packed. Doesn't seem fazed. Strange. Can you explain that, Colonel?'

The headmaster, holder of a PhD in pedagogy and mathematics, hesitated. Put the cards on the table? Wait? No point.

'Look, Mr Vich. Your son, and Aleana, a girl he likes, share an unusual form of emotional bond. Coupled with an unusual form of … detachment. Unpredictable in their reactions, shrinking from displaying feelings, neither is easy to decode…'

The headmaster loosened his Rosey tie.

'Now: I shan't expel your son or Moralli's. Amongst the few left at school during mid-term, their families otherwise engaged' – stern glance – 'the whole, er, misadventure can be hushed up.'

Most tables having been cleared, his voice resonated.

'However: I expect you, Mr Vich, to come up with disciplinary measures during the Christmas holidays. No Caribbean islands, no private jets, etc. I insist.'

Mercifully, the innkeeper, Charlie, came over and started chit-chatting, filling copious glasses with homemade grappa. Meanwhile, Hector Vich's mind was slaloming. Flashbacks and clashing feelings curled into a mental magma difficult to disentangle.

Charlie gone, Cedric's father threw the headmaster one of his hypnotic glances.

'There's a hotel for sale nearby. It's a shambles. I'll buy it, primarily to be closer to my son, guilty as charged for neglecting him. During the two, or is it three, weeks of the Christmas holidays, Ricardo and Cedric can be part of the demolition or restoration process, don't know yet, living with the workers, no heating, no hot water, hard manual work...'

'Is *that* what you call a punishment?'

Mr Moralli stood by the table, hands on his hips.

'Sit down.' Johan had reverted to his Colonel's voice.

'*Va bene*. A porto, if I may.'

He let his athletic yet dwarf-like frame fall onto the torn leather banquette.

'What a trip!' he squealed.

Voices make all the difference, thought Hector Vich for the umpteenth time. Johan's was raucous and authoritative. His own was ... whatever. Not to be overheard, anyway. The history teacher had an ageing castrato's voice. That said, it conveyed vitality. His laser-like gaze commanded caution. Just as well that Mr Johan was, by now, rather drowsy.

'Mr Moralli, it's an honour to meet you. It is well known that you are a pillar of the Rosey institution. I understand you have just come back from a memorial service in honour of the tenth anniversary of your late wife's death. So sorry.'

Not even the irate Moralli was immune to Cedric's father's charm. Yet, the man was a strategist, and he, Franco Moralli, unwilling to turn into a pawn on his chessboard.

'What do you desire?'

Vich's unexpected disarray mellowed the history teacher's barking but not biting heart. (Johan was by now snoring away.)

'Want? Nothing. Understand? A lot. Do you, sir, well ... approve of our sons' friendship?'

Moralli reflected.

'At first I was worried. Ricardo is the fish in a pond full of potential sharks, if you will forgive this primitive image.'

Hector Vich dropped his fork.

'I will not. Are you claiming that the so-called poor-little-rich kids can muster neither resilience nor resolve, their mental backbone atrophied by privilege? That they are bound to become spineless and rudderless predators and that...'

'Wrrrrong!' Moralli protested. Mildly pompous, the Italian's heavily rolled 'r's made his words sound thunderous.

'Look. My son's a narcissist,' he winced, 'who compares his image to that of his co-students. Most of them having such a different profile, in manifold ways, I think the first thing that drew him towards Cedric, a self-effacing boy, was their uncanny physical resemblance.'

Hector Vich pondered. He had seen Ricardo once or twice and indeed, they did look rather alike but then, don't all teen-agers? What if the teacher's son attraction had more to do with the generosity Cedric, presumably, showered his friend with?

As if suspecting this train of thoughts, Moralli jumped onto another.

'Absentee parents! The plague of our times! Nannies, teachers, what have you? Authority and caring are delegated, meaning...'

Vich, his eyebrows ironically circumflex, discouraged elaborating. The teacher shrugged.

'Esteemed Mr Vich. Would you like me to *truly* answer your question?'

Rubbing his watch, Cedric's father answered, 'please do'.

4

THE DOLL

Ced had called me explaining the situation, telegraphic style. There were payphones in our respective corridors and he only had few coins left. We agreed to meet at Nyon station.

There, he told me that Mr Johan and his father were having lunch nearby, that he had packed his stuff and that we'd no longer be together for a long time. Tears welled up my eyes.

Sitting at Ricardo's bedside, *ad hoc* I declared I'd become a spy. Cedric, standing by the window, kept silent. Ricardo, the inquisitive one, asked why.

'It requires indifference.'

'And what's so cool about that?'

'The art of being invisible.'

'Sure it isn't attention you want?' Ric sniped.

We were eating sandwiches I had bought. A week's pocket-money down our throats.

Ced choked and looked as if about to throw up.

'Don't be dramatic, man,' said Ric. 'Johan cannot expel me, meaning he can't expel you either. Besides, your father will pay for the bike's repair, or for a new one. I spoke with Georg. Cool cat. "Four-hour-long operas have been written with a thinner plot," he laughed, probably stoned. Bottom line: he'll press no charges, file no complaint, whatever you call it.'

'Both forms are valid,' I remarked.

'Dear Al!' 'Our walking dictionary. Bet you carry one in your bag.'

Not today but point made. Etymology, synonyms, you name it: I'll probably come up with an answer and if not, look it up in a hurry. I'm a maniac for definitions. At its core, a passion for precision.

'What d'you think will happen?'

'Some sort of punishment over Christmas, I guess... Can't be too bad for me as my leg will still be in plaster.'

Also characteristically, Ricardo cared first and foremost about himself.

I half-listened to their conversation about some tennis tournament or football match. But I observed what I had on so many occasions: Cedric was the giver.

He always tried to dissimulate his skills, his knowledge, his privileges. On Saturdays, when many parents came to fetch their kids for the weekend and Mr Vich would send his driver, the latter would be sent away: Cedric pretended to prefer the train... He'd wear second-hand clothes, all because Ricardo couldn't afford the prices in the local shops. He'd give private tuition to younger pupils, as did his friend who actually needed the extra money. He even agreed to donate blood – same reason. For Ricardo's birthday, he'd always think of something special but not too expensive: a first edition book, a framed drawing of some car, an old photograph of a legendary rugby team or actor, things like that. Cedric's delicacy was innate.

In exchange, so to speak, Ricardo transfused self-confidence. Lavishing praise, he helped Ced overcome his chronic shyness and self-doubts. Most importantly, he made Cedric laugh. He was a devil-may-care, if ambitious, companion to a seemingly carefree but deep-down worrier.

I meant to go for a walk, bicycles permitting, when the phone rang. Hector Vich was on his way. Please stay, Cedric entreated.

Moralli had told Vich about the boys' relationship. He had also spoken about me and about the 'trio' we had formed.

(Should anyone wonder why I was able to narrate the lunch taking place at that very moment: it was Hector Vich who, more or less verbatim, told me about it much, much later.)

When he sailed into the hospital-room, he looked so ... normal. Stupidly, I had imagined the hotel tycoon to be tall, dressed up to the nines, intimidating. None of the above. He opened the window to light a cigarette, a highly forbidden course of action. No hellos.

Then he examined me, taking his time.

'I see.'

'What?' I snapped, none too pleased to feel sprawled under a microscope.

'A lot. I'm told you nickname my son Amber, and Ricardo, Sapphire. Well, the colour of your eyes is the perfect mix: never seen anything so turquoise. Do you know that my driver has one brown, one grey eye?'

I pointed out that this phenomenon is called heterochromia. He seemed amused. I was struck by his eyes: copper with gold nuggets.

'So you're the semantic genius they say you are?'

They?

'Father, her brain is insured for more millions than Marilyn Monroe's legs!'

'Question is: what has she done with the dough?' winked Ricardo.

Hector Vich sneezed.

'All right boys, down to business. Your headmaster has agreed not to expel either of you. After all, no harm done to others, forgetting that motorcycle. Taken care of. Yet, as you can imagine, there will be a toll to pay. After some brain-storming, here is what we decided: three weeks of humanitarian work

over the Christmas holidays. In Kenya. There's an organisation called The Flying Doctors, or is it now AMREF? Point
is that, having no medical qualifications, you'll be sent to
refugee camps, or is it orphanages, well, whatever. You'll work
hard, boys and, need I add, in distressing surroundings. Have
I made myself clear?'

He had. Cedric looked relieved. Ricardo, sulky. Didn't like
to be bossed around by another's father: his own did little else.

'That's settled then. I'm also planning to spend most
coming weekends in Nyon to keep a closer watch on you,
Ced. Right now, must rrrrrun. My driver will take you two
back to school.'

Having given his son a brief but affectionate hug, Ricardo
a vigorous tap on the shoulder and me, the first hand-kiss of
my life, he vanished. The sensation of his lips made me shiver.
I sniffed my hand. The perfume of a future memory.

Cedric looked uncomfortable. I didn't: trains on Sundays
were scarce and I like to be taken care of. Also, I liked Mr Vich.

She's stunning and unaware of it, thought he. Fifteen or so.
No Lolita: more of a tomboy. Zero make-up, tennis shoes,
unkempt hair, no-nonsense attitude, androgynous figure. But
one day, this girl will be a heart-breaker. Hope she won't break
Cedric's.

Little did we know, back then, that I would, one day, injure
his.

'Well!' exclaimed Ricardo. 'Didn't I tell you, Ced? Case closed.
Cash is king!'

Outraged, I reacted violently.

'How dare you? He saved the situation, the obnoxious situation you have put yourself into! Honestly! You know that
Ced took the blame and should be bloody ashamed! Three

weeks in Kenya? It's more of a privilege than a punishment! I envy you, as it were!'

Neither of them used to me raising my voice, they shut up.

Cedric, however, was agitated. He paced the room, biting his thumb's fingernail.

'Listen', he finally said. 'When I was ten or so, my father and I went to Hyde Park in London. It bored him stiff, naturally. There was a little Pakistani girl in floods of tears. I asked her what the matter was. She sobbed uncontrollably. Someone had stolen her doll, her favourite doll, Dorry, a substitute sister of sorts. I tried to console her. To no avail. So I trotted back to my father, immersed in his *Financial Times*, and reported the situation. He jumped off the bench, went over to ask for her address. I thought he'd send her the nicest doll Harrod's had in store.'

Ricardo yawned. I urged him to proceed, impatient as is my wont.

'He did much more than that. He sent the little girl letters signed Dorry. First, she described school, learning a lot of things and making lots of friends. Then she travelled to Australia where she fell in love. Further on, as she wrote joyfully, she got married, the description of her romantic nuptials vintage Barbara Cartland. Written by my father! Finally, Dorry explained that, expecting twins, she was unlikely to come back but would forever love and adore Leila, the Pakistani girl.'

Twilight, by now, flooded the hospital-room with ochre shades.

'He never told me. His secretary did.'

Ricardo, not the sensitive kind, returned to practicality.

'How am I supposed to roam around Kenya with my cast?'

'Shall be removed in a month at the latest,' smiled a nurse who had slithered in and overheard us. Her smile was not directed at the patient.

5

KENYA

(Xmas 1973)

Some might remember Werner Herzog's 1969 documentary film, *The Flying Doctors of East Africa*. No great box-office hit. But Hector Vich, a movie aficionado, had been fascinated. Ever since, he had anonymously transferred generous sums.

In the late fifties, three British surgeons had created an organisation called AMREF (African Medical Research Foundation) to provide help in remote regions. Poverty, diseases and dismal hygiene, all compounded by lack of education, accounted for a catastrophic health situation. Back then, there was only one doctor to every 30,000 people – as compared to 1 to a thousand in Britain. A practically non-existent infrastructure made assistance by air the logical solution. Hence the name Flying Doctors. Mission hospitals were created. A medical radio network was developed. By 1973, training of rural workers had become a priority. It involved improving mobile and technical assistance, maternal and child support of utmost urgency, vaccine campaigns.

Ced and Ricardo would volunteer, decided Vich. They would learn a lot – not least, humility.

He'd accompany them, visit AMREF's headquarters in Nairobi, make sure the boys were entrusted with challenging tasks; then take a much-needed holiday.

Invite Aleana? She was intriguing, hence good company. What was her family situation? His son had no clue, or so he claimed. Being only children, 'the trio' considered secrecy – or was it silence? – a normal state of affairs.

Yes.

The man didn't know anything about my childhood, and nor did my two closest friends. The story might have inspired the kind of compassion I refused to inspire.

But here it is, in a nutshell: my birth was an intrusion. Walking into my parents' study, I always felt like an uninvited visitor, or else one who got the day wrong and is received for courtesy's sake. On my way out, I faded into a silhouette devoid of contour. My parents' hermetic love excluded me. With no umbilical cord to cut, I was born ... wild.

The forging of an identity depends on a given definition. I was robbed of it. Never was I called by my first name: nannies, who rotated in quick succession, addressed me as 'young lady'. Mother, though reluctant to engage in any form of attachment with 'the accident' (me), did not wish this accident to become unduly attached to anyone else (staff). Their common denominator was age and infertility: alien to filial love. Everybody else in the house (a prison) called me 'Miss'. Even my first name was a spelling mistake: my parents had thought of Adriana but couldn't be bothered to check the registry...

Children are no fools: what was I other than a paid-for responsibility and a well-dressed phantom? I never thought: when I grow up I want to be a stewardess, an actress or something. I thought: one day, I want to be young and have fun.

Mother and Father's blind fusion may be illustrated by occasions when, leaving by train, they would have me taken to the station at Bordeaux. While handkerchiefs were waved and tears shed, I stood on the platform looking like a doll. Nanny, whoever she was, would then buy me an ice-cream, as instructed.

Yes: when meeting no glance from interlocked eyes, children

feel shut out. Attention – or is it affection, as Vich would say? – will never be earned through presence. Only through invisibility. Boarding school, I fathomed, would be a life-saver, sanity-wise. It took shaving my hair off, among other none too subtle coercive manoeuvres, to be sent away to one.

How was Mr Vich to know that, come Christmas-time, I had to perform at my parents' annual 'happy-family' production, in which an important prop was *moi*? Mercifully, nannies had been dismissed and a television installed in my bedroom for my sixteenth birthday. Yet another screen.

On December 17st, Ric, Cedric and his father flew to Nairobi via Rome. (Two days later, thirty passengers aboard a Pan Am plane would perish after Palestinian guerrillas stormed the aircraft at Fiumicino's airport.)

The boys sat in economy class, much to Ricardo's dismay.

Upon arrival, they were greeted by fat and jolly eccentric Frau Semler. She whisked them through customs, then through the chaotic city's traffic, finally into an office resembling a local art gallery.

'I always wonder how we can do such good work drinking such a lousy coffee,' she grinned, pouring out gin and tonics. AMREF, she explained, counted on almost a thousand workers, more than a third of them Africans, its objective not a short-term but a lasting infrastructure, training being the essence, responsibility the spirit, the future a challenge, hence...

'Very laudable', interrupted Hector Vich. 'What are the boys to do?'

On she went, a little tipsy by then, about the most needy regions, recent floods or droughts, hic, mankind a big family, hiccup, commitment an apprenticeship and –

'Very well! Cedric and Ricardo will no doubt live up to your lofty expectation, Frau Sebber ... Keep them on the straight and narrow, *jawohl?*' he added brightly, imitating her German accent.

'Semler, *iv you vill!*'

After another sip, her tone became malicious:

'Why a holiday on Lamu? Why not a safari?'

'One of Jomo Kenyatta's countless nephews stayed at my Madison hotel and raved about the place.'

'Aha?' hummed Frau Semler, her short curls bobbing.

Hector Vich remembered the nephew's words well. They had been spoken with an earnestness the notorious playboy wasn't known for.

'On the northern Indian Ocean's coast, two degrees south of the equator, stands one of the cradles of Swahili culture and a crossroad of civilisations,' he had recited, erect with pride. 'As a trading post between Arabia and India, it was much coveted. First by the Portuguese; later by successive Omani sultans, in turn removed by the British at the end of the nineteenth century. Henceforth, Mombasa became the dominant port. Bad for Lamu's business but a blessing for its culture: isolation left the archipelago untouched by the nefarious effects of modernisation.'

Here, the nephew chuckled. Wasn't Uncle K standing for its virtues?

'Most locals never saw a car. There are no roads either, meaning not even bikes,' he further giggled.

Kenyatta had celebrated his ten years of presidency as well as the country's ten years of independence in October, and offered his cherished but useless nephew a Harley Davidson as an encouragement to remain in the States, i.e., far and out of the way.

Having left the boys in the care of Frau Samler, Slemrer, whatever, Hector returned to Nairobi's airport to board a chartered

Piper Cherokee. (By land, the trip would have taken several days staying in lodges overnight: out of the question.)

These were the seventies. Criminality was on the rise, terrorism rampant.

In March of '73, Black September had taken ten hostages at the Saudi Embassy in Khartoum. Three Western diplomats had been killed. Travelling to a Muslim country only two borders away from the Sudan, to a coastal town only miles away from Somalia, the hotelier had naturally expected hermetic gates, high walls, heavily armed policemen and so on.

None of it on Lamu.

Peponi's was half an hour's walk from Lamu village or fifteen by sea. The hotel's reception and bar were one and the same place. You were given no keys: there were no locks. The telephone, a square and black Bakelite affair, might have been an early Bell model. Lamu's operator, an old mamma fond of Peponi's Danish owner Aage ('you don't have a name, you have a sound') would give requests from number 29 a preferential treatment – meaning only two or three hours' wait for calls to Nairobi. To Europe, one or two days. Electricity was intermittent, depending on the generator's whims. Otherwise, gas lamps and candles were lit. No TV, no newspapers. An antique radio would deign to function once in a while, soon interrupted by swishes and crackles.

In the absence of cars, donkeys were the common means of transportation. Hector Vich, highly allergic to animal fur (remember?) preferred moving around by foot or on dhows, small sailing boats used as water-taxis.

Accustomed to pushing buttons, to racing around and to instant long-distance calls, he found himself set back in time. He had forgotten the sound of silence. Other than lapping waves, a distant muezzin prayer, cockerels crowing or dogs barking, the faint swishing of a fan and perhaps, at night, the muffled tunes of a lone hippy's guitar on the beach, nothing.

To all of this, Hector Vich adapted faster than he'd expected. A much-travelled man, he was familiar with the 'have a nice day' (or shrink session) of the Americans; with the Brazilians' dancing joie de vivre; with the Italian cunning friendliness. He had also endured fierce hostility in the Congo and kidnapping threats elsewhere.

On Lamu, he experienced a brand of gentleness and good-will quite unknown to him. Indeed: no need for locks of any kind. Muslim or Christian, white or black, well-off or poor, human beings seemed … genuinely pure. He had seldom felt so safe and carefree.

Relaxed? Not quite. There was the Vilma factor, as he called it – the one that had most probably been in the back of Frau Semler's well-informed mind.

'Hector Bwana', the Kenyatta nephew had winked some weeks ago, 'I'll have a surprise for you…'

Vich wasn't fond of surprises.

'Alone in Lamu, right? You need rest, OK? But you do like ladies, yeah? Well! Vilma. Indian, mid-twenties, beeeeeeautiful and good … body-relax. Manners, too, you know Bwana? I myself…'

No longer listening, Hector Vich had thought, why not? He fancied Indian women and favoured cash-transactions in such matters.

Vilma had been waiting, heavy kohl around her eyes, gold bangles around neck and wrists. Marble white teeth, a silky skin, a pleasant sing-song voice. So far, so good. The first three nights and days, she did not belie her reputation. Vilma was a serpentine bed-acrobat and, thank Vishnu, a hushed one.

But then she had discovered the donkey sanctuary. Her infatuation with the animals rang red-alerts and provoked frantic sneezing: Vilma would spend hours mothering 'the silly beasts' and smell accordingly, showers notwithstanding.

Exit Vilma.

Enter Bunny Allen. His arrival at Peponi's elicited an exuberant welcome and liquor-binge. In a sonorous voice, he recounted his latest adventures in the bush, encounters with lions, zebras, gazelles and so forth, or with indigenous tribes he managed to befriend. One could see why: Bunny was a big man of uncertain age with a sunburnt face lined horizontally, huge and calloused hands, yet gracious manners. When not roaming Africa or entertaining his Happy Valley friends, he'd be spotted poaching around Windsor Castle or casting his spell in pubs. With his earring, his gold chains from which dangled dangerous-looking claws or teeth, his parched face and exotic accent, they called him 'the gypsy'.

He and Hector Vich hit it off at once. The latter enchanted the former with his wit and multi-faceted culture. Bunny responded in kind.

The Marquis de Danet, another original clad in Savile Row safari-outfits, would sometimes invite them to his beautiful house behind Peponi's. It was built Makuti style: roofs made of multiple layers of palm-leaves mixed with chicken mash held together by mangrove poles; treated coral-sand floors; Zanzibar-made, exquisitely crafted furniture. Several Gobelins and a Renoir created incongruous contrasts. So did the man's, er, lady-friend, a flamenco dancer who would ceaselessly play Sevillianas on the gramophone. With her wide skirts and a low body lattice, she looked beguiling. Hector Vich noticed, in the fraction of a second during which the black mantilla covering her face slipped, that her complexion was that of an

English Rose. A fake and a fraud? he merrily wondered. On Lamu the improbable was always possible. (The charming, soft spoken Marquis who evoked one of Peter Sellers' gauche characters would, some years later, be sitting on the Olympic Committee.)

Frau Semler and Vich had agreed he'd call every three days.

When he eventually reached her, on Christmas Day, she reported: 'Your son is fantastic with the natives, Hector. People trust him and doctors respect him. As for children, they adore him, since he manages to present injections and operations as some sort of adventure. He's also very good at teaching. As to his friend: a born organiser. His efficiency has given us new ideas about logistics. Both boys are very dependable. One more solid than the other... You figure it out. So: all is well. I should think that you will find them a little changed when they join you in a week's time...'

About to hang up, she exclaimed:

'Good Lord, I almost forgot! Some girl called in a flood of tears. She said she was a school-friend and left a telephone number. Would you like me to fetch it?'

On his way to the tiny Catholic Church near the museum in Lamu Town, Hector Vich saw a young boy trip over a rope. He rushed over, took out a handkerchief to clean the injury and handed him to a woman with scared eyes (all the rest of her covered in a black *ninja)* with soothing words.

'What do *you* think *you* are doing, sir?' scolded a British officer.

'Well, the kid fell so...'

'Saw it. But sir, a *musungo* may only talk to a Muslim woman if proposing marriage.'

'Really?' laughed Vich. 'Most expeditious!'

'No laughing matter', boomed the officer, turning on his heel.

Later that evening, Dr Anna Spoerri, one of Peponi's icons and also an AMREF veteran, told him a chilling story involving a Muslim woman and a foreigner. Suddenly he thought of Vilma, throwing a basket-full of flowers into the sea, a donkey-baby having died: Indian tradition, she had whispered.

'Other than donkeys, do you know of any animals hauling carts or sledges, helping the blind or the police, respecting children, and, and ... Look at cats, bloody useless, selfish creatures!'

Did the crazy girl picture donkeys in the Antarctic or in the Bronx, disguised as huskies or Dobermans?

More sobbing had gone on until quite some money changed hands. For your furred friends, Hector had said, thinking: good riddance.

Was Aleana still crying?

6

NO MOSQUITOS

It happened!
The power of magical thinking, I thought.

The day after Christmas, knock on my door: my father sneaked his ostrich neck through it and announced that a friend's father was on the phone.

'From somewhere in Kenya!'

'So?' I answered coolly, my heart arrhythmic.

'Asked if we would let you fly down there for a week. Apparently an interesting place...'

'What did you answer?' I shrugged, my hands shaking so much I had to cling to my guitar.

'Well ... what's wrong with a spot of travel?' the not-at-all poor man ventured, unable to dissimulate his relief at seeing his daughter dearest removed from sight. 'All right?'

Hardly breathing, I said, yes Father.

Little did he know that I had found a way to learn a pretty extensive amount of Swahili and that I had been lying in wait for just *that* very phone call.

Practical matters were swiftly arranged as Mr Vich and my parents put their minds and money behind it.

Three days later, I arrived on Lamu.

Another planet.

Peponi's? Legendary, as I had also found out beforehand. It had, since the late sixties, been a magnet for hippies (many with Oxbridge accents), royalty (barefoot), rock stars (amongst them, the Rolling Stoned) plus every more or less well-heeled eccentric in between. Basically, it was a British enclave with a cosmopolitan flair on a completely unspoilt archipelago.

The silence. The peace. Hector Vich. Suntanned, debonair, a lot thinner than I remembered him, he looked like really, and I mean *really*, handsome. His copper eyes sparkled like gems, highlighted by that mane of ink-black hair.

How he knew it had been my birthday, no idea, but he produced a beautifully wrapped Guerlain flask for the occasion. '*L'Heure Bleue*', he smiled. 'To remind you of Lamu's indigo sky...'

That must have been meant for that stupid Indian girl, I heard someone murmur.

I did not care. Nor did I care for perfume. I had sworn, a long time ago, not to leave traces or trails behind. Scents were a no-go. But I was touched ... very.

Ced and Ric were due to arrive on New Year's Eve.

They did. It took them a while to re-adapt to the sybaritic atmosphere.

They had seen misery, sickness, famine, conflicts – at first hand. They had spent days without water and many a sleepless night. They had seen the firework of joy in a young child's eyes as he beheld the sight of the sea for the first time in his life; the same light in the eyes of the very ill wrapped in cool cotton sheets. They had been thanked with songs; hugged in bony arms; beamed at with wonderment. They might, or so they hoped, have saved lives having donated gallons of blood. (Coincidence or fate, Ced and Ric had the same, extremely rare blood group: AB-.)

By sheer luck, our stay coincided with Maulidi, the annual festivities commemorating the Prophet Mohammed's birth. The narrow streets, the waterfront and squares were thronged with women dressed in colourful *bui-buis*, men in embroidered kofias, children with henna-painted hands, all to the sound of parades and joyous yet devotional music. The dozen or so mosques bustled with activity, songs, dances, prayers: quite a cacophony. Gifts were exchanged, food shared, the fragrance of the dishes on display wafting through the air. On the last day of Maulidi, its climax: a magnificent procession of men holding the banners of their respective town or mosque.

Hector felt his leg tugged from behind. It was the little boy whom he had picked up after his fall. The boy pressed a small ivory comb into his hand then plunged back into the crowd.

Dinners at Peponi's were another brand of festivities altogether, with lavish trays of catches of the day and equally lavish pouring of cocktails. 'Half-drunk is a waste of money!' was the general idea.

During the day, we would swim for hours on end or walk for miles along the virgin, deserted beach lined with dunes. There was a cute Swahili boy...

Isn't paradise time suspended?

I swore that I would, one day, build a house there.

Years later, I did.

7

GRADUATION

(June '75)

The Kenya experience had changed my two friends in many ways. Superficially: Cedric let his hair grow inasmuch as school regulation permitted whilst Ric cropped his. Significantly: though the weeks in Africa had consolidated their friendship, the difference in temperament had accentuated. Ced, more than ever, the contemplative dreamer, the idealist; Ric increasingly restless.

As Frau Semler had reported, Ricardo was – and would always be – the efficient doer, good at organising but no good at coping with misery (*Beware of Pity*, by Stefan Zweig, was by now his bedside book). Cedric, in contrast, was gifted – perhaps plagued – with empathy and compassion. Yet, something odd about his behaviour had become striking: his camera came with him wherever he went. His passion for photography had become compulsive. Was he trying to keep emotions at bay? Interposing a filter between a raw sensitivity and an even rawer reality?

Hardly ever removing my sunglasses, wasn't I adhering to a similar pattern?

Other than that, not much to report between Christmas '74 and June '75 when the three of us were handed our Baccalaureate.

True to his word, Mr Vich had rented a house nearby Rolle, only minutes from the school. Ricardo's father's health deteriorating, the latter reluctantly agreed to his son spending most weekends there.

I was often invited but rarely accepted. After all, I had other friends, particularly a girl who was as much of a loner as me, Anoushka. We had something else in common: parents who ignored us. All she did, given time, was paint. Nush fascinated but also scared me. She seemed to have a third eye with which to see through people.

A Mitteleuropa thoroughbred, Nush's complexion and eyes, both a glowing caramel-colour, emanated exoticism. As did her 'mermaidy' body-language: her gestures were wave-like; now slow, now nervous, always undulating.

Her actual body, another story: she might have stepped out of a Cubist painting. From chin to ankles, from shoulders to hips, her figure was angular. Even her face, fleshy mouth included, seemed composed of isosceles.

But then ... Nush's eyes. Nothing languid about her eyes. They moved in a staccato rhythm. They scanned. They infiltrated. They made you feel defenceless, unmasked.

Nush was a mosaic of discrepancies. The sum was endearing. To me, at least. Back in school, that is.

Be it as it may, she and I liked to stay in the lovely cottage named the *section féminine*, 'co-education, not co-habitation' being another of Rosey's principles. Over the weekend, a rabbit-toothed, sweet and stupid supervisor would let us smoke and play full-blast music: the Doobie Brothers, Stevie Wonder, Barry White, David Bowie, Elton John's 'Candle in the Wind' and so on. We would wear dresses bought at the occasional flea-market and enact kitschy shows. Miss forget-her-name, an undemanding audience, joined in. When exhausted, we'd switch to Mike Oldfield's *Tubular Bells*, thus becoming deliciously melancholic.

Other girls devised elaborate scenarios to fake their parents' signatures on weekend permission-forms and had, or so they boasted, wild times with true or fictitious boyfriends.

I had a crush on an Indian boy, Radji Karputala. My not exactly expert efforts at rapprochement led nowhere. 'He only fancies fat girls,' Ced informed me. To eat myself into an over-inflated Michelin? No.

What else? We won the skiing competition against Aiglon, another Swiss boarding-school, for the second winter in a row.

Cedric would have won the singles tennis tournament, had he not decided to play lamely, allowing Ric to raise the trophy.

Georg Langon, the cool BMW owner and German teacher, smitten by Nush, wrote her a rather ambivalent, rather erotic, poem, which he forgot on his desk. (Would he have sent it?) Johan's anger was monumental. No second warning, he roared.

Hani Yamani, the Saudi petroleum minister's son, was suspected of having thrown a stick of dynamite into the 150-year-old fountain – emulating some Savoy prince or other who'd done the same: cool. In the midst of the oil crisis, Colonel Johan was never informed of the alleged facts.

Ced and Ric competed for the favours of an Aiglon girl: love all.

That Christmas holiday was the usual nightmare for me: parading as the prodigal daughter in a house I never considered home.

New Year's Eve was even worse. I was made to dress in full-regalia, meaning a silk curtain-like outfit ornate with ridiculous ribbons, and to recite a poem. I chose 'Invitation au Voyage' by Baudelaire. No one really listened.

Another six months to go until graduation. Other than Nush, we were all desperate to get out – out of the cocoon, out into the world – wherever that was, whatever that meant. 'Run too fast, fly too high?' Nush would dis-heartedly whisper.

Two weeks after Easter, Moralli wrote to Cedric's father. Given his antiquated knowledge of English, his letter's turgid style was comical.

Esteemed Sir,
Enigmatic Aleana, whose parents' baleful influence has limited her choices and chances, is headstrong. She once (shockingly, I permit to underline) quoted Evelyn Waugh boasting to dislike his seven children equally. 'Trouble is I have no siblings,' she expounded, tears in eye. Henceforth added, 'I sometimes wish that my parents died.' Yesterday, they did, God bless.

In a modest flash of thought and spirit, I wish to partake my disquiet. Would you perhaps watch over the young lady during the coming summer? She has nowhere to go – or may I venture, nowhere she wants to go to – after graduation. Mister Vich, forgive my infiltrating into alien lives but do contemplate that I am fond of the girl. Though feisty she is fragile and I, a fatigued fossil. Explaining why I send you this missive with delay. I had forgotten to.
Yours faithfully, —

Had Mr Moralli written this in a *London gondola* – as horse-driven cabs were once known? Vich's merriment was short-lived. Why had neither Ricardo nor his son told him? Why hadn't Aleana? And why had he, a father, sensed nothing? The history teacher was right: enigmatic was the word. Or was it? He couldn't find the word on the tip of his tongue.

On Whit Sunday, Mr Vich appeared alone, to fetch only me.

We were to have lunch. The boys were playing football somewhere.

No sooner seated:

'Why did I have to learn about your parents' demise through an intermediary?'

He looked uncomfortable. Unless his eyes lied, so did I.

After two glasses of wine, I told Cedric's father what I hadn't even dared to tell Nush, my kin in the abandonment department.

'Easter Monday, Mr Vich. The Bordeaux clinic where my mother hastened to die after Father's fatal car-crash. Only days later. Do you get strokes from loving too much?'

He filled another glass.

'Mr Vich...'

'Hector.'

Too many emotions had bottled up over the years and here was a person who offered release from pain. Why not let my defences atomise? Just this once.

'Hector. Look. I was taught fluency in four languages, but I was never taught to communicate. Whenever Mother and Father appear in my dreams, their bodies project a single shadow... Although they went through the motions of parental love, their attempts were in vain. In retrospect, I'm glad they spared me the farce of emotional pretence.'

Gazing at the tranquil Lac Leman and at Hector not rubbing his watch, I continued. 'When the gates of that clinic slammed shut, it hit me: their death was tantamount to deliverance. A release. On bail?'

It sounded cruel. Even to me. But impassive Hector merely waited.

'The doors were open, yes, but how or where to look for something I never knew, and therefore never lost? Will I ever miss it – whatever *it* is?'

Being me, aforementioned too often, I felt as lonely as ever – with a difference. I was not alone. As if on tip-toes, he ventured:

'In short, you're afraid.'

About to riposte 'Me? Afraid? Never!' I wondered: was I?

Confused, a bit. About my intelligence, no doubts to be harboured. About my talents, neither: I only had one. About the future? I'd sell my parents' house, vineyards, furniture, art-collection: nothing to hang on to. Whatever the sentimental value associated with them, it all was negative.

Then? The path of least resistance? So what? Le Rosey conditioned one to such a panorama. How many of my companions had parents who weren't divorced, families who weren't uprooted? How many of us weren't doomed or privileged enough to draw our future *journey* on quick – or slow – sands, with travellers cheques galore?

How cruel again! Many alumni had made dazzling careers. Many had lived up to their extraordinary *gifts*. Many had struggled, and hard.

'What will you do this summer?' Hector asked.

'No idea. But oh! "American Pie", know the song?'

'New York, New York' by Sinatra was more in Vich's league. Hammer it in unnecessarily?

'I see,' he said.

To take our Baccalaureate exams, we were transported by bus to Annemasse, just over the Swiss border.

We sat with all sorts of strangers on benches so hard that the scarce bones of my bottom cracked. Some looked panicked to the point of paralysis; some were scribbling hysterically and some, like me, showed no visible emotion.

This was, for the Bac A, our most important exam: philosophy. The question: 'Is character destiny, or is destiny the sum of our decisions?' I relaxed. My line of argument linear, it only needed circumlocutions and erudite references to warrant a three-hour essay. (Yes, character was destiny so long as genetics played the predominant role but then, shit or luck happens: education, influences, material and affective circumstances, good, bad or indifferent. In short, the aleatory interferes. From there on, an existence is a raw material to be moulded. Conditioned, certainly; damaged or not, depends. That was an issue I'd dwell upon. Be it only to fill space, I'd digress: is having an unbalanced personality a sound premise for one's equilibrium? Aren't more fragile personalities better equipped to cope with the toboggans of life, being used to rocking grounds?)

My conclusion: yes, character is destiny, inasmuch as a character will determine the decisions made later in life, the sum of which, etc. Then a question to the asked question: to what extent are correlations and causality related? I ended on (not so) flippant a note, citing the proverb: *Birds don't sing because they're happy. They're happy because they sing.* Attitude!

How had Ced fared? Turned out he had been given another theme: '"He who loses faith doesn't believe in anything any-more: he now believes in everything." How do you interpret this?'

'Not easy,' he grinned as we came out.

Ric had different problems: his was a Bac C exam, i.e. mathematics. No margin for fantasy there – just as well. Yet I worried. He was so insecure in some ways, his father's expec-tations looming steeply. Would he lose his nerve?

Nush? She was OK. Taking A-levels in what she knew best (French, Art and History) hadn't been a big deal. She probably snoozed on her bed, quite forgetful of our 'ordeal'. Nush was an 'I and Me' person. Kind, yes, but deep-down, unconcerned by others.

On June 24th took place *la remise de diplomes*. Other than Le Rosey blazers and ties for boys, or scarves for us, no funny hats, nor long tunics and speeches. Booze is what I best, if foggily, remember. Mr Johan wasn't all that sober either, once most parents had driven off. He even remarked on my blossoming bosom, cheeky old Colonel. We hugged. How I respected the man! He had, sorry to sound syrupy, tried hard to console me, as a parent would – or should. (Little did he know how relieved I had felt to have become an orphan.)

Hector Vich hadn't turned up.

Ricardo disappeared into the landscape with a very, very pretty lady – someone's elder sister, probably. Good! I had always wondered why a good-looking boy like him, with these hallucinating sapphire-blue eyes, hardly ever seemed interested in girls. (He might have wondered the same about me, but more about that later.)

Georg Langon approached Ced. The poor darling was casting expectant glances at the alley, a bottle of wine as his crutch.

'Time for a serious conversation,' our German teacher giddily declared. 'Wat iz it zat you learnt about zings like, em, heredity?'

'That if your grandfather didn't have children and neither has your father, you can fuck around in all impunity,' riposted Ced, doing his best to feign off-handedness.

'And what does that tell you about motorbikes?'

'That they're homosexual!' he slurred.

And so on. Georg and Cedric slapped each other's shoulders. Ricardo appeared out of the blue, dizzy in his own way.

Finally, we walked, or rather stumbled, down to the lake. As we reached its shore we heard an exuberant voice. Hector's.

'Apologies, my friends! Been delayed preparing a surprise! For all of you!'

8 – I

THE CRUISE

(July of '75 – Leonor)

'Life's too short to play it safe,' smiled the lady, her face un-decodable beneath a large hat and sunglasses.

Ricardo had noticed she'd been watching us and decided to find out why. Now all he could think of were her lips. Perfection. Their extremities slightly upturned, they conveyed mild irony – and a not so mild sensuality. She seemed to hover rather than walk. A former ballet dancer? He guessed her to be forty-something (her hands). She had what the French call 'du chien'. (What dogs have to do with class or elegance only the frogs know.)

'Madame, I noticed you observing our little group rather insistently. I'm curious…'

'Call me Leonor, will you?' That Sibylline smile. 'Look, it's just that I'm fond of young people and there aren't loads of them around, right? Forgive my indiscretion, would you, Ricardo? I know no one on this ship. As a matter of fact, I don't have friends – only drinking companions' – another smile – '… and … your friend, Cedric isn't it, reminds me of someone … I lost.'

So she knew both their names. Her last words unsettled Ricardo, afraid to have touched a raw nerve near a fresh wound.

'Leonor, might I invite you to the bar – a new drinking companion, with luck.'

What a disturbing charm, thought she. How alike the two

boys looked, other than the striking colour of their eyes! Was cobalt the right word for this one?

They sat on the bar-stools for a long time, Ricardo opening his heart as he had seldom done. He felt much at ease, which he seldom did. And never, ever had he been so tempted to kiss anyone.

In spite of the wood-panelled bar's penumbra, the lady hadn't removed her hat or shades. Shaken out of his trance by the bell announcing dinner's first serving, he pleaded:

'Beautiful Lady, come and sit at our table. Though I'm afraid there's hardly anything left to say. You know all about my special friendship with Ced, a whole lot about my past, quite a bit about the two girls with us, and...'

'Don't be afraid of anything, new companion dearest!' (They had sipped three whisky-sours each.) 'I long to resume our conversation but do prefer supper in my cabin. For you, another poker marathon, I presume? Be it as it may, we have another four days of cruising left – and as many nights.'

Gambling he had not mentioned. How come she knew that too? Too seduced and too drunk to dwell upon the matter, Ricardo stroked Leonor's soft hand and headed for the door with what he hoped resembled dignity. An icy shower later, Cedric irrupted into their cabin, looking exhilarated.

'What's the matter?'

Not that Ric was vividly interested. The image of Leonor occupied the little space in his mind not flooded by alcohol.

'D'you recall me harping on about *The Sea Cloud*? My father announcing a surprise – then telling us that, the iconic vessel no longer in service, he had booked us on this ship instead?'

Ricardo did. He also remembered how embarrassed he had felt to be, once more, once again, invited by Mr Vich. He further remembered Aleana laughing. 'No thanks, Hector. I'd rather pay for my own passage and invite Nush. She's been cut off. Her American mother's angry that she's not the Vassar girl she hoped for, and her father, a Poniatowski, incensed that she won't study law like her brothers, let alone learn Polish.'

The voyage was tactfully presented to Ric as an opportunity which he, Hector Vich, had a vested interest in.

'My son shows little interest in the hotel business,' he had said. 'No humanitarian cause, might I add. I've organised one year's employment in the Food & Beverage department of a prestigious hotel. If you do well, boy, the sky's the limit!'

The sky being Hector-The-Great? Ric couldn't help grumbling. How genuine was the man's generosity? But then, one had to sing for one's supper, as cynics say – with reasonable doubt, lest cynicism didn't exist.

Anyway, here we were. Ced and Ric in one of the 400 or so first-class spacious cabins, Nush and I in the opposite one, and Georg Langon further along the corridor.

'So?'

'So. D'you also recall me having dreamt for years about a transatlantic cruise to New York? About stealing the silly pistachio ice-cream cone brandished by the Statue of Liberty?'

'Man, why don't you save it for later? At least it'll be more interesting that what those awful Italians have to say.'

Abruptness. A trait Ric and I shared, among very few others indeed. Were our characters antipodal, I sometimes wondered? Never for long.

Over dinner, Ced could no longer refrain himself:

'I was so lucky as to have been invited into the Captain's quarters. He was second-in-command aboard the *Sea Cloud*!' he exclaimed. 'Can you believe it?'

Her antenna for imperceptible pain alert, Nush echoed:

'Do tell, dearest!'

Given his cue, Ced grabbed it hastily.

'Originally named the *Hussar*, she was the largest private four-master ship, with 3000 sq. feet of canvas. Built in 1931 in times already committed to steam and diesel, the vessel was conceived in the spirit of the great sailing ships of the nineteenth century. Imagine her voyages to the Caribbean, the Galápagos, Alaska and Hawaii, her decks now wandered about by iguanas, now by polar bears! Stalin's foreign minister, the Kings of Sweden or Belgium, the inevitable Wallis Windsor counted amongst the guests.'

Ricardo nearly dozed off while Cedric, eyes half-closed, described seamen balancing on ropes 150 feet above the sea, furled sails tumbling loose while ferocious winds lashed…

The Italian couple made their usual noisy entrance, waving around as if they were hosting the party. They sat down as Ced was describing the ship's later reputation as a 'floating bordello' when Trujillo's playboy son Ramfis roamed the Californian coasts flanked by Zsa Zsa Gabor and more characters with dubious rings, wigs, whatever.

'Ramfis!' exclaimed the fat Countess, enraptured. 'How very amusing for a South American dictator to name his son after a Pharaoh, don't you think *amorrrrre*?'

'How right you are, *bellissima*! He must have gotten it a bit wrong, but then what's the difference between Ramses and Ramfis in a banana republic!'

'Republic?' twitted the wife. 'How can a republic be ruled by a dictator?'

'Don't worry your adorrrrable head,' beamed the husband, patting the Countess' hand and nearly cutting his hand as he grazed her golf-ball-sized diamond.

Studying the menu, he had the politeness to mumble, 'You were saying, young man?'

'Talking about the *Sea Cloud*, sir. About to say how, chased across the ocean at gunpoint after Trujillo's assassination in

'61, the formerly named *Angelina* was abandoned east of the Panama Canal, see? Years of legal disputes later, invaded by moss, oxide destroying her brass, she was returned to the Kiel shipyards where she had been built almost 50 years earlier. Were it not stranded for repairs, we could have cruised on her! It was under *our* Captain's command! Can you believe it?'

The Countess looked baffled. What Captain? A man who hadn't even invited them, the aristocracy of Bellaggio, to his table? *Che vergogna!* Especially if the old man was somewhat of a legend!

Yawning at the table wasn't too subtly repressed.

'Dear boy! You evoke a style that went out of fashion with débutante balls and the foxtrot, light-ages away from the behemoths as mesmerising as multi-level car parks!' croaked the Italian.

Ced bit his thumb's fingernail, as sure a sign of impatience as his father's watch-rubbing.

'In a day and age where air travel dominates due to its cost-effectiveness, ocean liners would have become relics,' the Count continued perorating, 'had the Cunard Line not have designed a splendid ship such as this – running at the same speed as [blablabla], using half the fuel, [blabla], sleek and purposeful, and furthermore a two-class liner instead of three [bla]…'

'*Ma tesorrrro*', his wife cut in, as bored as the rest of us, 'how come the cruise takes six days instead of four?'

'Do you read, signora?' snapped Ricardo, now awake and kicking. 'That she would sail via Cork was mentioned in the brochure, on the tickets, probably in the newspapers. Besides, six days on Cunard Line's best ship won't kill you, alas.'

'Alas? What does that mean, caro?'

'Ala + s, that's you, dove dearest: more than one wing, the young man compared you to…'

'A *palomita*? How charrrrming!'

The Countess extended an ecstatic arm towards Ricardo. It hung in the air for a while. Her husband turned to Nush:

'Talking about Pharaohs, are your ancestors Egyptian? Well, what with that pitch-black hair cut Nefertiti-style, your parchment skin, the almond-shaped green eyes, cheekbones, the...'

'My *what* skin?' our friend exploded.

'Smooth, my dear, smooth is what my darrrrling husband means', the Countess crooned with feminine solidarity.

Dog, thought I. Another four evenings with these operetta cretins?

Hmm, thought Ricardo. What if I knocked on Leonor's door, presenting a bottle of champagne? No. Too banal. Strawberries? With cream?

Where the hell is Georg? thought Nush. Okay, I was a bit rude, not to say rudely dismissive this afternoon, but hey. He's grown-up.

Cedric was practising not to think. Not easy. Half his trunk was filled with books about Buddhism. Teaching one we are but star-dust in a celestial melody; mindfulness a source of enlightenment in accord with the cosmos, cosmos synonymous with order, and that ... to hell with it!

Trunks. They reminded him of Ric as they embarked on the *QE2*. First-class passengers being helped with their golf-bags, hat-boxes, manicured pets and impeccable teeth. Many second-class passengers were heaving their belongings down the gangways. Impervious to the Babelian tumult, Ric, dressed in an attire his uncle-the-tailor must have reproduced from some sepia photograph, looked grotesquely overdressed amidst tennis-sweaters thrown over linen shirts hanging over baggy trousers. What was he, Cedric, to do? Nush and Aleana feigned not to notice. Ric did. He rushed away from sight, probably blushing, presumed Ced, filled with guilty compassion.

This, now, was their third evening aboard the *QE2*.

Torpor had spread over its passengers as insidiously as a snake. The old-fashioned orchestra enhanced the sense of time rewound, slow-motion.

Not true for all.

Ricardo knocked on Leonor's cabin door, empty-handed.

She let him in. No hat. No turban. No sunshades.

In fact, other than crimson lipstick, very little.

8 – II

THE CRUISE

(July of '75 – Ping Pong or Zoo?)

How am I to know what happened in Leonor's cabin the night Ric was let in? I don't. But imagination is allowed some licence, right?

So: Leonor opens the door. She looks statuesque and at the same time, vulnerable. Did she expect him? Let's say she does. Ric feels strangely calm. They talk, delaying the urgency of turbulent desire. She says things like, 'I feel as though my life were a swing pushed back and forth by successive men'; or 'It's torture to know what you want when there're so many choices'; or 'I capitulated to drugs and booze quite young and still do, once in a while'; or 'I'm smart, not intelligent, you know? With nothing to lose, fear was the first to go.'

Her almost transparent tunic reveals her body's curves. By then, the mini-bar is empty. She opens wide the bay window of her sumptuous suite. The marmoreal sky reflects on an oily sea. 'Want some music?' No. He circles the space, jumpy as a thoroughbred at the gate. All he wants is to devour her enticing lips.

'Why don't you dare?' she teases.

Ric has fucked around. He's no puppy. But never has he made what is, for lack of a better word, called love.

Kissing Leonor feels like undressing her. He unbuttons his shirt and presses his chest against her bare back. The sensation is electrifying. So is the silence. They both hold their breaths. He holds the red-golden mane of her hair with one hand and with the other, caresses her neck. His fingertips move downwards until, kneeling, he turns her around. With his tongue, he continues his cautious exploration, something he had never done nor dreamt of before.

Leonor remains motionless. After what seems a fragment of eternity, he deposits her on the bed as one would a fragile statue. Unexpectedly, she bursts into laughter. Is she mocking him? No.

'I laugh when I'm happy, you know? Rather primitive, I know…'

What follows is porn minus the vulgarity. Having bitten his nipples, ears and neck, she licks his penis. They play the beauty and the beast in half-savage, half-tender ways. Later, breathless, ablaze and wet, they let their skins cool down a little, lying on the crumpled bed, limbs intertwined. After a while Leonor knots a towel around her waist and looks at Ric, her grey eyes pensive.

'Don't tell me I could be your son,' he giggles with the silly beatitude of the amorous.

Sleep overcomes her, hair spread on the pillow, slender arms on the sheets. Ric feels confused. She looks so waif-like, so unlike the woman who has displayed high-voltage eroticism. Torn in between the desires to protect and to rape her, he contemplates the clouds furrow through the night.

Later, they make love without haste. This time, Leonor also comes. Or does she? How to be sure? Suddenly it's dawn and she's gone.

On the deck, wrapped in a shawl, her scarf, hat and shades in place, Leonor shivers under the blazing sun. How long since she has surrendered so unconditionally to pleasure, in a profane yet chaste way? With a total stranger? Well. Almost.

Not only could Ricardo be her son, but he's her son's best friend.

Cedric was light-years away from suspecting any of this. He spent as much time as possible with the Captain. His curiosity about the ship, all ships in fact, was insatiable. After three days, he had acquired an encyclopaedic knowledge about yards, tonnages, machinery, engines, the differences between RMS, MV or MS designations, fuel varieties and so on. The Captain also indulged in colourful reminiscences, real or imaginary, of the *France* and the *Normandie*, keeping Cedric enthralled.

Of course, he had noticed his pal spending his nights elsewhere. Poker? Women? Why care? Before dinner, when not reading his Buddha stuff, he'd hang out at the bar with Nush, Leonor and me; then, with Leonor only. But my impatience must not get abreast of events.

Nush had tried, in vain, to rekindle Georg Langon's attention. Vexed, he had transferred it to a young Cuban (a he). Equally vexed, she decided to sketch a series of portraits and in so doing, met some interesting characters: a dainty old lady who had been a close friend of Beryl Markham, the celebrated Kenyan aviatrix; a former chef from Maxim's who adopted Gatsbyish airs; the inevitable caricature old families seem to breed, waxed bandit moustache under which drinks disappeared in quick succession and an affability which made one clinch your handbag included.

Most strikingly, a rare specimen called Elaine.

We had noticed her in the dining-room, surrounded by a happy, decent, normal family. Her plain, heart-shaped face had the kind of unnerving innocence of people who smile too much. Nush sketched her in red chalk, a spasm of disgust twisting her lips.

'Why on earth did you do *that*?'

'Third eye', she wanly answered.

Again, Nush scared me. She clicked her fingers, summoning a waiter. Not her style. What was going on?

The Italians had been removed from our table, *grazie a Dio.* The Countess spent her afternoons in the beauty-salon (waste of money); her husband, playing bridge (ditto), a Havana in one hand, a glass of port at close reach. 'Any game or sport that makes conversation impossible and dull wives tolerable is fine with me,' he confided sotto voce. Wink.

Ric? Exuding self-confidence. Belying the adage *chance en amour, malchance au jeu,* he was winning like crazy at poker. Lavish bouquets of white roses were delivered to a certain suite...

Leonor taught him passion without the encumbrance of sentiment. She also taught him physical synchronicity, symbiosis, synergy. The nervous attraction of the first encounter mutated into something more subtle, somewhat kinky. She'd produce a leash; handle him like a dog and pour champagne into a bowl for him to lap. Their skins had found an understanding their minds challenged. It was complicated but, based on complicity, not exactly perverse. It was about limits and transgression – my subjects of choice, as Mr Johan had once remarked.

Ric's personality, and, dare I say, existence, would be forever marked.

The evening before our reaching New York, Leonor made her move.

As observant as I – perhaps explaining her dislike of me – she was moved by Nush's melancholia, coated as it was with pearly laughs. Her guess? Nush would become a woman doomed to smother with the intensity of her clashing emotions. Approaching one of her canvases, she had been enraptured.

'Young lady, blue moons do exist: a blue moon is a second full moon in the same month. Did you know that Buzz Aldrin's maiden name was Moon?' Then, without transition:

'Would you help me?'

Sure, shrugged Nush.

Afterwards, she wasn't too sure she should have.

Dragged by Nush into the not yet opened bar smelling of stale cigars, annoyed at having his meditation ritual interrupted, Cedric sat down. Leonor removed scarf, hat, and sunglasses. Her grey eyes embraced the boy for a long while, without a word.

He squinted. Then gasped. Then raced outside, running in circles.

I watched Nush watching. I also imagined Ric, a bottle of Scotch rolling under his bed.

Only minutes later, Cedric bolted through the bar's glass doors like a space module re-entering atmosphere.

I dragged Nush away.

'Time for a game of ping pong, what do you say, old girl?'

'Why not head for the zoo, spinster sister?'

'Oh! Might I have forgotten to mention I lost my virginity to the Omani steward?'

'What?' Nush jumped. 'Wow! How was it?'

'Compared to – fucking what???'

We burst into uncontrollable laughter.

9

HECTOR VICH,
UNPLUGGED

Leonor took her son to Nantucket, her home since child-hood. Anyone who listened to her liquid voice would have marked her as Irish-born; her immigrant parents were, but she'd been made to feel American at heart.

The villa was superb. Bohemian chic to the minutest of details. A vast garden, elegantly neglected and scattered with dog kennels, sloped down to the billowy ocean.

Cedric's room had been awaiting him, he realised with a very un-Buddhist surge of emotion. It was decorated like a ship's cabin: navy-blue sofas, mahogany furniture and panelling. Even the windows had been redesigned as mock-portholes. Wrapped-up with elaborate ribbons: an antique globe and a compass.

'It is said to have belonged to *Sir* Francis Drake and is for you to keep so that you don't lose your head!' Leonor smiled with that mildly ironic smile of hers.

Ced, thrilled to bits, did not dare hug her. His mother, yes; but remote all the same. She had left him and his father ages ago, hadn't she?

She was careful. Took it step by step. Left him alone when feeling he wanted to be. Sometimes he couldn't help thinking, she treats me like a pet that must be domesticated.

Yet Ced liked her. A lot. He also admired her. A lot. God, was she beautiful! Tall, curvy, moving with grace, her voice soothing, her huge eyes peaceful. Her poise, so ladylike; her voice, so soothing.

Leonor mostly wore kaftans, which enhanced the impression that she breezed around, her arms like wings. But nothing compared to her hands on the piano. Beethoven only.

'Darling, there are five piano concertos and thirty-two piano sonatas! Enough for a lifetime, at least mine.'

'I thought the guy was deaf,' Ced ventured.

Her eyes a sad shade of grey, Leonor murmured:

'True. But the hearing problems didn't start until he was in his mid-thirties. Up to then, he had had plenty of time to compose masterpieces and to fall in love with some Josephine – the love of his life. She married another.'

Leonor massaged her fingers.

'How come he became death?'

'Deaf, *farling*, not death,' she laughed, seemingly addressing her favourite dog, a rather daunting Alsatian.

'Beethoven suffered from acute tinnitus. It's when your ears are invaded by continuous buzzing. Probably compounded by typhus. Back in the 1790s you were advised to immerse your head in cold water.'

'Jesus! Know the refrain, "Dear Doctor, what we die of is not the disease / What we die of, dear Doctor, are the remedies"?'

Leonor stiffened: 'No blasphemy in this house! I'm Catholic. And no jokes about medicine, in whichever…'

Regretting having raised her voice no sooner she'd spoken, Leonor lowered it.

'Honey, it just so distresses me. Beethoven contemplated suicide. At the première of the Ninth Symphony, in Vienna, he could no longer hear the applause. The vibrations of his own music were transmitted by a contraption in his mouth, teeth and ears being, imagine… There's a biography in your room. Do read it.'

Mother and son hugged, for the first time ever.

After a few days, they fell into the habit of going for a two-hour walk before lunch. They'd talk – well, she did most of the talking.

He learnt:

that she had been miserable as a child, her parents fighting incessantly, her sister jealous and hateful, her school-grades awful, provoking endless remonstrations;

that she had discovered smoking 'grass' early in life as a means of putting a distance between her socialite, WASPish surroundings and herself – then been jailed for a week by the local sheriff on her father's prompting;

that she had then turned to drinking, same motive, it being 'a legal drug';

that she had never been interested in boys, really. All her love-sickness had been directed at dogs – 'not only man's best friends, but lonely girls' too';

that she had, aged twenty, been sent to Switzerland to what was then called a finishing school, and hated it. One day, she met a handsome, very handsome, boy, slightly older than she. They smoked pot together. He seduced her because he lied very imaginatively. 'Your father was a mythomaniac and remained one for so long as I know. Did he tell you…

that he's a self-made man? His own father had been a hotelier somewhere in the Alps, then in Geneva. His wife discovered he betrayed her. Out of vengeance or despair – both? – she proceeded to squander whatever money there had been. Her sons had become artists: one, a sculptor; Hector, an actor intent on polishing patrician attitudes;

that his career had been a flop, mainly because he was considered arrogant and, to worsen matters, an intellectual;

that when they married, she had been madly in love but he,

only mildly. She had not told Hector how rich her family was. He had never told her how dire his own straits were, lavishing her with presents, hence accumulating debts. A marriage made in haste, not headed to heaven;

that Hector became very successful very fast, the hotel business requiring showmanship. To the detriment of their relationship, of course. A child was neither desired nor rejected: Cedric simply occurred. Leonor sought for solace and again found it in the company of dogs. She loved them, always had, always would, what could she say?

What Leonor did not reveal was that Ced had been a twin. His baby brother had died of heart failure minutes after birth. She didn't tell for two reasons. The first was fear, instinctive, motherly fear. The second, Ricardo. Ric, she realised with a shiver and some shame, had been *bound* to happen.

Ced's insomnia, twisted handwriting (while prematurely devoid of orthographic faults) or excellence at chess as a child had been ascribed to 'over-giftedness'. Other quirks enhanced the awed, if puzzled, consensus. Before going to bed he'd lay out clothes for the following morning: trousers, socks, shoes – but always two shirts. He'd divide food in two equal parts; then place the two halves in parallel on his plate. Whatever he bought with his modest pocket-money came in pairs, be it ice-creams (same flavour) or comic-strips. Whereupon he'd offer one of his purchases to whomever happened to be around. Asked to draw a tree, he'd sketch a trunk with identical branches at each side. A house would look birdlike, its two wings facing each other. People (couples) would always be trailed by a shadow – their exact if slanted reproduction. As to sports, Ced would only play games involving two partners – never team-games.

The Binary Boy, as he became nicknamed, remained solitary.

He had no friends. When asked why, he'd answer (not conceitedly, for modest he had always been): too thin, too tall, too blonde, too … something or other. Translation: too different from me. (Until Le Rosey and Ricardo, his near-clone.)

Leonor, the beholder of his unknown secret, had understood only too well. But she chose to leave.

Did I? she wondered.

Did she? wondered Cedric, watching her frail silhouette chiselled against the dark clouds in the distance. Did she not escape from a life that made her feel lonely all over again?

Badness me! she sighed. Twins. Ric. Have I allowed myself to sleep with a symbol?

Shit, sighed Ced. Doesn't my mother realise that I know her meetings with the gaucho gardener have nothing to do with plants? That Beethoven at all hours fulfils the same purpose? A fight against the *deaf-sentence* of solitude?

Time to go.

Packing, 'Hotel California's lyrics surfaced to his mind:

> We are programmed to receive
> You can check-out any time
> But you can never leave

The Eagles had deliberately written this as a double-entendre. Eagles!

10

NEW YORK

August 1975.
When Cedric walked into the suite put at our disposal (it was low season), he gaped.

I'd dedicated ten days to beauty-salons, hairdressers and shopping: my long hair was now permed and highlighted, my skin glowed under sophisticated make up and my turquoise eyes scintillated from beneath extended eyelashes. I was wearing a sleek dress and high heels. I had also gained weight, having discovered Eggs Benedict and binged on them. When had he ever seen me without leggings, sneakers or a soap-scrubbed face?

'Where's Ric?'

'Search me,' I shrugged.

'Wouldn't mind a body search,' Ced retorted cheekily.

'Haha. Well. Ric's become a TV addict. Hardly leaves his room other than to go to the fitness centre.'

Limp in a deep armchair, Ced ordered a bottle of Chablis and smiled. Those Vichs were bloody good-looking, no question.

'What's new other than revamping, Al?'

Where to start? I explored the city's mosaic-like, mammoth mess inasmuch as safety and the scorching heat had permitted, and was over-bubbling with impressions.

'Right beneath our windows, the Central Park Zoo. Its polar bear is legendary. Being me, all I can see are the bars... Forgotten when you clap eyes upon Time-Life building! Or

Grand Station! Ced! The Broadway shows! Museums and art-galleries with Nush! One becomes totally daunted by the oversized dimensions of everything. She hates the street system's grid and the centipede limousines. Yet she likes the Circle Line boats and bullied me into taking various rides with her. A bit boring, really, had we not come across an extraordinary couple... You'll meet them tonight!'

The wine made me loquacious. Glad for someone with whom to share my enthusiasm, I paced the room, milling my arms.

'Stepping out of this air-conditioned hotel is like diving into chemical vapour. It gauzes your sight! The neurotic effervescence is so thrilling you forget about discomforts. And at dawn – Ced, am I boring you?'

'No! You should write all that down.'

I had, of course. But talking isn't the same. Couldn't stop.

'Vibrant as it may be, this place is also spooky. But then! Then you go to Battery Park early in the morning and there, you really realise this is an island.'

This re-captured his attention. Islands were Cedric's passion.

Eggs Benedict were wheeled into the suite – they knew me by now.

'Where was I? Yes. Battery Park, a gazebo of sorts. Atlantic liners used to berth there. You can still imagine the muffled hoots... As the mist clears, it's like the printing of a Polaroid...'

My mention of islands had taken him back to the island of Nantucket. Heaths full of berry bushes and scrub oak, the town's Main Street, a mix of monumental houses with brick chimneys lining cobblestoned streets; lighthouses beyond the dunes and former whale-tanks – all of it composing a naïve painting, had it not been for the presence of his far from naïve mother.

How had she reacted to his precipitous departure? Though

Leonor knew where he'd been heading and Ced, her telephone number, both knew that neither would contact the other.

Missed opportunities? Sensing melancholy, I changed course.

'On a lighter note: can you imagine they sell ice-creams with bubble-gum flavour here? I mean, how *yak* can it get! Greasy hamburgers, watery coffee, chlorine-tasting water, *ouch*! I was brought up in France, remember?'

'Jesus Al, stop saying *remember*! It's a tiresome tic. We might drink like sailors but aren't brain-dead!'

Fair enough, but hey! I was seventeen. Stunned. Curious. Enthralled. So I indulged my élan, ignoring the rebuttal.

'Jazz clubs! Street artists! Soho! Meeting Rockefellers, Truman Capote, Gore Vidal, Andy Warhol or Tom Wolfe either at the "21" or at the "54"? How *wow* can this get?!'

'Who on earth took you to such places?'

Tell him about the Omani steward on the *QE2* who had turned out to be a student at Colombia University and the son of a well-to-do architect?

Fortuitously, Ricardo walked through the door. The boys slapped each other on the back, but one could see that Ric's heart wasn't in it.

'Hi man!' he coughed. 'How's everything?'

His friend, spontaneous as ever, told him about Nantucket, his bedroom, the walks on the beach, the conversations, dogs and all.

The 'all' made Ric react like a tarantula: Ced's tale had ended with a mention of his mother's 'toy-boys', whereupon he tossed the novel *Lady Chatterley's Lover* on the coffee-table.

'I now call her Lady L,' he smirked.

Dog Almighty. Music seemed the answer. I picked up my guitar and started playing some Django Reinhardt.

Salvation no. 2: Hector Vich. He too walked in without

knocking, delighted at seeing the constellation he was used to.

'Having a good time?'

Clearly he had no idea that his son had only just appeared, let alone where he had been. He might, of course, have garnered information from his employees at the hotel – not his style.

More wine. HV didn't seem to notice Ricardo's gloom. Ced made a persuasive job repeating what I had told him about New York, cheeky bastard. As his father turned to me – had he noticed my metamorphosis? – Nush walked in.

'Wonderful evening to you!' she cried out, arms extended.

Such joviality was utterly out of character.

Taking her aside I whispered, please calm down, we have what the Yanks call a bit of a *situation* here.

'No sweat, sweetie-pie.'

Fiddling with his watch, Hector Vich said:

'See you kids at dinner downstairs. Eight sharp.'

'Whaaat?' Nush fluted, definitely tipsy. 'Tonight, I'm inviting. The Algonquin. Pleeease, charming Prince, Knight in White *Amour!*'

Hector displayed a semblance of resistance, clearly amused. Flattery would get anyone anywhere with him.

'Dah-hr-lings', Nush continued, 'I've sold my first painting! For many dollars, oil-barrels, whatever! And do you know who to? Well, to THE Robert Mapplethorpe!' (Here she tripped over.) 'Oops!'

Ric was stumped. Mapplethorpe was one of the art market's superstars.

'Congratulations!' Hector waved. 'See you in the lobby.'

I dragged Nush to our bathroom and practically pushed her under an icy shower. Though happy for her, I was annoyed. Being my parents' daughter, like it or not, undignified behaviour did not amuse me.

The Algonquin, on the Upper West side, evoked Scott Fitzgerald, Dorothy Parker *et al* gathered at the famous Round Table. A different planet from Regine's (where the middle-class meets the middle-east, my Omani boyfriend had remarked. His snobbishness become unbearable, I had stopped answering his calls. Let him ride Gucci-hoofed camels).

Where was I? Yes. The Algonquin. Worn-out crimson velvet seats. Dimmed lights. Monocled, bow-tied waiters. To Nush's distress, Mapplethorpe was nowhere in sight. But the couple we had met on the Circle Line boat had turned up.

Marian Goodman's tone was guarded but warm. 'Some people are born naturally confident but I'm not,' the youngish woman who would become a grande dame among art dealers mumbled. Nush acted diffidently.

'Any advice would seem a step too far toward intimacy,' Richard Leakey teased, reaching for Marian's diminutive hand. 'But her taste is forged, believe you me!'

'Luck, my dear, is essential… Good health and bad memory help!'

Luck. *Le bonheur de malheurs évités se compose…*

I discovered that Leakey was heavily involved in Kenya's politics and he, that I was passionate about the country. 'Where we will meet again, Aleana!' he said, in his colonially inflected British.

Hector Vich remained uncharacteristically silent. Jet-lagged?

He would, later, confess he'd watched me all evening and thought, this girl's a ticking bomb.

It had begun to rain. Well: buckets of torrential water were hissing down the window-panes.

'Don't worry,' smiled Marian. 'At this time of the year, New York can be strangely tropical.'

She glanced at Hector. Though not touching his watch, he looked itchy.

'Paying the bill is the only sure way of escape,' he whispered cheek-to-cheek.

Which he did.

'Please excuse us,' he said, holding my coat.

Nush, always as pale as her outfit, spilt a glass of red wine.

'Who'd you think you are, other than a rude cash-machine?' she howled, drunk as a skunk.

'Better nouveau-riche than never rich,' Hector Vich snarled.

Without more ado, he took my arm and led me out of the revolving door.

On the soaked pavement, he heaved with relief.

'Ever saw the movie *Singin' in the Rain*?'

'Who hasn't?'

'Always your suave self, aren't you?'

'Sorry.'

'Better sad...'

'... than safe!'

He laughed and opened an umbrella that would have sheltered elephants. I trotted beside him. The scurry of people, the swish of cars slaloming among pothole puddles and plumes of geyser-like steam rising from the subway, all reminded me of my favourite painter, the painter of urban solitude.

This I told Hector. His reaction was unexpectedly emotional.

'Hopper... I knew him quite well.'

'Tell me!' I entreated, my aloofness down the – drain.

'OK, but let's sit in one of those B-movie bars, for a change!'

He did not say this in a vexing way. I nevertheless felt put back in my place: the spoilt-brat palace, as it were. Belonging to him, most probably.

Disregarding the traffic lights, we ran towards the first neon-lit place which looked open.

'She's my morally retarded daughter,' he told a barman scrutinising my face.

The guy twinkled knowingly and served two whisky-cokes as required.

11

HECTOR'S
ACHILLES' HEEL

'*Bon.* For reasons too tedious to get into, I was dispatched to my maternal grandmother's. A Baptist American granny with a taste ranging from pistachio-green to baby-pink. She lived in Gloucester, Massachusetts.'

Some pain-in-the-neck asked for *a bottle* of brandy. 'Half-drunk's a waste of money,' he slurred. (Where had I heard that before?)

'Do you take American Express?' enquired Hector, dead serious.

Having flummoxed the insolent intruder, he resumed.

'Aleana, America back then was another planet. America in the fifties, aged fifteen? After Switzerland? Wow, as you would say.'

(Have I mentioned that I had learnt karate? Well. When the pain-in-the-neck gave it a third try and snatched my glass in the process, I floored him. Hector didn't blink.)

'You were saying?'

'That my elder brother was spared the forced exile. Sculpture his passion, he asked me to investigate the art-scene if possible. It was. Among my grandmother's first guests were Edward Hopper and his wife Dorothy.'

Wow, I refrained from exclaiming.

'They had been married for almost thirty years. Pacific estrangement had replaced fusional passion. But the sense of humour was intact – and, darling girl, you will discover one day that this is what probably most matters… "Talking to Eddie is like dropping a stone into a well, except that it doesn't thump" she teased. He laughed. For some reason or other we started talking about boats. He'd been brought up in Upper Nyack and his knowledge of nautical subjects was mind-blowing. By the way, have you noticed that Ced has also been bitten by the bug? Ships and all that?'

'How old was he?'

'Who? Sorry. Hopper. Sixty something. Could have been my grandfather. Just as I could be your father, right?'

His eyes weren't paternal; that much I knew.

'I saw Hopper a few times afterwards. Following the large-scale retrospective of his work at the Museum of Modern Art, excessively solicited, he became a recluse bent on increasingly poignant depictions of desolate landscapes, silent spaces, lonely people… In some interview he lamented spending his days going to bad movies or reading crap instead of painting. A self-disparaging remark to get journalists off his back? His standards were too high… or rather his much younger wife's?'

Hector's hitherto animated face became still.

'Dorothy died shortly after Ed. The cause? Foggy.'

I considered asking him about Leonor. Better not. Ask him to tell more about his youth? Bingo! Fifth gear in half a second.

'What more exciting time or place to be alive than in the fifties as a teenager? Where 5 percent of humans had more wealth than the other 95 combined! The confidence, Aleana! Americans were candid, all of them: marvelling at progress and the future it held! Soon they would have underwater cities, space colonies, atomic trains, moving sidewalks, gyrocopters and … ice boxes! When you bought a new appliance, be it a toaster or a waffle-iron, you'd invite the neighbours to see it.'

His smile became, well, boyish. Sweet!

'Gadgets, big or small, were the rage! It was a kid's world: we were everywhere. Unsupervised and harmless. No seat belts, airbags, helmets, smoke detectors, or safety caps on medicine. It was assumed we knew that bleach was not a juice and that gasoline, in contact with a match, a bad idea. Sugar gave energy; red meat was full of iron and ice cream, of calcium. X-rays were so benign that shoe stores installed them to measure sizes. Cigarettes? Nicotine, like alcohol, soothed the nerves. I still remember billboards – billboards! – showing L&M cigarette-packs with the slogan, "Just what the doctor ordered!" Can you imagine?'

Which reminded Hector to light a fag and order more drinks.

'And then, television! I could tell you volumes about television… My friends and I saved two weeks of pocket-money, persuaded to be the first to receive colour TV. It was sent to the ad agency, a moving ceremony at the local post office, also the grocery shop. Well! Imagine our surprise upon receiving a thin envelope containing a plastic sheet divided into red, green and blue columns: "If you stick that onto your TV screen, you belong to the happy few to see it in colour!" the laconic letter explained.'

Hector laughed like the defrauded fifteen-year-old kid he had been upon realising the joke had been on him.

'Automobiles! You drove into restaurants, movies, banks, whatever, for the sheer pleasure of sitting in *your* car… It was all at hand, you know? Jobs, credit, music, bagels! Even travelling. Bear in mind that aeroplanes remained vastly expensive until the sixties. As for sex, ha!'

Again, nostalgically starry-eyed:

'Our excitement at stealing catalogues depicting women (light-years before *Playboy*-centrefolds) showing their girdles with a half-naughty, half-guarded smile! Bras looked like chastity-belts moved up a few levels … Jesus!'

Just to say something, I said, 'Well, he had little to do with it, did he?' Proving once more I should shut up more often.

Unexpectedly, a lone tear vacillated on his eyelid.

'The simplicity of desire, Aleana… The simplicity of desire! To be so happy with so little!'

In the penumbra of that bar, it crossed my mind that what Hector Vich lacked in terms of darker colours (remember my *penchant* for the bronzed skin-types?) he more than made up in other shades: from the azure, the radiant sort, to the ultramarine when he had the blues, the deep sort.

I put my hand on his. It felt warm but tense. Sitting on a rickety stool, his legs crossed, he did not jiggle his free foot. I liked that. People who twitch their feet drive me nuts.

'Ah, Aleana', he resumed, composed again, 'I could tell you so much more… The movie – palaces! One got much more dressed up than people do to go to the opera nowadays! Such a treat… John Wayne! Lana Turner! Ronald Reagan! Clark Gable! Well. Of course, there also was the paranoiac fear of communism, of the nuclear bomb, with Korea and all that…'

Without transition:

'I've never seen such slender and gracious hands as yours. Too bad they contrast with your indomitable, rotten character!'

Our eyes intertwined and our arms locked, we stepped out of the gritty bar. No more rain.

A few steps later, I exclaimed, 'Shit! We forgot your mega-sized umbrella!'

'So what? Do I look like a banker?'

12

BEING, THE BEGINNING
OF BECOMING

I t's September 15ᵗʰ 1975. Our last evening in New York.
Hector Vich flies back to Geneva. No goodbyes.

Ced, Nush, Ric and I do the tritest thing: up the Empire
State Building, we swear to meet at the very same place in
exactly one year. (What's the melodrama with Cary Grant and
prim-and-proper Deborah Kerr called? It'll come back to me.)

Encouraged by Marian Goodman, Nush decides to stay in
New York to pursue painting. With offers of introductions to
Roy Lichtenstein, Franz Kline and the like, Nush can't believe
her blessing.

The School of Journalism in Paris has accepted me. At
Christmas, turned eighteen, I'd be able to sell my late parents'
belongings. Then the world would be my lobster – haha.

Cedric decides nothing. Does he hope for a call from his
mother? Ric encourages him to fulfil his dream: go Greek
island-hopping. His father vetoes the plan. His son is to study
the Hellenistic world first.

Ric? Hector Vich, as aforementioned, had organised a job
for him as the F&B assistant in another Madison Avenue
hotel. A first step, but no small one, towards the responsibility
and recognition he had craved since adolescence. A token of
trust, he trusted it to be an homage to his trustworthiness. A
poker-player, he resolves to play his cards right.

Hector Vich's no fool. He produces a joker – a black one: Leona Hemy. Other than having lost prime property in a legal battle ('Shit happens and clean Switzerland produces plenty,' she had declared in a press release), she resents Vich for having divorced a woman on the grounds of her excessive love for dogs. It is known that she has drawn a will leaving the bulk of her fortune to a canine foundation. Her own pet is called Taxi. She loves to summon him when walking in a park or on some beach.

In her mid-fifties, her ego as inflated as the boy's ambition, she's a feared personality. Above a stout body, her square-jawed, ice-cold face makes decryption impossible. She's also a hotelier known for her bossy streak, rough language, and weakness for dandies. She takes an immediate liking to him. (Leona? How close a name to Leonor, thinks Ric. Her dog-mania adds irony to coincidence.)

The tycooness seizes Ricardo with velvet-gloved claws. 'I'll eat him for breakfast when the time comes.' Meanwhile she'd use him to collect damaging information about HV. The latter thinks likewise. Both know that Ricardo's no babe, adding titillation to the game of double-deceit – triple, perhaps, were the boy to play one against the other.

He's an opportunist, that much is clear, but he's not a bad sort. While the going is good, he mostly wants to move on. Learn. Food and beverage he soon ticks off. Maintenance soon bores him too: understood. But finances – that's something else! Especially when turned into what's called creative accountancy: 'cooking the books'.

He will climb ladders fast but forget how to walk in the process.

One year later: September 15th, 1976.
Empire State Building.

Nush, Ced and I had prepared a festive picnic. French champagne, Swiss Vacherin, and so on. When Ric appeared, so late Nush's eyes had welled up with tears, we had trouble in hiding our shock. He looked exhausted and emaciated. He didn't marvel at the postcard sunset or beam at his school-friends.

'This building belongs to my boss.'

'Is that supposed to a hello of some sort of…?' sniffed Nush. I was stunned.

'*This* place, owned by *one* person?'

'Yeah.'

Finally, Ric relaxed and after an hour or so, we were happily giddy and giggling like in not so old times.

His last year was told in more or less the same terms as above. We wondered about the Hector vs. Leona bit and the implicit conflict in loyalty it implied, but the ever-protective Cedric gestured us not to ask.

We had been studying in Paris – he at the Sorbonne, me at the School of Journalism. Paris was a long story, too long to tell right now. Ced's view of it was photographic and day-lit; mine, of a more underground nature. I'm a night-bird and a jazz fan.

Nush's adventures were by far the most colourful – as a painter's should be. (Oh. Have I mentioned that she had 'inherited' my sexy Omani flirt?) It was Ali who introduced her to Peter Brook. She being a Polish princess and he the son of Jewish immigrants from Latvia, their first encounter was … frosty. But her good-natured charm soon seduced the maverick theatre director. Marian Goodman, herself of Hungarian origins, made sure it would. Brook was preparing a film, *Meetings with Remarkable Men*, based on the book by the Greek-Armenian mystic, G. I. Gurdjieff. It would star Terence Stamp, among others. Would she help designing the sets?

How far from a severe, stifling upbringing in Vienna could

you get? At merely twenty? Though shy as ever, Nush had acquired a halo of joyous optimism.

'D'you know that Peter produced *Salome* at the Royal Opera House in London some years ago – with sets by Salvador Dalí? Dalí! And now, he asks me to…'

The four of us embraced and started dancing in a circle, singing 'Lady Marmalade' at the top of our voices:

> *Voulez-vous coucher avec moi, ce soir,*
> *Voulez-vous coucher avec moi?*
> *Gutchi gutchi yaya, gutchi gutchi dada*
> *micha chocolate yaya !!!!!!*

The lift-boy told us it was time to go. Ric helped me re-pack the picnic basket.

'Can we talk alone somewhere?' he whispered conspiratorially.

13

TRISKAIDEKAPHOBIA

The irrational fear of the number 13
=
Chapter skipped.

14

IRIS

It happened as Ric travelled to Paris via Madrid to negotiate some deal or other.

'Ambling around Barajas airport, I spot a spectacular redhead sitting in the bar facing the duty-free shop. A bit too skinny ... apart from her boobs,' he grinned, throwing a sidelong glance at my décolleté. Thanks.

'Elegant in a non-logo-label way, somewhere in her twenties, a look of bored affluence, strikingly pale with almond-shaped eyes. These were gazing at the ceiling. Weird, but I like weird.' Ric lit his second cigar – since when did he smoke these nasty things?

'Actually, Al: I don't mind steaks cooked medium or rare. I read in three languages without a preference for either. I do prefer the atmosphere of the Vich hotels to those boutique ones, but seriously, give me a down pillow and I'm fine. Italian food? French cuisine? Thai tit-bits? No problem. But when it comes to women, it's redheads only. Leonor's imprint.'

Had he not looked so forlorn, I would have been tempted to remark a) that he liked elder women, his mother having, etc. and b) that he had become one hell of a spoilt brat. What if the pillowcases weren't crisp linen, old chap? And the cigars not Montecristo's, hmm?

'I follow her into the duty-free shop. She meanders around with the demeanour typical of beautiful women: decisive steps, casual attitude, disregard for others. When a sales girl offers help, she politely but adamantly dismisses her. Whilst the girl is harpooned by some guys less interested in purchases than in killing time, the S.R. loses none. She stealthily picks up a perfume, then another; pastes some sort of bandage on the anti-burglary stickers, opens a package of La Prairie make-up and replaces the empty box in the bat of an eyelid; slips an alarm clock from its display into her blazer's pocket with confounding nonchalance and, smiling at the cashier with a steadfast glance, strolls out.'

'Wow!' I exclaimed. (I'd been overdoing the *wowing* lately.)

'Further on, she picks up a few magazines as if assuming the press is hers for the taking and heads towards the boarding gate without so much as looking over her shoulder. Exit the Spectacular Redhead.'

He looks genuinely amused.

'Last call for the flight to Palma de Mallorca. Shit. Mine delayed, as usual with Paris, I examine the mirrors and cameras the S.R. had been observing with what I had assumed a vacuous look. No random venture. Clever girl.'

'But a thief, Ric!'

'Yeah. So what? Aren't we all, one way or another?'

Speak for yourself.

'Anyway, an idea occurs to me. I snatch a scarf from some shelf and rush to the gate. Too late. "D'you know who it belongs to?" the employee asks, running one finger through his spiky hair. I describe the redhead. "*Uyyy?* Miss Iris Banes. She's a frequent, *vamos*, a constant traveller. Does the advertising for Iberia, see?" I flash my most ambiguous smile. "OK, OK." After some computer-clicking, the employee croons, "no problem, *guapo*, we'll send the scarf to Mallorca. To her private address. Who might I ask are you?" "An honest man", I grin, the irony lost on the man wiggling his hips whilst taking my card. Jesus! Why are most of those airline guys homos? And frankly, what are all the cameras for?'

Why bother answering that they're always blind spots? My imagination began racing.

We were sitting outside Mortimer's and noise has always helped me to concentrate. Luckily, Ric was now chatting with acquaintances at the next table.

I try to visualise Iris. A Charlotte Rampling look-alike? Why not? With a matching voice? Let's see.

She's thin but something indefinable suggests it hasn't always been that way. Her abundant red hair is flamboyant: might it be dyed? A pointed chin enhances the impression of determination her keen eyes project.

What makes her steal? It is a game? A challenge? A disease? An antidote to boredom? A revenge? Was she robbed of something essential, at some point? Let's suppose she was very poor – perhaps abandoned? Dropped on the steps of some Scottish convent while winds lash the moors? No. Another try: she's the illegal daughter of a Roman aristocrat who, blackmailed by the Mafia, is forced to ship her off to an Ottoman harem? Just kidding. OK. Let's say she used to be fat, yes, even obese. For whatever reason, she's entrusted to her grandfather, a defrocked priest who lives in Baden-Baden or rather, in its casino – he's a compulsive gambler. Iris' elder brother, Philip, a junkie, is on the run. Addiction runs in the family, and –

No, tztz! Let's now say that Iris grows up with an aunt. Julie, or perhaps Juliette, who has no idea how to handle kids, having had none herself. She's mocked at school. They call her a freak, they call her a whale. The cruelty of kids is no object for speculation. Then there's the piano (or violin) problem: Iris desperately wants one. Her aunt, definitely called Anastasia, won't allow it. She hates what Iris most loves: music. Iris retracts into her world, which is full of anger. Or could it be lyricism? Does she write pamphlets or poems? One way or the other, rebels are loners. Her only male friend is a communist masseur who converts Iris to vegetarianism – if you look long enough, you're bound to find a *rapport* between the Reds and greenery. In order to buy a Steinway (unless it's a Stradivari), she robs a bank.

No-no-no! She's no Bonnie and there's no Clyde: Iris resents men. That contempt boys had shown for her former self was just too hurtful. Fuck them – or rather not, precisely. Will she marry some sugar-daddy all the same? For security's sake? Is that why she's so well-dressed and haughty? I doubt it. Dependency, be it only financial, doesn't match with…

'What on earth are you brooding about, Al?'

'Nothing darling!'

Even at my age (given my background) I know that this answer satisfies most people. Relieved to be ignored, I let my fantasy meander again.

Let's rewind: Iris, we hypothetically established, had been extremely fat. Her aunt, a star-studded cook (at La Goulue in NY? Taillevent in Paris? The Mandarin in Hong Kong?), meaning well, fills her with the very thing that is the source of Iris' problems: food. Iris cannot refuse. Eating is presented as a means to show gratitude. Eventually, finally, mercifully, she is granted a scholarship at university. No longer obliged to sing for her supper, or swallow in order to sing, Iris will starve herself into a size zero. But habit is a bitch: the abundance she now refrains from stuffing into her stomach she'll stuff into her bags or pockets. Then comes an encounter which will make her heart leap or sink, either way, make her coordination disintegrate and life take a turn for the…

'Al!' Ric pulled my sleeve. 'Snap out of it *for a moment*!'

I complied and engaged in a supine conversation.

My imagination, however, was re-ignited upon remembering Hector's nostalgic whisper: 'The simplicity of desire,

Aleana, the simplicity of desire...' I also remembered him quoting Kierkegaard: 'Had I followed my pleasure and chosen what I had a talent for, police spy, I should have been much happier than I afterwards became.'

No philosopher, I decided to help Ric all the same. Not altogether altruistic: I was intrigued. I'd find her.

But then again... Might I also find out that Iris Banes is the third daughter of a completely normal middle-class family, no rape history, no fratricide or other unfortunate mishap? She's never been fat. In fact, her perfect figure catches the attention of a model-scout in Liverpool. She learns to roll her gait and to hold her head high, is successful and well-paid, gives up smoking but not her childhood hobby, stealing turned into a sport, then an irredeemable obsession, in short, into a disease, as are all addictions. Hmm.

15

ACEDIA, AMARK, ALARM

Hector Vich had always resented being tagged 'an intellectual'. When had he first come across the word *acrasia*?

His charismatic English teacher had transformed literature into enthrallment. He had turned The Romantic Catastrophe into a movie featuring the likes of Coleridge, Shelley, Byron – not precisely the sort of protagonists teenagers would be drawn to in terms of plot or suspense. Undaunted, Mr Fox presented poets as other young men worried about unfulfilled aspirations, unkept promises, unachieved desires. 'To any sensitive adolescent, the future's overhung by might-have-beens,' he'd smile. '*Weakness of will* need not be a lifelong curse.'

Might his son, like Hector back then, be haunted by the fear of unworthiness? Embracing uncertainties, content with half-knowledge? Was he pressuring Cedric? Had he made a mistake forbidding him to explore the Greek islands?

'Ced seems devoid of ambition and, generally speaking, of impetus,' he reflected. 'At least, he isn't into drugs, drag-queens or arson.' Something.

Ricardo, in contrast, is the facts and figures type. He knows where he's heading and favours the bee-line. As to Aleana … strange girl. Both daunting and moving. She obviously cringes from showing vulnerability. But then there are her eyes, always a bit sad, always somewhat absent. Does *she* know what she wants? Is she a good influence on Ced, who adores her? Was having been ignored by parents whose love excluded her crippling?

Je te porte dans moi comme un oiseau blessé – the line from an Éluard poem resurfaced in Hector's mind: 'I behold you like a hurt bird.' Wingless, no; her wings were intact, and so were Ced's ... but when and how would they deploy them? Would they ever? Were both teenagers' fertile imaginations disabling in the sense of putting goals and dreams out of the realm of volition? They affronted reality, deprived of affection early in life. Would they long for attention – or crave for what Aleana called 'invisibility'?

Leonor had left when her son was only six, or was it seven? Not only had he, Hector, been absent too frequently thereafter, but pretty unconcerned too. He remembered a tiresome do-gooder-matron inquiring:

'How's your son?'

'Cedric? He's nine, that's how he is.'

'And?'

And nothing. What else? Ced was a kid and that was that, as far as he was concerned. The lady darted him an icy glance and stomped away.

Memories. Doubts. Self-reproaches. Being a father wasn't easy. Nobody claimed it would be. (How, by the way, was Mr ... *Materelli*? No. Moralli. He should call Le Rosey to find out.)

Hector longed for some Vilma or other to help him forget about thinking. He headed to the next bar.

This year, however, no Kenya – nor meeting on the Empire State Building on September 15th. Stuff had happened.

Back at the ranch, or rather in the family château near Bordeaux, I sign all there is to sign in order to sell properties.

By now, it's Easter of 1977.

Ric now works in Leona H's London Park Lane Hotel. She has taken residence there, for tax-avoidance purposes, though she hates the place and the people: exasperatingly polite. The richer the Brits, the dumber, in her opinion. That's one problem; another is the Brits never getting to the point – supposing they get it in the first place.

Bitch, thinks Ric, discarding the thought in a hurry. After all, it's thanks to her that he now lives a life of luxury outside Mr Vich's patronage.

Two events take place at The Hemly Park Lane the first week of September: one a medical congress, the other a Saatchi & Saatchi conference.

'Let me introduce you to Dr Amar Khoury!' Leona squeaks. 'After multiple liftings I'm so cut I need a good paste!'

She emits an ingénue's laugh, outstretching her arms to the handsome thirty-something man wearing a pink cap.

How is she to know that Ricardo Moralli and the surgeon, widely known as AmarK, had met in Kenya two years earlier?

Flying Doctors considered AmarK a pioneer; tribes worshipped him as a magician. Frau Semler, in between 'refreshments', would address him as *Maestro.*

The surgeon had developed new methods for facial restoration. Treating patients with genetic malformations, he realised that the extraction and isolation of certain cells presented a chance for organic development with permanent results. Although the acceptance of stem cell transplants was still years off, their introduction was revolutionary in the mid-seventies, as was the array of possible uses.

In Kenya, these very explorations had done 'miracles' for maimed, handicapped or wounded. Ric recalled a kid suffering from a tumour situated on the orbital roof – AmarK's skill restored his eyesight. Implanted cells had spurred dramatic bone growth in another child and his grandfather's degenerated skin, falling apart, had regained elasticity.

'How are you, my boy?' AmarK beamed, genuinely pleased. 'Fancy meeting you here again! How've you been? How's your friend, er…'

'Ricardo's working for me!' Leona interrupted in a proprietary tone. 'Now. Can we get down to the matter at hand, it being your hands' (eyelash flutter) 'and those implants of yours? I need you to iron out the ravages of stress, as…'

Here she paused with eager expectation. Dr Amar Khoury, dedication to science and obvious irritation notwithstanding, was also a businessman. Hence he raved: 'Leona! My beauty! You look not *one* day older than…' Etc. etc.

Ricardo, bored stiff, saunters to the bar. Facing the huge bay window, he sits down and watches the full moon gliding into sight.

'Nice ponytail. How was Woodstock?'

The redhead from Madrid airport.

'May I join you?'

He stutters, please do, please…

'Thanks. Moon-dreaming?'

'Yes.' He's desperately thinking of a way to engage in scintillating conversation but his mind strikes. She peels a banana.

'You like bananas?' he asks. (How's that for engaging in, yes, quite.) 'My name's Ricardo.' (No improvement.)

'Mine's Iris. How was your flight from Madrid?'

He gasps. She laughs.

'Haven't you noticed my panoramic vision? I saw you too, of course.'

Her totally relaxed manner unwinds him. A second whisky-sour helps.

'May I confess something?'

She shrugs. He shivers.

'The other night I dreamt of you.'

'Oh? Do tell.'

Weariness in her voice suggests she's heard that line before and more than twice. To hell with it.

'Here it is. I'm jostling my way around the stands on Portobello Road market when I spot you haggling over the price of an imitation Birkin bag. The Senegalese gives in. Fifty pounds. You hug him. A contrast in colour to behold. I'm jealous. You hail a taxi: it crosses Castilla's rolling and barren landscape dotted with decrepit fortresses. You mock the resemblance with Antonio Banderas contending he's gay. Banderas? The taxi-driver? Me? It's blurred. Now, in a church, you light a candle. Next scene: you're sitting in a café Faubourg-St-Honoré, sipping red wine with the same vacuous look I've seen at Barajas airport. A group of Japanese pours out of some bus and streams over the threshold of Hermès. You knot a Hermès scarf around that flamboyant hair of yours; wrap a shawl over a haute-couture dress, rather looking like Audrey Hepburn in *Charade*.'

'Nice'.

'I follow you, how did I get there, no idea, knowing what you'll do. Adopting the same attitude as in the duty-free shop, you swap the fake bag for a fifteen-thousand-pound authentic one, in less than a split second. Swarms of croaking Japanese provide the necessary confusion. Just for the kick of it – I imagine – you engage in conversation with some selling girl while expertly removing the security chip with what looks like a nail clipper, but it's a scalpel. You then stroll out of the shop, aloof as royalty. When I finally reach the door myself, I run around like a beheaded chicken but can't find you. Then I do, sitting at the same table opposite Hermès and having a good laugh ... at me.'

Breathless, Ric reclines in his armchair, rather pleased with himself.

Iris, not losing a beat, tosses him a sardonic glance.

'Very inspiring, but lopsided. I would have replaced the false Birkin with a real Kelly.'

'More distinguished, yeah?' he snickers, wondering if her Oxbridge accent wouldn't be equally ... borrowed.

'More fun too.'

Though his body feels limp, Ric's furious. He has invented that dream to mesmerise, well, to at least intrigue her, and, as mentioned somewhere else, fantasy isn't his forte. So he thinks, bloody hell, *tout ça pour rien*? His gut feeling, however, tells him, hush. If you snap at her now, you lose her forever.

'Where are you staying?' he asks (instead of and more importantly: how long for?).

'At some friends' house in Kensington.'

'Oh? Are you here with your ... family?' Ric mumbles.

'Me? A family?'

Another unsettling laugh.

'Mine, a demented question?'

'I'm much too dyslexic to stay in love or produce kids, Ricardo.'

That *does* take the wind out of his sails.

'Really?'

'Really.'

What if he had meant her parents, cousins, or other relatives? Why an answer aimed at stressing she's single?

Iris removes her glasses, not dark but kind of orange, and then it hits him, and hard: she could be Leonor's twenty-year younger twin.

She would have slithered away had the doc not appeared.

'Sit down, will you? We have plenty of time before dinner and for you to freshen up.'

Turning to Ric: 'Let's have a drink. That woman will kill us both, mark my words. Vanity compounded by authority *and* the other way round – terrifying!'

So Iris was staying with the doc.

'You're off the hook for tonight,' he continues gleefully. 'Leona went to see her astrologist, poor guy. Have dinner with us. You seem to know each other, right?' he smiles, now facing Iris who, for a change, shows a semblance of emotion. Looks like reticence.

'Kind of… We met in Madrid, some time ago, but…'

'Perfect. That's settled then. Let's go. Can't stand this glitzy place anymore.'

AmarK's house was lovely. His wife, Lati, a diminutive, cat-eyed lady, meowed, 'Shall we let the gentlemen have a smoke in the library and have a girlie chat, Iris dear?'

She was clearly in charge. Question marks were *pro forma*. So was her voice, Ric fathomed.

Dr AmarK's study-library was what you'd expect in terms of ostentatious understatement. Wood-panels, Chesterfield sofas, silver cigar-cases. Nothing special in fact – except for the bookshelves. There was something seriously strange about them. A myriad of volumes leaned against each other in a way defying gravity and logic.

'Ha!' boomed Amar. 'You've noticed! I'm not surprised. Haven't you told me back in Kenya that your father's pride and joy are his first editions? Well, boy, have a closer look.'

Ric did. The Doctor chuckled.

'Well. I once came across the memoirs of a friend of Chateaubriand, Joubert-forgot-his-name. He only read when strolling round his park, tearing off all the pages not worthy of his admiration: what he considered forgettable he considered disposable of. The story so amused me that I decided to adopt the habit. You can appreciate the result: hundreds of books with only a few pages in them. Hilarious, don't you think?'

Raised to revere books, Ric didn't.

His host, realising that expounding the more subtle aspects of his philosophy wasn't a good idea, didn't. One last thing, though.

'Listen. Before we sit down for dinner, I must, as a friend and as a physician, warn you: beware of Iris. She's toxic.'

Alarmed by Ricardo's almost tetanic spasm, the doctor hastened to banter, 'By the way, what about a haircut? But right now, another drink?'

16

HOUSEBOAT EVENING, WEIRD

They were sitting on the terrace of the Café de Flore Boulevard St Germain, basking in the pale sun. Ricardo was pouring his heart out to his friend, narrating the whole story – well, not quite. He left out the girl's hair colour, his dream and her name. Yet confessed to be smitten. Coming from him, it was akin to admitting felony.

'I can see why the doc was shocked. I must have turned as ghostly as … back in Menengai.'

Ced recalled the Kenyan evening only too vividly. They had rushed into a mud-and-daub hut to help with the delivery of a baby. Too late. The stillborn's entrails had been devoured by giant siafu ants. Ced had hugged the sobbing mother crouched on a straw-mattress. Ric had vomited all over the place. Now, like then, Ced felt little sympathy for his friend.

'Honestly! How could the doc warning about some girl you've only met once provoke panic?'

'You don't understand!'

Such was his distress that Ced, whose mind could normally cut corners, realised that something ineffable escaped him.

'Tell me then,' he gently needled.

Tell that he couldn't help identifying Iris with Ced's mother, his one-time lover? No way. Instead, he recounted the dinner at AmarK's house.

Iris had gone to bed on a pretext of nausea. (Nausea?) After some small talk with the doc's wife, he had steered the conversation onto the subject of Iris.

The girl was much younger than her demeanour and appearance suggested: in fact, only two years older than he was; her mother had committed suicide when she was only seven. Her father had been a butler in some grand house somewhere in America.

She had neither finished school nor attended university but had managed to become an intern in an advertising agency and get promoted fast. 'Success is access' was her motto, Lati said. Another one: 'There's no bad luck – merely sloppy planning'.

'Access to what?'

'To power, presumably, but … what kind of? Not the kind money buys, don't think. She's already earned loads of that.'

Though not at all hungry, Cedric had wolfed down the venison.

'How come Iris is staying with you?'

'She's a repeat-patient, can't you see?' the wife not precisely purred. 'By the way, ever heard of someone called Elena, Lora…'

Ric chocked: 'Who? Why?'

'Oh, nothing, just a conversation over the phone we couldn't help but overhear. Rather bizarre. Never mind.'

Suddenly and not convincingly, AmarK hit his forehead.

'No Lorraine whatsoever. Leona! That Hemy woman!'

'Anyway Ced, as I walked back from Kensington through Hyde Park, I burst into nervous laughter. What a fool.'

What exactly was he talking about?

'C'mon', Ced nudged. 'Gotta surprise for you!'

His friend let himself be steered along like a sleepwalker.

On the way, Ced put a forever protective arm around Ric's shoulder. His friend could be disarming, exasperating, impetuous. But a fool? Dreamily, he recited:

They called me a fool, they called me a child:
I found an angel of the night;
His voice was low, the look was bright;
He looked upon my crown and smiled.
The voice was not the voice of grief,
The words were hard to understand.

'I vaguely remember that poem from school. You're not suffering from total recall, are you?' Ric rather mockingly chuckled. 'It's a plague.'

Upon reaching the gangway to the barge, Nush and I rushed to meet them.

'Finally!' we cried out in unison.

Champagne corks started flying and stars sparkling above the Eiffel Tower. We were sitting on kilim-covered sofas at the *péniche*'s bow, the autumnal breeze wafting through the air – when Nush jumped up.

'Ela!'

No one except her had heard a scooter screeching to a halt.

I, seldom speechless, swallowed hard: the girl Nush kissed on the mouth was none other than the 'insignificant' Elaine from aboard the *QE2*, the one who'd posed for the portrait that struck me as so disquieting.

The boys, never having seen the portrait, could not measure the metamorphosis: the plain girl had become a punk before the word would become trendy. Her now platinum hair was Brylcreemed porcupine-style. Other than leather boots stamped with the Chanel logo and a macho's Rolex, Elaine's attire matched her look.

Her smile, however, was as innocent as a lamb's.

'Hi Ric! Gotta surprise, naughty you!'

'Another?' he joked half-heartedly.

She produced a small painting from behind her back. It depicted the Empire State Building.

'Isn't it fanta-bu-lous? Nush overpainted one of Cedric's photographs…'

Ced averted his glance from the collage. Scary. The tower seemed to implode, the moon above it, to dissolve.

Ric felt ashamed. He had forgotten all about their pledge to meet on September 15th in New York atop the…

Embarrassment sharpens envy. He steps aside and broods. Al inherited a fortune. When not dabbling in journalism, she buys then restores a 1930s *péniche* and turns the houseboat into a gem: enlarged windows, cedar-panelled interiors, a hidden TV, underfloor heating; and yes, even a telephone line and a drinkable water supply. The Moroccan furniture tries to enhance the impression of bohemia. Come again! A floating home makes sense: Al has always liked being able to take off anytime, anywhere. Removable anchors are her ideal. She always has a suitcase packed and, when travelling, never completely unpacks it – just in case. Again: cash is king. Ha. Irritatingly, she'd be prone to hum, *Day and night my toils redouble / Never nearer to the goal / Night and day I feel the trouble / Of the wanderer in my soul.* Yeah? Really? What toils? As to Ced … his phenomenal capacity for concentration, equalled only by an elephantine memory, has always turned learning into a promenade. Then: what trouble? Zero. Daddy ultimately foots the bill. And should he not, then Leonor will – a thought painful to endure…

Loud music ejected Ric from his smarting.

Nush had introduced a tape into the recorder. The weirdest medley. 'Knockin' on Heaven's Door' by Bob Dylan was followed by Sibelius' *Valse Triste*, alternating with one of Abba's silly songs, then *Melancholy Man* by the Moody Blues. All the time, the ambiguous girlfriends had been leaning over the brass railing, fondling and smoking non-stop.

What was meant to be a joyful get-together was turning into an ambiguous mess. Ced replaced the tape with Rod Stewart's latest hit, *Tonight's the Night*. In the kitchen, he retrieved two bottles of Margaux from his parka.

Ric returned to the prow where he didn't find me in the best of moods.

'How've been, beautiful?' he mumbled with what he hoped to sound like affectionate interest.

'What's there to say? Anything unlikely to bore you? That I destroy at night what I restore during the day (my health)? That I enjoy Journalism School? That it teaches you stringent discipline?'

'Great!'

'Yes. Great. We're given articles from all sorts of magazines to verify – right down to the most anodyne fact, and all with the utmost precision. Something I've always liked. Ced and I seldom meet. We lead different lives. He's the academic and the...'

Ricardo feels left out. Once more. Those two drift. He struggles, constantly always afraid to fall short of expectations. His father's, first and foremost, but also his own. What do they boil down to? Independence. And independence, to the poor schoolboy surrounded by rich kids, means *money*. Yet: can it buy the insouciance innate to his friends? Only in roundabout ways might it be acquired.

He joins the other girls. Still leaning by the railing, they look seriously gone with the wind. Nush's voice is monotone and weepy.

'Ric! The joy from painting is gone... All this bullshit about artists being blessed by despair, the igniting spark of burning inspiration and all that – a myth. Even if torment kick-started the engine, you need peace to keep the pace… Love-sickness is the only constant in my creativity.'

Seriously? Her girlfriend seems devoted. Naturally, she reads his mind.

'It's not just that men and women alike are scared by the intensity of my emotions, as your mother, no, sorry, Ced's mother said on the *QE2*, or that my parents consider me a failure. Batteries don't recharge the way they should. I mean hey, I still am, let's face it, stunning!'

She lets go of a mirthless laugh.

'What happened? Your paintings were full of spark.'

'No kidding. You *looked*?'

She approaches Ric as if to hug him; then recoils.

'Yes. I wanted to introduce motion into what is and remains a static art form. I wanted to inject vibration into atonal surfaces. But I reached an impasse, just like the Vorticists or Futurists did… Using superposed and treated materials to create relief, I had hoped I would create horizontal levitation.'

She could have spoken Chinese. Yet, he said, meaning it:

'I loved those paintings.'

'The wrong people would. Sorry. They were gimmicks. Fashionable a season or two, forgotten soon thereafter'.

Having overheard that last bit, I felt stumped. More than what Nush said, it was the way she said it that was anguishing. She talked as if describing someone else, someone alien. She talked like a dipsomaniac would.

'What about you?'

'Ah. Nothing to write home about, Nushita…'

When had he last written to his father? Ric realised, shame compounding shame.

Elaine pulled him a few feet away.

'We smoke opium, handsome.'

Opium?

'You're not literary, are you? De Quincy? Baudelaire? Freud? Our revered Jean Seberg? No bell?'

What was everyone talking about? Nush stumbled away. Elaine threw him a sharp and stern glance.

'Look man. I think you're a self-pitying wimp,' she stuttered. 'There're too many guys like you. Which is why girls like Nush turn to girls like me. Why d'you think we smoke opium instead of sniffing coke? 'Cause we need to numb the pain of disappointment, not get more alert to it.'

Strangely, Ricardo liked the mad girl. *What you see is NOT what I am* was written all over a pretty face, sadly smudged by vulgar make-up.

'Deeeear, ever heard of Vietnam? Of Malcolm X? Of Martin Luther King? Of Watergate? The IRA – or injustice at large, for that matter? Don't think so. You're just some dopey Pink Panther unaware Black ones exist,' Elaine now giggled hysterically, nearly losing her balance. 'The world isn't about your little social complexes and big luxury hotels!'

She reeled over. Nush ignored her.

'Take no notice, Ric. She thinks the world's a rubble, the universe a debacle, and so on. We're all accidents yet happened.'

Hitherto in the wings, I now fumed: 'How bloody dare you?'

'Great evening,' sighed Cedric. He had been lying on the deck a few feet away, half-listening, half-agonising. Ambling by, he rubbed his eyes as if he'd been asleep.

'What about a nibble?' he cheerfully asked.

I practically pumped gallons of mineral water down the girls' throats.

Unexpectedly (who said the unexpected always happens but the inevitable never does?) dinner was … cool. Nush apologised for her misbehaviour: August spent with her parents in Vienna had been an awful experience. Elaine sprinkled the account with self-derisory touches. Both described their life in Greenwich Village with glee: their brunches in Caffé Dante on MacDougal Street; their frugal suppers on threadbare carpets in some atelier or other; their own loft with wide-planked floors, walls smeared in paint or hung with photographs, wearing muffles and hats for lack of heating in the winter or nothing at all in the summer. Amazing how happy they sounded, having looked so miserable a while ago.

By the time I produced a Tarte Tatin, its apples caramelised to perfection, the atmosphere matched the candlelight. Whilst Ced admired my 1930s pen collection – a Parker Vest Pocket Duofold, Onotos, a fabulous De La Rue Pelican in sterling silver – I took Ric aside.

'Remember I promised to find your mysterious Iris again? Well, I did. She does own a house in Palma de Mallorca. And she loves auctions. One is coming up next month in the Formentor Hotel. I wouldn't mind attending. There'll be vintage fountain pens. Shall we go together?'

Ricardo took a deep breath. Hector Vich wanted to buy the formerly sumptuous hotel. Could he pull it off – and meet Iris again? His mind was racing when the telephone rang.

I rushed back to the table, probably white as chalk. There were no two ways of saying what I had to.

'Ced. Your father's been stabbed in New York. His condition's critical. The phone's in the kitchen…'

17

RESHUFFLING OF CARDS

Having hung up, Ced resentfully asked:
'Why is it *you* they called?'

'They tried you first.'

'Yeah. But how come they had *your* number?'

'Because you never answer your phone, perhaps?'

Not nice but no lie. The St Luke's Hospital had told me I was listed as a next of kin. It surprised me as much as it would have shocked Ced.

Nush and Elaine had fallen into a comatose torpor. I learnt from subsequent research that opium, like morphine, is first and foremost a painkiller with sedative effects; yet, smoked and mixed with booze, it can enhance imagination and trigger (creative?) hallucinations. Was this what had driven Nush to hanker after the drug? Or had Elaine, most possibly a devil in disguise, fed it to her in order to gain control?

Ever pragmatic, Ric booked four tickets for the first flight to New York the next day – which was actually today, September 16th, 1977: the two girls had repeatedly slurred they wanted to go *home*. Good riddance.

Ced and Ric entreated me to come along.

No way. Though Ric seemed even more shattered by the bad news than Ced, I couldn't help but wonder: with Hector gone, wouldn't his whole card-game crumble?

Anyway, I declined. The Clinic lady had told me that, though critical, Hector's condition was stable. He was fit and in his mid-forties. He'd recover. Other than that, I felt it would be, say, uncouth to appear at his bedside.

This said, I kneeled and prayed in front of a lone candle at dawn – and that, really, isn't like me.

Hector Vich did not die.

But Mr Moralli did.

Exactly a week later.

Ric ran to Central Park and spent hours running, half-watching the astonishing mosaic of cultures happy to dance and sing in their native tongues. Belonging to none, he felt not only a rootless orphan, but a shit. He had let his father down.

Hector, his sense of humour unaffected, recalling Moralli's letter ages ago, wondered: were Moralli's last words *toodleloo*?

Ric flew back to Paris, no direct flights to Geneva available. I fetched him at the airport. The guy was shattered. We drove to Le Rosey in the most opaque of silences, until reaching the gate.

'Did you love your father, Ric? Deep down?'

He darted me the most contemptuous of looks (rightly so) and snapped:

'Only three kinds of people tell the truth, nothing but the truth: children, the drunk and the imbeciles.'

It was bliss to return to Rolle. I much looked forward to seeing Mr Johan again.

His sonorous voice was tinged with heartfelt sorrow.

'Ricardo, welcome back...'

Arrangements were made and Mr Moralli buried next to his wife in the picturesque Nocelle cemetery above Positano, south of Napoli. Other than Ricardo, Colonel Johan in full regalia and me, only a dozen or so remote parents attended.

The lunch following the burial was sinister. Ric was clearly no one's favourite person. The food was awful, the wine acid. On top, it was drizzling.

'Let's walk back.'

Walk? The staircase carved into the side of the mountain, about 2,000 steps, was as steep as a wall. But no sooner had the rain abated and a rainbow spread its arch, the sky seemed to cascade down to the sea streaked by the white of boats.

'This view looks like eternity!' grumbled Mr Johan, not prone to lyricism.

18

FORMENTOR

Formentor Hotel, Mallorca, mid-October 1977.
Ric and I are shown into a lovely bungalow: the owners
have been informed of Hector Vich's offer and have decided
to accommodate his negotiator in style. Who do they think I
am? His lover? I rectify: a journalist. More bowing.

Tomeu and Juan Buades (victims of a heli crash in 1973)
had transformed the ship-like hotel, built in the twenties
over wide acres on the peninsula at the northern tip of the
island, into a legend. It had attracted guests such as Edward
VIII, Churchill, Chaplin, Scott Fitzgerald and honeymooning
Rainier and Grace. The magnificent gardens skirted a kilo-
metre-long, white-sanded beach. But its glory was dwindling
as fast as the funds required to restore the hotel's lustre.

Other than conferences and the Formentor's annual Literary
Prize celebration, auctions and banquets kept the place afloat.

The October 25th Christie's sale had been widely advertised
– by Saatchi & Saatchi, for whom Iris worked.

Ric bought make-up remover and a lovely dress. His intention: clear. His instinct: far from.

Later on and until midnight, the preview would take place
in several halls of the vast hotel. Strolling around, he had been
baffled by the lax security and the bazaar-like atmosphere.
Although neither the jewellery nor the objects were of tran-
scending value, a trained eye would be fast to spot rarities …
the eye of a discerning kleptomaniac?

'A flappy tunic and oversized hat made Iris look majestic, yet eerie. Her none too feminine silence – *nota bene!* – enhanced my fascination,' Ric would tell me later. 'I even managed to think of next to nothing.'

My guess: she so very much reminded him of Leonor that he felt numbed.

Elongated shades of majestic pine trees dappling the beach, scents embalming the air, they went for a stroll.

Iris kicked off her shoes; removed the turban; shook her flaming red mane and ran towards the sea. Ric half expected her to dive into the waves fully dressed. She didn't. All the same, the few people around stopped to watch.

Tomes could be written about voices – what they reveal, what they provoke, what they dissimulate and sometimes destroy. Iris' was *enveloping*.

He started walking leisurely, leaving it up to her whether to catch up or not.

'Can't you wait for me?'

'The wild must be left free.'

That hurt look.

'You're disconcerting,' he sighed, not slowing down. 'One moment you act as if you needed no one in the world; the next, as if in desperate need of protection…'

'Reassurance.'

'The difference?'

'When you hanker for protection, it's because you feel helpless. When you crave for reassurance, you want to be needed.'

His account verified that Iris had indeed been ugly and obese as a teenager. Bulimia had shrunken her into her present silhouette. Dr AmarK had then fixed her nose, lifted her boobs, liposuctioned remaining fat, etc. She had acquired an upper-class drawl imitating her father, the British butler much in vogue in ... Nantucket. There, for decades, he had been Mrs Vich's employee – and confidant. I pictured Iris growing up as a servant's daughter, never ceasing to admire and to envy the laid-back lady whose intimidating beauty she would forever try to emulate.

Dazed, Ric had forgotten about the auction preview. A small crowd at the hotel's entrance provided a swift reminder. Suddenly he felt guilty about the thought at the back of his mind, it being to observe Iris' attitude in the presence of gold and glitter. Yet...

The showcases that attracted Iris' prolonged glances did not contain the most valuable pieces. Ric had studied the catalogue and contemplated buying her something. A bit vulgar? (I wouldn't have minded him bidding for the Waverly Cameron from 1901, or the early 1930s Waterman Patrician in jade resin my heart was set on, but, no object of desire myself, fat chance.)

'Allo my darlinks! How wonderfool to see you!'

Benita! I beamed with pleasure.

'Allo Ricardooh! Luking for a rink? Just juking,' she added hastily, reacting to my grimace.

We found a table at the bar. Next to us, an overdressed woman accused her companion, and not *sotto voce*, of being responsible for the burglary in their house the previous summer and heaven knows what else. The bottom line was that she *needed* these Bulgaris, otherwise... Judging by the man's tepid protests, surrender was impending.

'How are you, *ma chérie*?' I asked Benita, my closest Parisian friend. I adore her. An alcoholic with a quicksilver mind and wit, she was fighting a nasty cancer and had, lately, won another round. We reminisced about our wild nights in La Caveau de la Huchette. Boring to Ric and Iris.

'I wouldn't mind having another look around,' the latter yawned – a bit too ostentatiously.

'Diamonds are *some* gurl's best alleeye,' croaked Benita.

No love lost between these two.

Iris glanced at various pieces with apparent distraction. They bumped into the couple who had been in the bar. The wife was standing in front of a tray full of earrings while her husband looked the other way in resignation. Ric muttered, 'Poor guy!' To no one, as Iris had vanished.

He returned to the bar where an exuberant man had joined us. Introductions were made. Benita whispered, 'Gabriel was my srink years ago. Now ve only drink togeser. Less expensive, more fun.'

When Iris came back and decoratively crossed her long silken legs, Gabriel pretended casual interest.

'What does a pretty girl like you do when…?'

'I work for ad-agencies. Presently, a consultancy job for big retail chains in Spain.'

'How fascinating!'

Gabriel observed her with mixed feelings – or was I imagining things again?

'It is!' she echoed with vehemence, the irony lost on her. 'Do you know that 40 percent of people who change address will also change their brand of toothpaste? More seriously: in twenty years, there'll be twice as many sixty-year-olds as newborns… Age pyramids determine the positioning, or shelving, of products. Formerly, the principle was simple: place superfluous products at eye level, the necessary ones elsewhere. But you can't expect 'oldies' to bend down or stand on their toes to buy tissues or milk. Nor do children influence their mother's purchases the way they used to: health consciousness. In addition, product-loyalty isn't reliable any more. I could go on and on...'

'Vould you perhaps nut?' interjected Benita.

'... you'd be amazed at the war waged by brands to conquer a prime location' (here a pause – Benita).

Gabriel scratched his jaw. Something was on his mind and it wasn't demographics.

'At how much do supermarkets estimate their loss from theft?'

Ric and I nearly spilt our drinks. Not batting an eyelash, Iris answered that the percentage was dwindling fast, due to increasingly cleverly hidden detection devices.

Did I detect a wink?

'Surprisingly, losses incurred by duty-free shops are amongst the highest. Why? Because of the assumption that no one in his right mind would steal in a place swarming with police.'

'Is sat so?' chipped Benita.

'Yes. Given the exorbitant rentals, they gladly scrimp on the running costs of cameras.'

I was amused. Complex and damn attractive, Iris fascinated me. On Gabriel's prompting, we rose to leave. While throwing him a grateful look, I captured the stern one Benita addressed to Ric. Point taken?

19

SHEBAM! POW! BLOP! WHIZZ!

The dinner lacked the *je ne sais quoi* that warrants the word magic. Iris was a good storyteller. Yes. But would it be fun to travel with her? Would tonight be a first stop? To which magnetic pole?

'A coffee? A sidecar?' Tilting her head, she whispered: 'What about a room?'

Gliding down the long corridor to the room, they kiss, now delicately, now avidly. In the room she says, 'Not so fast. Any chocolate in the mini-bar?'

A woman on a permanent diet craving for chocolate is opening up to pleasure, isn't she? Iris unwraps the Toblerone's long package as if peeling a banana.

'You have dancer's legs. Beautiful…'

'Would you lick them if they were ice cream?' she whispers in that husky voice of hers.

Then she cautiously, very cautiously, unzips her dress facing the bay window. Mesmerised, Ric slithers towards her. Holding her hair with one hand and brushing her skin with … he stops sharp.

The first night in Leonor's cabin. Is he going mad, or does the whole scene not smack of a remake – a remake with a double, perhaps a stunt?

He takes her savagely. No preliminaries, no after-play. She responds in kind. They do not fall asleep: they pass out.

In that quilted limbo in between sleep and wake, Iris dresses as gracefully as she had undressed; slips into her high-heeled shoes, buckles matching her emerald-coloured skirt; pins her red mane up... A strip-tease in reverse gear and slow-motion. When she closes the door, Ric feels an overwhelming sense of relief, followed by anger, followed by fright.

Iris had come well prepared. Make-up, a change of dress and all. Had he been a marionette, an instrument? In what wider scheme? He showers and bolts from the room.

At the reception, the hotel director gestures in a state of great agitation – yet nothing compared to the woman throwing abuse at him. The previous evening's shrew! Her husband tries to drag her away. To no avail. She's a lot stouter than he is. Finally the man shuffles to the bar. Good idea.

'Would you mind closing the door?' the guy mutters. 'Can't take that racket anymore!'

In his sixties, dressed with care and soft-spoken – Swiss from the sound of it – he seems a nice man. While they sip Bloody Marys, Ric asks how long he'd be staying.

'Staying? Bidding at auction tonight, while you're at it? No way! My wife's driving the entire hotel crazy.'

'Anything wrong?'

Dervish-style, he swirls to face Ricardo.

'My nerves are on edge since Giselle started looking for those earrings of hers. She turned the whole place upside down.'

'Don't all rooms have safes?'

'Young friend, safes have nothing to do with it. What happened is that at yesterday's preview my wife removed her earrings to try God knows how many others on. With so many people roaming around, you can imagine. They're gone.'

'Sorry to hear that...'

He emits an unexpected chuckle.

'Since I can't be blamed, no obligation to indulge in yet another whim! I mean hoho, *oderrrr*? How many emeralds does a woman really need? Aboriginal stuff, that's what I'll buy in the future!'

Whereupon he starts rambling on about his business in such detail that Ric's almost glad when the virago storms into the bar.

'We're off,' she declares shrilly. 'This dump's history!'

After a desolate handshake, the elder man is removed. Ric waits a cautious amount of time before venturing to the reception.

Paco Mendez, the director, looks shaken.

'We got away lightly. Hours of tantrum are preferable to litigation.'

'I wouldn't be surprised if that woman lost a lot of things,' Ric smiles. 'Hysterical ones usually do.'

'Comforting words. Thanks. Had a pleasant stay?'

Ric raises a manly thumb.

We had agreed to meet atop the promontory shortly before sunset. A breathtaking view. When Ric appeared, he was scratching his arms. Frantically.

'A feline night with the tiger? Allergic, perhaps?' I teased.

He collapsed on a rock, uttering not a word. His sunglasses hid his eyes, eyes hypnotised by the sea.

The vision made another surface; Iris' buckles matching her emerald-coloured skirt. Christ!

When you remember one thing, you tend to remember connected ones: Iris' targeted look when passing the showcases; the fact that in the bar, she had been facing the nerve-wrecking woman; her swift disappearance. It all added up.

Ric longed for a parachute. When *falling* in love, it helps.

Why so hypnotised? Her sensitivity *a fleur de peau*. Not to mention her velvety, incandescent skin. And then, well … the voice.

Still: having seen what he had at Barajas airport; half-dreamt what he had thereafter and now suspecting what he did, another doubt started nagging: wasn't her almost carnivorous eroticism an ersatz for gluttony? Addictions, by definition, are triggered by imaginary, not actual, needs. As AmarK had remarked: whatever the addiction, the chances are that one slips into transference, meaning, in Iris' case … swallowing men?

Were men, to her, robbed objects taken hostage?

Or might she merely be a conniving lunatic, full stop?

'You're all right?' I asked with genuine concern.

'No. I'm a simple guy and some things are simply too complicated,' he answered faintly, heading for the cliff.

Only years later would he see Iris again. At Cedric's wedding.

PART TWO

20

A BIRD, A CAGE

Some birds search for a cage.

Nush had been my closest girlfriend at school. Other than admiring her for various reasons, her scaring me for many others, she inspired protectiveness. Not that she came across as weak. No. Rather because she seemed too intent, too intense about almost everything. '*Je suis une exagerée!*'

Indeed. The abrupt swings from that exalted nature to a deep dark one were disconcerting. A tactile person, she now shunned the slightest physical contact, be it only my brushing her hand or shoulder when talking. Music no longer made her wiggle. She would keep the curtains drawn at all times.

Shortly before leaving school, Nush had drawn a double-faced Janus turning his back to a three dimensional mirror.

'A self-portrait', she had shrugged, before tearing it to pieces.

'Next one, a trisexual drama-queen?'

'Why not?'

Since that peculiar evening on my houseboat in Paris, I had tried to keep in touch. (All things come in threes. I'll come to that.) However: whenever I called her in New York, Elaine would answer and explain that she was either sleeping, or painting, or out. Out of what?

My letters remained unanswered: intercepted?

I had moved to Arles, not far from Avignon, driven by my passion for gypsy culture and music. (I'll come to that too.)

Be it as it may, I flew to New York in early September '81.

Would we all make it atop the Empire State Building on the 15th? I had sent messages all over the place. No answers.

Walking into the gloomy atelier near Bleecker Street, fears assailed me. Nush looked and felt like a simmering volcano. At the same time, unsubstantial. Was she on heavy drugs? She denied it, hand on heart. Not even joints, she swore.

I complimented her on the reviews of a first solo exhibition, many nearing eulogy – no small feat in New York, especially reacting to 'neo-post-expressionist portraits'. A bit *passé*, some said, had it not been for her innovative techniques mixing or superposing latex with oil, glass-dust, paper-glue – search me. I'm no expert.

Nush hardly reacted. She looked at Elaine, sitting at the other end of the atelier. I looked at her too. When our glances locked, I cringed: she had the kind of eyes that make you want to turn away. Not hostile. Not mean. But ones which take everything in at once.

I walked to the open kitchen and unpacked the meal I'd bought in some gourmet shop, suspecting that Elaine made sure I'd overhear their conversation. Whilst Nush's voice was muffled, hers was strident.

'Did you tell your friend about the last exhibit?'

'Course not. Please don't, Ela!'

'Sure. Did you pay the rent or must I, as usual…'

We kneeled down on Japanese tatamis, legs splayed and I, most uncharacteristically, did not utter a sound.

I resented what I sensed. Had Elaine gained absolute ascendency over *my* sweet Nush? Like the victim of a sect, she seemed to have surrendered her inner compass. Her sparkle, spirits and stamina had dwindled as candles would. Was this dependency sexual? Didn't think so.

Though ill-disposed towards psychobabble, I couldn't help wondering: had Nush blended the figure of a dyke-dominatrix with that of her authoritative father? (Granted, on the Warhol & Co scene, the former was furiously fashionable.)

When Elaine went to the loo, I felt the pressure whoosh out. Nush smiled her naïve smile I knew so well. The rest of her still jangled. She whispered:

'Why's everything so complicated, Al?'

'Don't know, *chérie*. It just is when you let it.'

To defuse suspicion, I hung around for an hour or so and raved about Nush's new appearance.

'Surely thanks to you, Elaine?'

'Absolutely! With her raven-black hair and her complexion, Nush looked too exotic. Egyptian, as the buffoon Italians on the *QE2* said, or too alike Anaïs Nin as they said here. You have to fit in to move on, see? And what's more artful than the Renaissance?' she giggled. 'So here we are: from Nefertiti to Botticelli!'

Nush's new Venetian-blonde curls fitted her like me, a boxing-glove. Ridiculous. Ditto with her biker outfit – but enough said.

Back at the hotel (The Vich Madison, need I specify?) I asked the concierge to print out all the reviews pertaining to Nush's latest exhibition and to find out Ms Leonor Vich's telephone number on Nantucket.

Another week until September 15th.

Time enough for a bird to escape its cage?

21

CRISS-CROSSING

Ric circled the room, rocking on his heels.
'Hi Al honey-pie! Whadsthemadder?' he drawled,
Texan boots matching the accent. When he produced a cigar,
removed its tip with a silver-cutter and lit it with a golden
lighter, I freaked.

'Has the Carter era turned you into some sort of nutcase?
Hey! This is *us*! OK, we're six years on from Le Rosey, but it's
still *just us*.'

He removed his grotesque bow-tie, looking like a kid caught
with his finger in the jam jar.

'OK, cowboy, a stiff one coming up!'

Some vodka down our veins, we relaxed.

'What's the trouble?'

'Nush. We must help. Fast. And by fast I mean – now.'

When I exposed my rescue plan, Ric didn't raise an eyebrow
or twitch a foot. Like Hector Vich, he had perfected the tech-
nique of delayed reactions.

'Would you come to Nantucket with me?'

He smoothed his shirt; then smoothed his face; then said:
'Yes.'

Next evening, we arrived at Leonor's house.

Ric gaped. Here was his 'Mrs Robinson', six years and
twenty pounds later. She hugged him with bland affection.

Her charm; her poise; that half-ironic smile of hers were
intact. Her hair, as flamboyantly red and her lips, as mesmerising

as ever, failed to ignite a sparkle. Has my heart, Ric wondered, become frigid? For years, he had remained true to his predilection: redheads. Married ones: less time-consuming.

Time! His obsession.

He wore two watches, just in case. On whatever subject, his sentences would be sprinkled with clichés such as 'time's the essence'; 'they don't know what time of the day it is'; 'don't have time on my hands'; 'time's flying'; 'there's no time like the present' – and so forth.

Bottom line: time was money. In other words and other than health, the point.

For if Ricardo had learnt something in Kenya with The Flying Doctors, it was that poverty and illness were not for him.

So whatever *time* he did not spend working or cavorting with hurried redheads – the burning of calories upmost in his mind – he spent in fitness-clubs.

'You *do* look incredibly fit, darling!' cooed Leonor. 'And suntanned! How d'you manage?'

Ric had persuaded Hector to open a Vich hotel in Houston, a hotel conceived by himself only. It had met with great success. And in Texas, you spent a lot of time outdoors. Barbecues and all that.

As I think to have mentioned, Leonor had taken no shine to me during our cruise aboard the *QE2*. Now, however, we exchanged conniving glances, obviously thinking along the same lines, their being that Ric had found it a lot easier to integrate in Texas than in New York, where his Latino look and none too WASPish demeanour had limited access to the clubs and people which, in the Big Apple, 'mattered'.

Houston was another story. The mere fact of being European

had made it easy to become the toast of the town. Gold-buttoned blazers and casual Todds, plus kissing ladies' hands and bowing to gruff husbands, did miracles. He was now surrounded by a coterie of admirers. The decoration of the Vich hotel enhanced his aura. The famous Italian Mongiardino had been entrusted with most of it; the more elegant among Ric's conquests, with more feminine touches. Both Leonor and I could picture him strutting about, at long last feeling princely.

We were sitting on the veranda. Fading sunrays fell in oblong swatches around us, the sound of a Beethoven concerto mingling ever so faintly with the waves skimming along the beach.

All good and well: but we had come for a purpose.

Leonor intercepted the impatient look I darted Ric.

'Let's have dinner, shall we?'

The vast kitchen, the centre of which was a huge fireplace, glowed. Leonor asked Ric to help her with seasoning the crab-meat and me, to explain the situation.

I depicted it the best I could. Perhaps too extensively, since I started describing Nush at Le Rosey, then in Paris, finally in New York.

As Leonor and Nush had bonded on the *QE2*, no need to dwell on our school-friend's contradictions.

I described the scene on my *péniche* three years earlier and our get-together three days before in her atelier.

To portray Elaine proved trickier: I mistrusted my bias against her. Remembering Hector Vich's words, ages ago or so it seemed, I finished by saying: 'In short, I am afraid.'

Leonor let it all sink in.

Ric mumbled:

'Well, if that girl washed her brain, she probably cleaned Nush's accounts too...'

'Do shut up!' Leonor chided without delicatesse. 'Money isn't the issue right now, can't you see?'

Had she smacked him, the blow might not have made him recoil as her words did. Just as well that a small Labrador, looking like a guilty clown, his muzzle full of red paint, came waggling in. A silly dialogue between the dog and Leonor ensued. Her confab concluded, Leonor sunk back into in her wicker chair.

'I'm no shrink, darlings, nor a melodramatic person. But my guess is ... what is it? Mind if I prepare a joint?'

As we didn't, she did.

'That Elaine woman strikes me like as a dangerous manipulator. I remember her from the cruise too: plain she was and plain she probably remained, technicolour hair, piercing or tattoos notwithstanding. Lacking personality, she feeds on Nush's – Nush who tantalises, disquiets, seduces, all of it totally unawares – as opposed to her shadow, inverted commas, only *too* aware. Jealousy is poison. Does Elaine crave attention, thus try to make Nush pale into insignificance – no: lower her to her own, *common* denominator? She changes her exotic appearance to that of a blonde-bimbo, calling it Botticelli when it should be called Barbie. Hooks her on opium. Persuades her to stop painting portraits, knowing full well that this is where Nush's talent lies and that she, having none, will be eclipsed.'

Leonor blew smoke-circles, eyes half-closed. Her languid attitude, her husky voice, her gracious hands were bewitching, not only to Ric.

If only to break the spell, I resumed.

'Do have my doubts about the homosexuality bit too. Could be another act staged by Elaine to elicit interest. There's neither tenderness nor erotic tension between these two – at least in my opinion.'

'Does it matter? This Elaine woman is controlling. That's masculine enough.'

I thought Ric would jump. He merely sighed.

Suddenly, Leonor straightened up.

'I shouldn't have smoked this. It triggers visions. The one I just had I don't like in the least. Aleana, you're right. We must deliver the bird from its cage before it becomes a jailbird who'll stop at nothing in order to escape. Ric, please bring paper and a pencil!'

She started rolling the latter on the former with her fingertips. Just as Hector did on occasions.

'Ric darling, could you find out what bank Nush uses and what her balance sheet is?'

'Easy. I opened an account for her at Chase. Years ago.'

'Oh?… Hmm.'

'Aleana: could you roam art galleries and find out what role Elaine plays in managing her … career?'

'Yes.'

She smiled at me.

'Do you know, pretty girl, that you are just my ex's type?'

'Me?'

'Yes. You should and, my dear, will have an affair with Hector. Wait. We'll see. In the meanwhile, shall we go to bed? Tomorrow, I'll accompany you to New York. Wouldn't mind having a closer look at this infamous Elaine. Good thing you came. Goodnight.'

Good + good = ?

Ric leapt out of the door, direction beach.

22

ANOTHER DAY AFTER

I sunk into sleep feeling like a caterpillar and woke up butterflying in the golden light that flooded the room. A strawberry milkshake was brought to my bedside. Wow.

Had Ric knocked at Leonor's door last night? Had she worn little but crimson lipstick? Hopefully.

Beneath the toughness, Ricardo's a softie. It's not just money-wise that we, his schoolmates, were privileged. His father, however well-meaning, had been quite an emotional tyrant. In his son, Moralli had detected a potential he both boosted and resented. The boy was handsome, very; tall, irreverent and insolent. The teacher never had any of it. Only the strikingly sapphire-blue eyes suggested parenthood. Also, the reverence for books.

I digress. Merely to say that I had wished, in a way, for Ric and Leonor to rekindle their ... what's the word?

Strolling into the drawing room, a long swim later, I saw no sign of bliss on his face, no love-bites on his neck, no. Ric was reading the *Wall Street Journal* like a retiree without slippers. Appearing with a basketful of flowers and a wink, Leonor wished us good morning.

Good? Again? Things became a bit tricky after that.

Ric spoke about Texas with obnoxious awe. Leonor laughed, pointing out Texans' coarseness matched their teenager girls' dreams – big boobs followed by expensive liftings. Ric retorted that her Nantucket crowd was no better. Sure, she replied, but not so shallow.

'Ha. No parading of pseudo-benevolence and mega-bucks in these rarefied surroundings, perhaps?'

'Why not drop it, dear? Let's go for a walk, shall we?'

'Okay,' mumbled Ric, his ravaged face telling a tale.

'Join us?' Leonor pleaded.

'No. Going fishing.'

Rather rude. But I was fed up. Let those narcissists stumble around, be it on the beach or in life. Did they care about Nush, *really*?

As a distraction, I prepared the kind of salad only home-grown vegetables can produce.

Of course we later had lunch, as civilised people would.

Of course we drank a lot, as sad people with raw nerves do.

Of course we remained very lucid because alcohol, in its first phases, does that to one.

Ric and Leonor talked like people knowing that words don't matter and won't help anymore. I hazily thought that we all shared a perverse tendency for non-fulfilment.

The butler kept filling our glasses. The *butler!*

'Charming man', I quipped, my neurons re-aligned.

'Oh darling, that's my faithful Banes. A jewel more precious than any Jeeves!' Leonor exclaimed. 'Had to let him go some years ago as his daughter was problematic, stealing stuff or whatever, but then he wasn't the culprit, was he? Can't tell you how happy I was when he asked whether he could come back.'

Oh shit, thought Ric. Oh Dog, thought I.

Talking of dogs, three of them crept onto the terrace, tails in between their legs, ears leaning backwards, limping.

'Poor sweethearts!' Leonor wailed. 'All of them prey to some virus, can't remember its name. Good thing I've found this vet, Dr Something-or-other, with this incredible homeopathic cure...'

'Enough!' exploded Ric. 'You don't know the name of the

disease affecting your half-children! You can't remember the name of their saviour-doctor! Do you remember mine – or your son's, for that matter? Do you?'

His exasperation bordered on hysteria.

Leonor looked at me. I looked at nobody.

'As to homeopathy', he continued, absolutely ablaze, 'cut the crap! You might drop lovers like Nush pops pills but let's be serious for a moment. There's no cellular foundation connecting the eyes to the tongue or the feet to the brain!'

'What about homois-pathos? Consider the etymology…'

'Save semantics for the dupes,' Ric barked at me. 'You're tiresome!'

Hadn't ever seen him take a stance with such blatant disregard for collateral damage. Ric roared on:

'Oscillococcinum is prepared by incubating small amounts of duck liver and heart for fourteen days, then by filtering, freezing and rehydrating the solution into sugar granules. If any molecule were to survive this kind of treatment, its concentration would involve 400 zeros.'

'Please drop it, Ricardo,' Leonor pleaded. 'One day, dear, even you might discover loneliness and then, who knows, even you might seek the love of pets…'

We all sank into a gap-gulfing silence.

Her words would, in the distant future, lead into a trap that, in turn, would lead to Ric's ironic demise.

Our rendezvous atop the Empire State Building was only five days away. No time to lose, love lost or not.

Banes slithered in, shadowless; the perfect butler *par excellence*.

'Ma'am, Mister Cedric is on the phone.'

'I'll get it!' Ric cried out; cried out as if rushing for a lifebelt.

23

THE KISS

Ric and Ced joined forces to find out what was going on with Nush's finances, displaying the complicity of their schooldays. The three of us met in the evenings to exchange notes, in some bar or another. Then, the boys and I would part ways.

My 'mission' in this rescue operation had not proven as titillating as some of the less phoney specimens in the art-circus were most amusing. Less so, what I found out.

The consensus, in that lingo of theirs, was that Nush had shown potential and originality but that, in a steady diminuendo, her inspiration had become 'fractured'. Some said that she was too influenced by trends, hence inhibited in her convictions; others, that the emotion had drained out of her work, it having become too contrived. Time and again, I heard comments such as 'so thick with concept that the medium is robbed of message'; 'the raw sensitivity had been replaced by chin-stroking Works of Significance, the latter blurred by portentous abstraction'; 'fierce without bite' – stuff like that.

Another consensus pertained to a more personal level. Friend or fiend, Elaine's influence on Nush was considered eviscerating. Her whole persona too laboured to be credible.

When I reported the above to Leonor, the epitome of composure, her body twitched. We were eating Eggs Benedict in her room at the Carlyle (she wasn't going to stay at the Vich Madison, was she?) and, when I added the information Ric had forwarded, she threw her head backwards, forcing her eyes to swallow back tears.

'Right. I'm meeting Elaine tomorrow. I called and pretended to be a museum curator from Edinburgh, scouting new talent and all that. Another two days before your Empire State Building get-together, correct?'

'Yes.'

'How romantic!'

Hmm. Undercurrent tensions could torpedo it all. Notwithstanding their present 'old-pal-trip', Ced and Ric's lives and temperaments continued to diverge.

Nush and I had also drifted apart. Though they often change direction, I follow straight lines. Zigzagging in a geometrical, if you like, way. Her trajectory was more of a labyrinth, all turns and traps.

Leonor asked if I'd stay. We could watch a fun movie. I declined gracefully, hugged her wholeheartedly, thanked her profusely but had other plans.

Hector was waiting. In the same gloomy bar as some years before. 'I'm a sentimental fool become a man of habits' he had chuckled over the phone.

This time, the waiter threw no oblong glances before producing booze.

'The fifties are back!' grinned Hector Vich, seamlessly resuming our former conversation with his usual nonchalance.

'Oh? Meaning you're about to get pimples again?'

'Ridicule never killed anybody.'

I turned my back on the mirror above the bar, faced Hector and was once again struck by his looks. He must have been in his mid-fifties by now, but those tiger eyes and fine features framed by still ink-black, abundant hair kept reminding me of Gary Cooper. The fifties indeed!

'What makes you say that?'

'Many things. Musical revivals. Movies like *Grease*, *American Graffiti* or TV series such as ... search me. Homages to the back-then idols. And of course, puritanism under the 'everything goes' façade. The decade of Watergate and polyester reveres the Eisenhower and Elvis era, haven't you noticed? Last not least, the fifties are coming back in the guise of Ronald Reagan's America. But enough of that...'

He laughed apologetically.

'Let's go to the Carlyle – tonight's their jazz evening, and you do love jazz, don't you?'

Oh-oh.

'Actually, Hector, my musical taste has much ... evolved. Gypsy music is what...'

'You must be twenty-two or three, right? Four, perhaps. You know I don't keep track of time too attentively. But Ced tells me you're not easy to keep track of either. Has love bitten you at last?'

Tell him about my life in Arles? Explain I had embraced the gypsy lifestyle, been accepted by their community in spite of my appearance (blonde, narrow hips, in other words, the Ava Gardner antitype) and taken two gypsy orphans under my wings? Add that I had had no lover for two years, gypsy ethics intractable as regard to intermingling intimacy?

What for? On the other hand, why not? Hector's were no mundane questions. He cared. So I told him as much as I could without getting maudlin. In front of the Carlyle, he stopped sharp. There and then, he kissed me. A kiss I shall never, ever forget.

Woody Allen was performing. The saxophone has always been one of my favourite instruments, and Allen one of my least favourite people. But bliss transformed everything into a sugary haze. Hector's arm wrapped around my shoulders, I felt protected. Safe. Let me transgress my principles by saying: happy.

At some point, Leonor's words sneaked into my mind. 'You should and *will* have an affair with my ex' – or something like that.

Leonor. Elaine. Nush. Should I tell Hector about the situation? No.

We walked back to the Vich Madison where, obviously, he was staying too. Tricky? Shame on me for thinking it might.

'Lovely evening, Aleana. Thank you.'

'Did I not bore you?' I asked, genuinely worried.

'Boredom is the disease of the *blasés*. Which we are not.'

'I don't know what to say…'

'Just as well. Looking for words, you stumble on ideas. Better sink into sweet dreams, sweet girl.'

Raising an imaginary hat, he walked out of the door again.

The telephone on my bedside table was blinking.

The message: 'Big kiss. Benita.'

Another kiss! I spread on the bed and laughed, remembering our farcical scheme in June, a month after Mitterrand's victory at the French elections. Lots of people had panicked: the future regime boded ill for tax evasion, a national sport. French presidents, no sooner at the reins, acted monarchic. No scoop. But an intellectual, truly socialist sceptre-holder? Aouch.

Though penniless, Benita intended to hold on to three Old Masters which had been in her family for generations. Short of starving, she'd never sell a single one. Having turned forty, old age round the corner, according to her, security, hitherto at the very back of her mind, shot to the forefront.

'Whoever it was who sung "Life Begins at Forty" must have been geriatric,' she declared, refusing to blow out the candles on her birthday cake.

Drinking heavily on the terrace of some café while watching a triumphant demonstration near the PS headquarters, we devised a scheme.

We'd rent a Mercedes (important, insurance-wise) and cross the border to Switzerland three times, same place same hour, me presenting my press credentials and mentioning, by the by, that I was writing an article about the United Nations (which I indeed might). The morning of the fourth day, a friend of ours would call the border-post and, channelling Deep Throat, denounce a certain Mercedes with a certain number plate, smuggling valuables into Switzerland.

Sure enough, when we arrived, the car was almost dismantled. Benita ranted and protested exuberantly, screaming it was her nephew's birthday. I wriggled my hands, explaining my job was on the line were I to be unpunctual, begging the customs officers to let us go. Having ripped the fabric off the seats, X-rayed the wheels and whatnot, they apologised – to me. I believed they hoped to have seen the last of Benita.

Next day, they waved us through, almost saluting. Need I say that the three canvasses were rolled-up and gift-wrapped confetti-style on the backseat?

Good fun.

24

BEAUTY NEEDS BEAST

Leonor sits in the far corner of an Italian restaurant in Soho, her hair drawn back into a ponytail, catalogues from a myriad of auction-houses by her side. She observes people come and go, mostly wearing torn jeans and tilted hats.

A young lady walks in, wearing a dress rather out of tune in the surroundings. She approaches the table.

'You must be Mrs Vikonor?'

'And you, Elaine?'

'Yes,' she smiles.

What? This dainty girl, the vivid image of good-health, the famous ogre?

'Bet you expected me to look different? Bet you've heard quite a lot about the punky tandem Nush and I formed, right?'

'Well, Miss Camp, I must admit that...'

Leonor reaches for a cigarette. To hell with not smoking before lunch. The girl doesn't smoke, even apologises not to.

'Not even the odd joint? A little opium perhaps?' Leonor ripostes mischievously.

'Info is intox in New York's art-world, Mrs Vikonor. Shall we order? I'm buying. Please call me Elaine. The surname Camp is an invention. Part of the gig, see? Of course you don't...'

While they study the menu, Leonor's mind wanders. Isn't the girl supposed to represent Nush, looking out for possible exhibitions? Is her honesty an attempted sabotage? Her auburn hair a wig and her demure attire, a disguise?

The waiter having taken their order, she asks the first of these questions.

'Oh, it's simple. I have resigned – resigned as Nush's alter-ego and resigned myself to the fact that her chances of a breakthrough in Europe were groovier. Nush's not tough enough for the scene here.'

'As opposed to you?'

Though Leonor's voice is friendly, not so the undertone.

'Tough? Let's say I'm more resilient. You see, I'm coming from boring folks in conservative Iowa, led an uneventful life, lack of passion or ambition helping. In short, I'm an average girl with pleasant but unremarkable traits. Had I not met Nush on a cruise some years ago, I probably would be married to the guy next door.'

A broccoli soup is half-slammed down in front of them.

'Why has a swell lady such as you chosen such a shit place for lunch? In order to put someone like me at ease?'

Leonor weighs her words carefully.

'Look, Elaine. I have of course done some research. Surely you're aware that your reputation is slightly, er, more than slightly that of a … fringe-virago, forgive the…'

'No sweat.'

A silky silence follows. Then:

'Mrs V, am I wrong in presuming that you know Anoushka? Personally, I mean?'

Leonor drops her spoon and removes her glasses.

'No. But haven't seen her for years. I found her extremely attaching and when I learnt about the … somewhat depressing developments, it was always in relation to your influence and lifestyle.'

'Both nefarious, right?'

'Not my choice of words.'

'So I bet you expected some sort of sinister women-eater with black nail-polish on crab-like fingers rolling into this joint, a pun, on spiky skates?'

'Unfortunately, my imagination couldn't quite muster that picture,' laughs Leonor, beginning to feel amused.

'Imagination! Something Nush has in excess and I totally lack. That's why I was so seduced by her – and then, by the role she invented for and imparted to me. This wasn't going to happen in the residential suburbs of Des Moines, was it? And yes, I'm bisexual. Sorry.'

After a forkful of overcooked, spice-less *spaghetti all'arrabiata*, Leonor folds her napkin.

'Let's have a decent meal, shall we?'

Elaine insists on paying and Leonor on taking a taxi to the Café Luxembourg off Broadway. Casual but damn good food.

They both order spare ribs with ratatouille.

'Elaine, my turn to be sincere. I'm no museum curator from Scotland. Old enough to be Nush's mother. Her own, as you know, being emotionally absent, I worry. What's going on?'

Elaine goggles. Shock in her eyes is diluted by sorrow.

She cups her oval face with her hands. Leonor, feeling guilty and once again disconcerted, takes them in hers.

'No harm meant.'

'It's not *me* you harm, lady. I so very much hoped Nush might be given an opportunity as far away from here as possible! As to me? I want out! I want my life back! In fact I packed and left that awful atelier yesterday. But I *do* love Nush, get it? She made me feel useful for ... ages – but then the ages become too dark. The trigger was a mirror: one day, I saw the bitter lines Nush had anticipated in the portrait she'd sketched on that cruise, when I still was ... banal and tranquil. *Spooky.*'

'Why don't you write?' Leonor asks. 'Talking as you do, you might have a real talent...'

'Nice try but drop it, Mrs Vi...'

'Leonor, please.'

'Whatever. Should I ever put pen to paper, I'd be a ghost-writer. All you heard about Elaine, the dyke; the savvy negotiator; the opium lotus – all of it's a ploy devised by Nush. In order to overcome her shyness and self-doubts she needed a demon – or a sort of boulder, if you like. All of it virtual, understand? I'm an invention. I'm a cartoon-character. And I'm tired.'

She wolfs down her spare ribs like a very famished person indeed.

Had everyone got it completely, radically wrong? Was Nush the vampire, Elaine the victim? Two things were beyond doubt: she was no means a beast but Nush, by all standards, a talented beauty. It being so, why had she felt compelled to manipulate that simple girl? Why this complex set-up, this make-belief, sinister farce?

Leonor decides to bring up the subject of money. It might cast some light on the rest. First she orders two Irish coffees and tells anecdotes about her dogs. Might Elaine want one of her puppies? The girl's eyes light up at the suggestion, but cloud over a moment later.

'I need time *not* to care about someone else. Not animals. Not even of myself. No masks, no mothering, no ... yeah. Travelling would be nice.'

'Do you have any money, honey?'

Elaine shrugs.

'Some. I accepted my cut of the sales while the going was good. Hey! Who made the phone calls, helped hang the paint-ings in the galleries or pestered their owners? But all fair and square.'

'Has Nush any left?'

The girl darts Leonor an indignant glance.

'For your info – and let me suggest you have a lot of detox to do – I never had direct access to her account. She paid me cash. But boy did she spend it! Ever seen her shoe-collection? Well. Imelda Marcos would pale with envy. An enigma, since she always wears boots or nothing at all, but then I gave up understanding her quirks a long time ago. Then – that mother of hers. Emotionally absent, you said. Hmm. She sure is alive and kicking on the phone. Nush used to transfer quite a lot of dough to her. Seems the father's a stingy jack-ass. A prince, yeah, but, Jesus, no king of hearts! May I have another coffee? Scottish, Irish, anything other than Polish!'

Leonor looks at her pack of cigarettes. And lunch isn't even finished. She asks for the bill. Elaine tries to snatch it.

'No way, dear girl. Go spoil yourself a bit.'

'How I wish you didn't suspect me of wrongdoing. As a voice-over, I never fumble my lines, but right now, it's just me, see? No lines, except around my eyes. And if you're interested in Nush's finances, find out who that Italian school-friend of hers is, forget his name, but he controlled her account.'

She begins fiddling with her watch. Bells in Leonor's mind ring. Shrill bells.

'May I eclipse, evaporate, exit? So tired. Don't know why, really. Who said: "You're so young and *already* have done so little"?'

It was Oppenheimer, the so-called father of the A-bomb, muses Leonor, watching the lonely, very lonely girl, escape.

25

SEEN THAT
MOVIE TOO...

The Empire State Building reminds many people of many movies. *King Kong. Much Ado About Nutting* or *Mouse in Manhattan* (two animated films!); *West Side Story* among others.

But for hopeless romantics, it's *An Affair to Remember* with Cary Grant and Deborah Kerr that springs to mind. The main protagonists have met on a transatlantic cruise. He's a gigolo-would-be-painter and she, a do-gooder of some sort, typical Kerr. He promises to sort his life out and they pledge to meet exactly one year later atop the ES Building. He honours the pact.

Not doubting him, so in love is she (choubidou) she rushes across 34th street in such an amorous haze that she's hit by a bus and left a paraplegic. He waits until midnight; despises himself for having been trusting and would have become a cynical renegade had he not discovered the truth. Happy ending (chimpoum). A 1957 Hollywood weepie.

Now: September 15th, 1981.

I'm the first to arrive on the 102nd floor, narrower but less touristy than the observatory deck on the 68th. Though no longer the tallest building in New York since the World Trade Center was completed, the Art Deco skyscraper remains emblematic.

Other than blankets and food, I'd brought the kind of stereo equipment people carried on their shoulders back then. In it, a tape on which I had recorded songs meant to highlight this special occasion.

First and foremost, 'New York Serenade' by Bruce Springsteen. (Even today, let me assure you that its first four minutes are amongst the most mind-blowing melodies I've ever heard. *Do*, let me insist, listen to them!) Then, of course, Elton John's 'I've Seen That Movie Too' – followed by all sorts of tunes pertaining to our schooldays or to the city.

The first to arrive, at 7 pm on the dot, was Ric.

'Why aren't I surprised, as they say?'

Ten or so minutes later, the lift door opened again. Nush. In a wheelchair. Pushed by Leonor.

For a split second, I believed it to be a sick joke. A dodgy *clin d'oeil* to the Deborah Kerr character?

Leonor's appearance slashed such thoughts. No hat, no sunglasses, no beaded kaftan: instead, leggings and a huge sweater than had seen better days. So had she, by the look on her face and her messy hair. Yet, as always, she moved with poise.

'Huloooo daaaarlings! Sorry to intrude, but naughty Nush needed a little assistance.'

She caressed our friend's cheek ever so gently.

Ced must have walked up the stairs. We hadn't noticed his presence. He looked at Ric, who looked impassive. Then at his mother: she hugged him tightly.

'Only a few bones in the feet are fractured, quite badly that is. She'll be able to walk in two months or so, though maybe with a limp for...'

I hastened to replace my self-made tape with one of Marvin Gaye's, having forgotten it started with the track 'What's Going On'. No good. On the other hand, its rhythm was catching and besides, anything was better than awkward silence. While we laid out the semi-traditional picnic, Leonor retrieved make up from her handbag and applied it to Nush's face. When they joined us, she looked positively stunning.

Whatever they say about booze, the next hour made me contemplate alcoholism as a serious improvement on breathing: after the initial knot in our throats (neither of us even pretended to swallow the version of an accident) we had a great time. And I mean: great. Even Ric, no longer tense and taut, started not only enjoying himself but also making us laugh – Nush included. We were by now listening to Madonna, waving to the beat.

'How come so many chicks are just Material Girls?' he grinned. 'By the way, did you know that Georg Langon is supplying the Hell's Angels with motorbikes? Can you imagine our former German teacher with that crowd?'

'He did seem to have an inclination for tough guys, didn't he?' I joked, remembering the episode on the *QE2*.

Aouch. Double-friendly-misfire. I had forgotten how hurt Nush had been and also, that she had become a proclaimed lesbian. (To not think before talking: one of booze's double-edges.) Leonor – who had been persuaded to stay in spite of her attempts to leave us 'alone' – cooed:

'Men? Who needs them, right, Nushita?'

Brooding silence.

'Hell no!' I chuckled. 'Nice men are ugly and the handsome ones, not nice.'

'Quite!' quipped Leonor, quick to take the bait. 'And then, the not so handsome but nice men have no money...'

'In which case they're after ours! Even when thinking we're not beauties.'

'Precisely! Problem being that the heterosexual, nice and rich men who think we're beautiful, are cowards!'

She and I giggled like kids. Nush shot us a revolver glance.

'C'mon, Nush! Just … *kidding!*'

She sniffed. Tried to smile and after a while, succeeded.

'Forgive me. My legs hurt…'

'Don't pull ours!' Ric scolded in one of the abrupt mood-swings he was prone to. 'Pull yourself, legs included, together.'

Surprisingly, his harsh words had a sobering effect – calling for the uncorking of another bottle. Hitherto slumped in her wheelchair, Nush now sat erect.

'Elaine, my muse, has left me.'

Leonor mumbled she'd climb the ladder to the building's spire, the door left open, a privilege not to be missed. She probably had slipped a tip to the maintenance guy, just in case.

'So?' Ric asked, somewhat disdainfully.

'Wasn't she some sort of witch?' echoed Ced.

'Says who?' snapped Nush.

'When?' I asked.

'Three days ago', she again sniffed.

'I see,' said one of us.

'NO! You don't. You can't!'

This whole story was beginning to enervate me. Elaine had been no shrinking violet; that much I knew. But then, nor had Nush.

'What happened? What the hell's going on?'

She knew me. Beating around the bush? No option.

'I used and misused Ela. When I spotted her on the *QE2*, I knew I would. Deliberately or not, I really couldn't say, I transformed her into the portrait I had sketched. My third eye, as you used to call it, Al. Malefic. The Dorian Gray horror-tale backwards? *Tu comprends?*'

No.

'What about you, Ced? You, the photographer who compulsively filters things using distance?'

She curled into an embryo position on that sad chair.

'Look. I was good, damn good at portraits. I'd sketch people on the bus, in the park, at bus-stops. Strangers. I *pictured* their lives. Where were they heading for? Why? What did their home, office, wives, husbands or kids look like? How did they make love, if ever? Be it obese guys; whores; Wall-Street yuppies; Nigerian or Taiwanese; ex-Nazis or potential psychopaths – my fantasy took it all in, all at once, amalgamating *visions*. In my atelier, I'd spend nights trans-painting these … intuitions.'

Nush used her scarf to blindfold her eyes.

'Ela was a translator, if you will. No creativity whatsoever, but a shrewd observer of my observations. I stumble and stutter when it comes to abstraction. So: she became my voice. But she had to look the part. Hence, *I morphed her into my masterpiece…*'

For a moment, we thought Nush had fainted. Not so.

'One afternoon, I caught her in bed with a coward.'

'A what?'

'A man, dummies!' she hysterically laughed. 'First I thought it was another woman. Petrified, I stood at the door before realising it was a Viking-beatnik guy, see? So engrossed were they in love-making they didn't even notice me. In short, having stolen her soul, I was now robbed of perspective.'

Perspective? Like in horizon? Had the cruelty of her narrative dawned upon her? Hit her, perhaps? There was something ghoulish beneath all of this. I followed Leonor's example and climbed up to the building's spire. Unfortunately, we could hear all that was said below. Leonor looked aghast.

'… I became dependent on exerting power. But let me add that experimentation, in every which way, excited Ela. Don't forget: she was a plain girl with a plain encephalogram when we met.'

'That's a damn nasty thing to say,' grunted Ced.

'The truth tends to be,' Nush riposted dryly. 'I had my hair dyed straw-blond. On the way back, I stopped at the optician to have my eyes fitted with lenses so they would look arctic-blue.'

She squeezed her wheelchair's handles.

'Too late. Too bad. I had lost her.'

'Well', hissed Ric. 'At least the end is over.'

Wishful thinking.

'Then I'd I meet some of the very same strangers again and *saw* that they had become as I had depicted them: injured. When I told Elaine, she just shrugged: "Time to change register. Your Frida Kahlo period is over. Emulate your other hero, Rothko."'

Two painters who had committed suicide.

Finally, Leonor and I walked down the stairs again.

'Your friend Elaine will be fine,' Leonor smiled.

'I bet,' sighed Nush. 'She's more resilient than all of us put together.'

'Her exact words.'

'What? When?'

'I had lunch with the girl. Not the slightest bit bland or brainless.'

The most laden of silences fell like a rock.

Time (possibly the wrong one) to insert my tape. Elton John.

> I can see by your eyes you must be lying
> When you think I don't have a clue.
> Baby, you're crazy
> If you think that you can fool me:
> I've seen that movie too.
> So keep your auditions for somebody

who hasn't got so much to lose
'Cause you can tell by the lines I'm reciting
That I've seen that movie toooooooo...

None of us, upon parting, suggested we'd reconvene at the same place, same time, next year.

26

A TALK IN
CENTRAL PARK

Cedric and Leonor had agreed to meet at noon the next day for a walk. When Ricardo asked if he could join them, his forever kind friend, though reluctant, said, naturally. It was one of those marvellous, early Indian-summer days, a peacock's tail displaying crimson, yellow and brownish splendour.

Ced, still unaware that his mother and Ric had had an affair.

Leonor, unaware that I knew.

Hector Vich, obviously unaware he'd bump into them.

Ric, Ced and Leonor met at Central Park's zoo (rather appropriate, given their untamed nature) and strolled towards the Mall, the promenade where loners sit on benches reading the papers. They ambled on to the Bethesda Pavilion, then toward the Bow Bridge, where they leant against the parapet, watching ducks and swans gliding on the lake. Birds were already flying south.

'Shall I invite Nush to Nantucket?'

'No, mother. She needs a normal life. Something challenging...'

'Is challenge what you'd recommend for a suicidal girl skirting improbable normality?'

'The improbable is always plausible. You should know, Mother dearest!'

Nearby a couple was kissing. Further away, another couple

feuded a heated argument. An inspired-looking group seemed frozen in yoga trance, unless it was transcendental meditation. No mugging or murder in sight. Good vibes are few and far between in this city, thought Ced, missing Symi, its sanity and its lighthouse-keeper.

'Remember AmarK?' asked Ric.

'Of course!' muttered Ced. 'Why?'

'Because I called him last night. You know me: I'm a practical guy. I need answers. I told him about Nush. I told him that we, her long-time friends, had not seen it coming. To cut a long story short, I begged him to ... *explain.*'

'I need an ice cream!'

Leonor's cuckoo too, thought Ric, a certain part of his anatomy stiffening.

'Right. Dr AmarK started by pointing out that he was no shrink and that Freud, comma, Sigmund, had himself committed suicide.'

'So?'

'Theories diverge. Analysts, psychoanalysts, scientists, call them what you will, do agree on one fact: most suicides are reactions rather than decisions. It's statistical. The survivors won't explain their act in terms of rational assessments. If people jump from heights, drown, hang or shoot themselves, it's generally because agony's become so unendurable that it's no longer the inner danger that most scares them; it's *the terror of surviving* it. Impulse overpowers thought.'

'Oh do shut up!' Leonor twittered. Like her son, dire reality wasn't what she most valued. She longed not for a Greek island, but for a bubble-bath and a cuddle from some dog or other – perhaps a gardener...

Impermeable to all else but facts, as usual, Ric went on.

'Biology is about the avoidance of pain and ultimately,

death. But suicidal people are fearless. Fearless!'

'What on earth do you mean?' asked Ced, confused.

'According to the Doc, suicidal people opt for the less terrible of two terrors.'

'Don't we all? It's freezing!'

Leonor rushed off. Neither Ric nor Ced followed her. The former pursued his tirade.

'Ninety-four percent of those who commit suicide signal their intention – talking about it, withdrawing their savings, writing cryptic letters – without eliciting the alarm they intend to. Four out of five, i.e. eighty-one percent, of their closest relatives or friends fail to take these signals seriously. Can you imagine?'

Did we wish to?

'Anyway', continued Ric. 'Most people who intend or succeed committing suicide are under toxic influences, drugs, alcohol, and so on. What does that tell us? Other than almost thirty – yes, thirty! – percent of the family members of those who attempt suicide killed themselves?'

'Listen, you two. It gets jazzy: the great paradox of the brain is that it can't feel pain.'

'What?'

Ric paused for effect.

'The organ which is the seat of pain, joy and love is *insensitive to injury*. That's why brain surgery can be conducted without anaesthetics.'

'Stop!' Ced exploded, suddenly incensed. 'What the freaking fuck do *you* know about any of this? You, treading on my father's thick carpets, sleeping under cashmere blankets, waiting for me to admit – wait no longer – that I'm not cut out for the...'

'For what? Art? Responsibility? Taking care of Anoushka, whom you've been infatuated with forever? Get real!'

Cedric had heard enough. True, his school-flame used to enthral him. But later on, she terrified him. Too unpredictable, too erratic, too ... different.

He remembered Aleana telling him how flattered Nush had been to be included in The Factory's deranged crowd for a while. Andy Warhol, she had posited, was a monster. Having conquered fame because of his eccentricity, his innovations, his militant homosexuality coupled with the claim to be a virgin, he defended artifice. To his credit, he detected talent and promoted artists such as Basquiat, Julian Schnabel, Francesco Clemente, to name but a few later defined as the Transavantgarde, she had reluctantly conceded.

Just when he'd hoped she'd shut up, Aleana had gone one further, comparing Nush to Edie Sedgwick. The pedigree and beauty of both had fascinated the albino Mephisto too. Their background, fortunately, was far from the same.

Edie Sedgwick's wealthy father had three nervous breakdowns prior to his marriage, after which he was diagnosed with bipolar disorder. The family doctor advised him *never* to have children. He produced eight. Edie was the fourth. 'Given so many tranquilisers, I lost all my feelings, persuaded to be insane.' Some doctor! Her brother Minty was an alcoholic by the age of fifteen and committed suicide ten years later. Another brother, no sooner released from a mental hospital, crashed his motorcycle into a bus. Edie, also institutionalised on various occasions, died from an overdose.

'Thanks for sharing this most uplifting story,' Ced had fumed.

'Since when do you listen?' Aleana had hushed, reaching for his hand.

'Hullo!' boomed Hector Vich, emerging from behind a bush as if he'd been lying in wait.

What the hell was *he* doing in Central Park, a lollipop hanging from his lips? And why would Leonor, now clad in a fur coat – genuine fur – reappear at precisely that moment?

'Oh dear! Serendipity, I presume!'

'Ever so clever with words, daaaaarling!' she crooned. 'And how well you look!'

'The prerogative of prehistoric men.'

'Quite. Always been so good at moulding the past to your purpose, *chéri!*'

'Forget yesteryears!' re-smiled Hector. 'I'm in love. Love!'

'Does the unlucky one reciprocate?'

'She doesn't know it. Yet.'

27

PACKING. PAST CARING

Wheeling Nush into the beauty salon was like posting a parcel. Post-traumatic shock? My instructions were clear: a facial, a massage, the re-dying of her hair to its black colour, a manicure: I needed about five hours to sort out her life – meaning erasing her former one.

American efficiency is impressive. The removal company contracted to fetch her belongings and ship them to Nantucket arrived on time; a specialised enterprise to clean and repaint the place, also. Yet I had time, perhaps too much of it, to go through Nush's stuff. Should I pretend not to have perused letters addressed to no one in particular, I'd be lying. Same with her sketch-books, all too often depicting mutation and mutilation.

It takes a lot to rattle me. My upbringing had infused me with steadfast nerves. Never have I cried out for help. Nush, it seemed, had done little else. Having read what I did, studied her work, I felt … *boulversée*. Shattered and moved.

When the landlady asked me to sign the due papers in exchange for an undue amount, she had the vulgar impertinence to say: 'Well! Goes to show that nuttiness doesn't make happy, whaddyasay?'

I pushed the woman out of the door. Nush was just a girl, a lost girl ensconced in some inner turmoil. Possibly, the only world she knew.

Sitting in the empty, white-washed atelier a little longer, a lukewarm Coca-Cola in my hands, I could hear Hector saying:

'Money simplifies life. Beauty complicates it.'
Tender Had Been The Night.

28

LIFE & SHORT

Leonor wasn't stupid, but none too subtle either. A born care-taker, yes; but mainly of dogs. Deep down, she was a loner who preferred silence or Beethoven to intimacy.

Four years would go, race or drag by before we would be reunited.

Again on September 15th. By now, it's 1985.

In the meantime, we did meet; but never all of us four ex-Rosey friends together at the same place or time.

By and large, Nush had abided by the rules: living in the guest cottage, the girl wasn't allowed to enter Leonor's house unless calling beforehand. Canvasses, brushes and paint had been provided in order to keep her at bay.

Yet, Nush was a musicals aficionada and would listen to *Porgy & Bess*, *My Fair Lady*, *Singin' in the Rain*, *Cats* and lately, *Les Misérables* – a recent blockbuster – on a loop.

That did it. One evening, Leonor stomped across the lawn and screamed, 'Enough! *Cats* bad enough but *Les Misérables*, honestly! You're far from being miserable yourself, let me point out, whilst I can't even hear the sea anymore, such is the racket the wind wafts over.'

That *night*, Nush played Liza Minelli's famous *Cabaret* song, 'Elsie', full-volume non-stop.

The day she died the neighbors came to snicker

'Well, that's what comes from too much pills and liquor!'
But when I saw her laid out like a Queen
She was the happiest corpse, I'd ever seen...

It never crossed Leonor's mind that the girl's insolence was neurotic. Of Ric's tedious exposé in Central Park, she mainly remembered that first suicide attempts more often fail than not; second attempts more often succeed than fail. Were stringent rules bad for a psychic convalescence? Delicacy was of the essence. Patience, the quintessence.

As conciliatory as her son, she decided to take Nush for slow walks, her legs still in need of care.

Alas and again, Leonor didn't see the writing on the wall: Nush had fallen in love with her (call it a transfer) all the more obsessive for not being requited. She furthermore committed the fatal error of having sex with her. Once or thrice. Out of curiosity. And fatal is not a word employed lightly here.

Every so often Nush left, only to return weeks later without warning.

If only Leonor had read *Beware of Pity* by Stefan Zweig, Ric's bedside book.

PART THREE

29

FOUR YEARS, FIVE PAGES

R ic worked and travelled, both incessantly.
He convinced Hector to swim counter-current, create small hotels, forty rooms or so, called Vich-Clubs.

The themed concept was crowned with tremendous success in New York, Houston, even Los Angeles: the Art-Vich (each room decorated on the theme of painters, be it Modigliani, Matisse or Mondrian); the Music-Vich (same with scores by Bach, Schubert, Vivaldi); the Time-Vich (with an impressive collection of antique clocks, sand-clocks, sun-clocks or replicas of Dalí's *montres molles* displayed in the rooms) were soon lauded across borders.

Hector's own favourite: the Library-Vich, with book-lined mezzanines; suites with book cabinets; spiral staircases flanked by *trompe-l'oeil* leather-bindings – and so on. A large segment of its clientele was the adulterous charmed by discretion.

But the only hotel Hector became personally involved in with a passion was the Vich-Lodges in Kenya. Opposite Peponi's, on Lamu.

Slowly but surely, Ric fomented the plan to be independent. He was assiduously vied for, having become a symbol of refinement; considered a dandy who collected rare wines, quattrocento sculptures and cubist paintings. Not to mention sumptuous redheads, each rarely seen in his company on more than a very few occasions.

Rich and famous in his own right, Ric remained frustrated. He had expected more elation from satisfaction.

One afternoon, he bumped into Nush in Greenwich Village. 'How's life?', 'What's new?' and more such scintillating dialogue followed – until Nush had enough. 'Let's have a real conversation, shall we?'

They had drinks in the Plaza's atrium.

'So. What's the story of your life, lately?' Ric asked, more out of concern than of real interest. 'Glad to notice you're hardly limping anymore...'

'Knowing you, I'll spare you the ordeal, Ric. What's the point, anyway? One always tells of a break or a breach: from a person, a country, a self. One always narrates the end of a story. Same here: I paint ruptures. Tricky to explain, darling, I know, but...'

Her words had triggered an idea. He invited her for dinner, later on.

For the occasion, Nush wore a copper-red wig. They never mentioned Ced.

Cedric's life warrants more and better than generalities here. He still wrote letters. At least to me. Excerpt:

My passion for islands isn't new, nor my disinterest for the likes of me. Even during my days at the Sorbonne, I favoured the company of the elder. Since then, I've roamed the Greek islands, staying here or there, without goal or haste, gathering the nectar of the ephemeral. I took photographs: not of monasteries, but of monks; not of ships, but of sponge-divers – *bref*, of people only. Every face is a map, every wrinkle an equinox. Days are pretty much alike. I'm not singular either. Love? Well, the occasional bella, bellissima on a holiday is, of course, a welcome diversion. Hey! But also in this respect, I favour the company of women whose multi-faceted or multi-layered destiny might tailor that of many less ambitious ones. Women to whom all will ever remain inaccessible, incomplete – as will their tomb or their statue. It's a misfortune to be born with immoderation in one's soul – a misfortune without which there might not be remarkable destinies. Islands, not surprisingly (!) seem to attract permanently unstable, perpetually unsatisfied ladies who'll divorce five times or never get married, despising lovers either too dull or not demanding enough. Curiously, some of the most attaching women can be found amongst these … I like tales. I revere mythology!

Γεία, beautiful Al – and try to avoid Troy.

When writing these lines, Ced was blissfully unaware of what would hit him soon thereafter.

He finally settled on idyllic Symi. One of the more than a hundred islands composing the Dodecanese, Symi is among the smallest and least populated. In the seventies it became plagued by an outburst of leprosy. Not, mercifully, the contagious and seldom curable kind, but the nodular variety.

Trained in Kenya, Ced took over. He hugged and helped the ill, conveying that it entailed no danger of contamination. He single-handedly built an adobe house that would become a meeting place. Meanwhile, having cabled his father, specialists were sent. The Panormitis monastery organised an Orthodox ceremony in his honour, followed by a dance and bonfire staged by kids on one of the shingle beaches that indent the steep rocks. He had been adopted. His speaking Greek had of course helped.

Ced was happy.

Every now and then, he took the rackety ferry to Rhodes. There, he'd rent a motorbike and criss-cross the island with his camera, looking for interesting faces, human contrast and, if possible, a pretty girl to flirt with. It was good to feel a stranger. One who, admittedly, enjoyed a gastronomic treat and pillows once in a while.

It was in one of Rhodes' best restaurants, the Tamam, that he spotted a spectacular girl. Both being alone and reading, they ended up introducing themselves.

'I'm Iris,' she smiled.

His honey-coloured eyes and her Venetian-red hair matched to perfection.

Meanwhile, Ced's father was experiencing an explosion.

Had he not called Aleana a ticking bomb at some point? Well.

In his late forties, he felt like an adolescent again.

She had shattered his cynical serenity.

Yes. Tender had been their first night in New York, and tender their subsequent encounters. Yet the girl – a young woman by now – was ferociously elusive.

She still owned that houseboat in Paris but, other than that, little else. When in need of clothes she'd buy some, then give them away. Did her reluctance to remain attached to anything extend to any ... one?

Hector Vich, handsome and generous, clever and amusing, wasn't used to being treated with distracted detachment.

Believing that any problem can be solved once understood, he had people research gypsy culture – why had Aleana embraced it with such uncharacteristic passion? Their report: that particular community in the Provence or the Camargue stemmed, more or less directly, from the Baliardo family – its prominent and patriarchal figure being Manolo de la Plata. The latter's hero: Django Reinhardt. Their successors: the Gipsy Kings.

Become famous and wealthy and offered suites in six-star hotels, they remained reluctant to part for even a short while and would gather, be it in a small bathroom, to play the guitar and share whatever food.

Aleana had learnt to play the guitar very young. As with everything solitary, she excelled at it.

Solitude! Only children, especially those bereaved of affection, understand it will ultimately come to that.

Hector's conclusion: gypsies, often suspected of being thieves or bandits, abided by a most rigorous code of honour among themselves – especially, towards women. Their families often encompassing four generations, they moved together as a clan. To Aleana, Hector fathomed, they represented what she had always craved: a sense of belonging. Unconditional solidarity. Plus respect.

He would give all of it to her, given time.

What Hector could not have pictured was the emotional impact gypsy music had on Aleana. Taught not to complain, not to show distress, not to express frailty, Aleana often cried.

She cried remembering her distant parents, now forever gone. She cried because of period-cramps. She cried because her lighter had run out of gas. She cried because she wasn't a teenager anymore, but also because those times were no paradise lost and the present, none regained. Because she had never been to Vladivostok and never would. Neither tired nor sad, she felt ... vanquished. So she just cried.

30

CONTAGION

Ced was the first to arrive on my *péniche* on September 15th, 1985.

Ten years after our first rendezvous on that date. Ten years after our leaving Le Rosey.

Three popes have succeeded each other; the Pol Pot regime finally collapses more or less at the same time as the Shah of Iran is ousted by Ayatollah Khomeini; Indira Gandhi is assassinated; Sadat and Begin sign a peace treaty at Camp David whilst terrorism makes the headlines with alarming frequency. (The Egyptian statesman himself gets killed in 1981.) Arch-conservative and heavily-permed Margaret Thatcher becomes Prime Minister of the no longer so United Kingdom (after royal war hero Mountbatten is also assassinated, allegedly by the IRA) and socialist Mitterrand becomes France's President.

Reagan and Thatcher are ridiculed on posters depicting them in each other's arms, storm and fire in the background, Scarlett and Rhett style, with 'Gone With the Blast' as the caption. (They would laugh all the way to posterity, having restored prosperity and confidence.) Afghanistan is invaded by the Soviets; the Lebanese Civil War rages; the Falklands War is a quickie; the Iran–Iraq War, the outset of a domino-drama… Simultaneously, the end of the Cold War seems in sight. Soon, the Berlin Wall would be pulverised.

On a more flippant note, long and liquid lunches are still in fashion. The moon has almost become an English garden.

Prozac helps calm nerves; the likes of Donald Trump glorify coarse ambition. Other late seventies icons: jittery David Bowie, junkie Janis Joplin, punky Lou Reed. They're soon to be overshadowed by Jackie (now O); by provocative Madonna (a Catholic, as it were) or spooky Michael Jackson. Will techno-rock and heavy metal relegate the Beatles to some Jurassic Park? AIDS, now an epidemic, puts a brake on sexual permissiveness. Genetics and technology advance in quantum leaps.

The first half of the eighties was one of these 'plateau' periods following frenzied phases of excess.

Caution became the golden standard – even amongst us, the young. In 1985, our 'trio' (quartet, including Nush) were all twenty-seven years old. Psychedelic drugs are out: too dangerous. Liquor would do. Through satellite channels, we saw 'live' 524 people perish in the worst air-crash ever in August of that year (short flight from Tokyo to Osaka). Only years later would we get used to zapping; not only in terms of TV channels, but also in terms of attention spans.

But back to September 15th, 1985, on my houseboat.

Play a compilation of the group Ten Years After? Naah. If you listen carefully, their songs are sad. Even though saturnine Nush wasn't around, forget why, I opted for 'Plan B' and introduced another tape: 'Saturday Night Fever'.

Whose mood couldn't be uplifted by such cheerful crap? We had started dancing merrily when the phone rang.

Oh Dog. Not again! What now? I swayed into the kitchen.

'Are you related to Anoushka, Princess Poniatowski?'

'Kind of. Why?'

'The person has been caught on CCTV shoplifting. No relatives in the US. Gave us this number. Might you pay the fine? She let rather expensive gloves slip into her handbag. Inadvertently, she claims.'

Money was transferred and Nush told to wait for us in the flat Ric had rented on 58th Street. He was fed up with hotels, as a dentist might be with *Jaws* movies.

A few days later, we flew to NYC, determined to act casual.

Upon walking into the duplex, a splendid buffet flanked by candles and flower-bouquets awaited us. Effusive hugs were exchanged.

How was life in between New York and Nantucket? At the mention of the latter, she swirled around as if she'd seen the devil.

Various innuendos had led me to believe that Ced's mother had thrown Nush out, accusing her of harassment. But then, good-hearted as ever, she had invited her back – on the condition Nush stop insisting on something she neither wanted to give nor to receive.

'Lower the volume,' Ric commanded with what seemed apprehension. 'Must listen to my answering machine.'

Phones hadn't been bearers of joy, lately. This one was on loudspeaker.

'Inspector Flic here. Must convey … very bad news. Been trying to reach you for hours but it being Saturday … Mr Vich's, first name Cedric, mother was found dead in her kitchen here in Nantucket. Suicide it seems. Ever so sorry to leave such information on a … machine, but we urgently require your, er, presence … assistance…'

We exchanged petrified glances.

Nush rushed to the bathroom: from the sound of it, to vomit.

Inspector Flic's call was eventually returned. We learnt:

… that Leonor's lifeless body had been found around noon by the gardener;

... that TOD ('Time of death') was estimated at between 9 and 10 the previous night;

... that it had already been established that her blood showed a high content of alcohol (0.9, corresponding to a bottle of wine, baby-food to us) plus traces of dextroamphetamine or one of its derivatives. ('Sorry?' 'Medication for ADD. Can't elaborate. I'm no medic.')

Leonor had cut the arteries at the hollow of the elbow with a kitchen knife – not her wrist with a razor-blade, Flic added with a sigh. (Too banal?) According to the cook, employed for almost twenty years, she had been troubled and nervous recently. Mrs Vich had left no note – but, as only her fingerprints showed on the knife's handle, there was little doubt to be harboured...

Doubt? Little?

The Inspector sounded truly concerned.

He had taken the trouble to check the timetable of the next day's ferries to Nantucket. (Direct flights, back then, weren't only few and far between but, on September weekends, fully-booked.) We could make the 10 o'clock from E. 35th Street, arriving at around 6 pm.

Meanwhile?

Ric, the decider and doer – couldn't think of anything to do or say.

Ced looked semi-catatonic. When he finally spoke, he sounded absent.

'Shouldn't I have told her that I'm getting married in three weeks tête-a-tête? Not long distance?'

Nush, having re-emerged from the bathroom, green as a lime-sherbet, exclaimed:

'You – what?'

'Getting married. Is it a crime?'

Nush looked at him with ... *blind* eyes.

We persuaded our fragile friend not to come with us. With nowhere to go, apparently, she asked the boys whether she could squat at the flat for a night or two.

Me she ignored as if fearful. However endowed or plagued by a third eye, mine, if only two, can be pretty sharp.

31

LOVER DIDN'T DO IT

Upon arriving on Nantucket, Inspector Flic, a stout and severe-looking hulk, filled us in. The butler, whatever his name, had taken his yearly holidays: family matters in England. He had left on Thursday, his presence on the flight confirmed. The cook/maid, a veteran fixture in the household, had taken Friday night off. Her sister, who lived a few miles away, was celebrating her 70th birthday. Verified. As to the gardener: he was off duty every day at 6 pm and drunk himself into a stupor in a bar where, this particular Friday, he passed out and was carried to a motel to sleep it out: checked and double-checked, witnesses and all.

Ced became impatient:

'I want to see my mother. Now.'

Flic disliked the tone.

'Look here. First the house. Yours, henceforth.'

A most tasteless innuendo.

White-clad men with hygienic masks swept the kitchen floor; the gardener sipped a milkshake, probably Alka-Seltzer flavoured, and the old cook dozed in a corner, her face bloated from weeping.

'You were right, Inspector. No point. Let's go.'

A morgue is a morgue – a universally gloomy, aseptic, neon-lit place. Ced was offered the option to go in alone. He refused. We were family, he explained.

To see a purple-grey body, retrieved from a refrigerated drawer like food from a freezer made supposedly cool me freeze in shock. Sorry for the facile pun.

Leonor's arm was cut, deeply and precisely. The thing (yes, a classic): it was the wrong arm. Left-handed Leonor was unlikely to have butchered the hollow of her left elbow.

Dog Almighty. Observant as I always have been, trained to have become more so as a journalist, I cast a puzzled look at Ced and Ric. No reaction. The one who could have confirmed what I thought was Nush – her visual memory a second nature.

An extremely suntanned man approached.

'Good … excuse me … sad evening. I'm Detective Jonas from homicides. Might you be Anoushka Poniatowski?'

'No sir.'

I spelt out my last name. He didn't need to write it down.

'Aleana, may I? Been researching you. My job.'

No trenchcoat, no half-chewed cigar; yet his manner irresistibly reminded one of Peter Falk's Colombo – in thinner, taller and better.

'I believe you suspect what we know.'

'Possibly,' I muttered, not sure on what foot to dance or stand.

Ced and Ric looked confused.

'Very well. You people must be hungry. May I suggest dinner? On the taxpayer's bill!'

The guy was *sympathique*. And starving we were. Unwilling to talk and unable to rest, we had watched videos all night.

He took us to downtown Nantucket, near Steamboat Wharf where we had docked only hours earlier. A bubbly place: lights gleaming, ships looming and humming above the quay, the smell of earlier rain, gasoline, and wood smoke mingling with that of the salty ocean. A car ferry from Hyannis was gliding in. We settled at a table on the restaurant's terrace.

The irony of the name Jonas on an island famous for having been America's whaling capital amused me. Not appropriate in the circumstances, but the homicide guy winked, ordered seafood and lit a cigarette.

'Mr Vich, Cedric if I may, could it be that you never noticed your mother was left-handed? Nor you, Mr Moralli, Ricardo? From certain letters we have found, it seems you were acquainted with the victim, ain't it so?'

Ced looked dumbfounded, flabbergasted, whatever the word might be. Nonplussed? Wrong time for semantic subtleties. Would look it up at some point. At this one, Ric jumped up as if out of an ejecting seat.

'Back in a tick.'

What a ridiculous expression.

The exchange that ensued was an interrogation without hostility or emotion – at least not on the detective's part. Peppered with piecemeal information, it spurred my imagination into, once again, a gallop.

Right … No: left. Leonor, left-handed, could not possibly have cut her left arm with the strength required to sever the deeper veins. Besides, she was extremely clumsy: 'I'm useless at anything manual,' she'd shrug, 'other than playing the piano. Fortunately, dogs don't mind!' (Young men left unmentioned.)

Dogs!

Her favourite, the only one allowed in her house, had been found poisoned. The Alsatian was called Garfield: vintage Leonor. Trained as a watchdog, he could be ferocious – ditto the cook, the gardener and acquaintances.

'Pointing to premeditated burglary?' ventured Jonas, with a gratifying 'no-dumb-blonde' glance at me.

Let's speculate. Someone kills Leonor. Let's posit that the motive(s) is (are) personal. Poisoning the dog is meant to throw the investigation off-track. Approach the dog without being attacked? Must have been someone well-known. Like, perhaps, the cuckold neighbour's son-in-law? The old cook's sister's nephew? He owes ugly Auntie Gertrude money. She's jealous of Gwendoline (do we choose our name?). She lives comfortably with a generous lady; is given clothes; hardly ever needs to cook as the lady's on an endless diet – so: Gertrude sees and seizes an opportunity. Let him, nicknamed The Leech, do the deed. He's immoral, amoral, what's the difference, and while he's at it, he can steal her jewellery.

Garfield? The Leech wears clothes perfumed with Leonor's *Dior J'adore* and brings a chunk of sirloin. Hmm ... Alsatians aren't easily fooled by some Tootsie. Besides, the nephew, Alphonse or Alfred, is a coward and a profiteer: he'd have gone to the police to denounce the cunning aunt in the hope of being rewarded (in cash). Fat chance, I thought, admiring Detective Jonas' thorax and clever hands.

The gardener? Nah. He's a drunkard and a gigolo. Why on earth kill the redhead egg? Unless she'd contemplated firing him, having set her eyes on, say ... Jonas? Tztz. He must be in his forties, antediluvian in Leonor's eyes.

The butler, who usually does it in dated Agatha Christie novels: further away than across the Atlantic, impossible.

I emerged from my fantasies just in time to overhear a most puzzling piece of the puzzle: the boots.

It had been raining on Friday evening and all through the night.

When the police arrived on the premises, they observed the footprints of a pair of boots. Size 14! Huge. Way larger than anyone aforementioned. Meaningless of course: a murderer won't wear his own shoe-size, will he? The seriously interesting bit: footprints were traced towards the kitchen door – but none, ziltch, zero, leaving the house from whatever angle.

Judging by the depth of the imprints, the boot-wearer must have been heavy: about 220 lb. Again, incompatible with anyone remotely suspicious.

At this point, my brain not only galloped: it went on steeplechase.

Hurdle no. 1: an empty bottle of red wine. Leonor hated red wine. She only drank whisky-sours and champagne.

Hurdle no. 2: ADD medication? *Please*. Her only concession to pharmaceuticals had been anti-cholesterol pills.

Hurdle no. 3: the alarm system. She'd personally switch it on before the 9pm news. Why hadn't it been?

Hurdle no. 4: Garfield the dog. How come he hadn't even barked before swallowing poisoned meat – handed to him by an intruder?

Hurdle no. 5: whoever walked towards the house, entered it, and then killed Leonor must have gotten out. On a kite? Swooped away by a helicopter? Evaporated like a djinn?

The detective looked at me, Hector-like. Too late, man. My formerly frigid heart is now immune to any other man's charm.

Ced having come back and calmed down, we lingered on, listening to street musicians.

'I've taken the liberty to reserve three rooms in a hotel around the corner,' Jonas said.

Ced stretched out his hand.

'How very ... delicate. Thank you.'

'What about our bags?' asked Ric.

'In my trunk.'

'Good thinking,' said Ric, hoping that this Jonas guy wouldn't think *too* much. Since he probably already had, then that he'd shut up. Why should his friend, Leonor's son, learn about the fling? Torrid, yes, but fleeting. Ten years ago, for fuck's sake.

Jonas, naturally, had inquired whether any of us had been on a ferry or on a plane days before Leonor's 'demise'. We all might have had a motive: Ced, the inheritance. Ric, unfinished business with a tease who'd treated him like a pet and dismissed him like a toy-boy. Me? She was Hector's ex-wife. *My* Hector.

After a foamy bath, I took half a Lexomil.

No sooner swallowed, I stood upright on my bed.

Pills. Where had I seen a whole bunch of them?

Boots. Who wore boots and nothing but boots, regardless of season? But: why of Centaurus dimensions? Possibly because some shop was left with no others?

Red wine. Who drank red wine for breakfast?

The dog. Whose smell would be familiar enough for Garfield not to react aggressively?

The alarm. Who other than Leonor's staff knew its code?

To each, to every, question, one answer: Nush.

Let's see.

Nush's no criminal. Yet, acting out of character or on impulse...? She has the keys, that much's established. Leonor's had enough of Nush's bipolar and bisexual behaviour. Her good heart, however, prevents her from banishing the young girl. (Artists are artists, right?)

On to the next step or hypothesis:

Nush arrives on Friday afternoon, unaware that Leonor's staff have all gone. Garfield waggles his tail. She despises the dog as she despises anyone responding to Pavlovian reflexes. And I'm one of them, she sighs. She wants Leonor to take a final decision: take me or leave me. Love me, or don't. But nothing lukewarm: that I cannot take. Leonor wonders: was it not she who, on the *QE2* had said: 'To seduce is to devour'?

She cajoles, opens a bottle of Pommery, even puts on the

radio in the hope that distraction might calm the girl down.

'I want an answer. I need a decision. Focus!'

Leonor ducks the confrontation. She wants to watch the news, followed by a comedy, dinner tray on her knees.

But Nush *desperately* wants Leonor to understand. What exactly? Not too sure. Something decisive must happen. Now. Leonor tells Nush to have a rest, is about to pick up her tray and walk up the stairs.

'Don't let me down! Don't leave me alone! Please let's have a last drink!'

Leonor, thinking Nush means a last drink before going to sleep, reluctantly agrees. Little does she know that alcohol, in conjunction with dextroamphetamine, causes confusion.

'I'm dead,' she giddily winces after a while.

'Not yet!'

In a rage, an uncontrollable, a tectonic, a crazed rage, Nush picks up the knife that's been lying on the kitchen table (is it her fault?) and cuts Leonor's arteries – at the inside of her elbow.

A wrist is sacred to a painter.

So far, so freaky.

What about the dog? Did Nush, sobered up by the sight of blood and the consequence of her deed, look for the rat-poison under the sink, retrieve some meat, mix the both and hand it to Garfield? Has the ADD medication made her sharp enough to enact a diversion-manoeuvre?

No. Plausible, but unlikely. Or likely and implausible.

The Lexomil begun to jiggle my brain.

Donc – as the French say every other second.

New scenario. No serendipity. Sheer and sober premeditation, up to the sharpest knife removed from some drawer.

But … why would Nush want to harm Leonor; possibly

watch her bleed to death? Because another rejection is just one too many? Because if she can't have Leonor, no one will?

Getting to Nantucket, on a rainy mid-September Friday, easy: whereas leaving from NYC, Providence or Boston, the ferries are packed – yet you normally get a last-minute ticket. No one with a hood or a cap would look conspicuous. From the dock to Leonor's house, a ten-minute walk. Let's say it's around 7 pm: people are home or out. In any case, not in their garden.

Nush is aware of Leonor's habits: she'll be in the kitchen listening to Beethoven, cutting salami or some fattening stuff she only allows herself on the cook's nights out.

Leonor is annoyed to see her. Being gracious, she sits down and lets the girl's abuse, followed by pleading, wash over her. Closing her eyes makes it easy not to listen. Nush goes to the fridge, takes out meat and surreptitiously mixes rat-poison with the blood that Garfield, she knows, loves to lap.

'Thanks!' says Leonor. 'Almost forgot to feed him!'

But when the clock indicates ten to nine, she's had it.

'Go to the cottage, will you? Sleep. We'll talk tomorrow. Sober.'

'There *will* be no tomorrow!' screams Nush. 'Nor do I intend to be sober!'

Then, the knife … the arm … the…

In her condition, shock erupts into a geyser-like spur of concentration. She pours the rest, mixed with the Pommery, into a funnel she inserts between Leonor's lips. Slipping her hands into the gloves – stolen with or without premeditation – she cleans what has to be cleaned (not Leonor's fingerprints, obviously); puts the oversized boots back on and leaves the way she had come.

The trick: she slips into the boots putting her toes where her heels should be. Upside down, if you will. Explaining why no outwards imprints were found. Also why the weight had been over-evaluated … and why nothing had indicated a limp.

Getting back to NYC in time for our Empire State Building rendezvous? No big deal. The ferries to the mainland, early on a Saturday, were equally crowded. It was still raining.

The silhouette of a weirdo with hunched shoulders comes back my mind. His ashen hair framing a ghostly-white face struck me. Hobbling around the 102nd floor, looking neither up to the sky nor down at the streets, with the air of someone who knows that there's little difference between life and death, he had paced the same floor as we had, way above the hum of so-called normal life and then, suddenly, spat into the void.

Remembering him, I remembered something I'd noticed in Nush's former atelier. Wigs, in all variations. I'd thrown them into boxes with a collection of boots.

Half asleep, or asleep already, I laughed. Why a dilettante journalist instead of a gothic novel writer? Who had said, 'Coherence is the last refuge of the unimaginative'? When it's not Oscar Wilde, this sort of a line is usually Bernard Shaw's. Then I stopped laughing.

What would I not have given to be under fluffy covers – with Hector. He hadn't returned my calls.

I had left messages all over the place, meaning in five countries. Not used to feeling lonesome, I felt lost. Damn it! Was I regressing back to an adolescence I'd never actually experienced?

Finally about to sink into sleep, I thought, no wonder that the expression is 'love at first sight'. Blindness helps, for sure. Otherwise, more people would take a second look in a hurry. Whereupon my overwrought mind was invaded by a nightmare.

God was a Cat, after all. Not killed by curiosity, but by

vanity. His eyes kept switching colour. He was an albino cha-
meleon who smiled to no one.

32

ON THE PLANE

'Mr Ricardo Moralli?'
Early on this Monday morning, September 17th, the hall of Nantucket's hotel had been invaded by Finnish tourists going 'hohoyhoy'.

'Your Pilatus is waiting at the airport.'

Some plane! An old jet-prop fitted for amputated dwarfs. Some airport too. Not unlike the one in Lamu. Well. It was just the two of us. Ric had to go to New York, business meetings and all that. I wanted to go back too. I needed to see, rescue, confront – all three, perhaps – Nush. My monstrous scenari had left me with a bitter aftertaste of remorse.

A four-hour flight. No mini-bar. Opaque clouds prevented me from gazing at the coastline. Exhaustion was kicking in. Ric would certainly read the papers, starting with the stock-market section. Wrong. He tossed them on the floor.

'So', he said, smiling warmly. 'How are things with you and Mr Vich?'

He retrieved a flask from his pocket. 'Brandy. Might help.'

Since when was he interested in the lives of others? I threw him a sidelong glance. His eyes were closed.

'Since when?' he unknowingly echoed.

Though recoiling, I removed my sunglasses.

He squeezed my hand. Meanwhile, my memory zapped through anthologies of poems, in verse or prose, in languages dead or alive, hoping to find adequate words. I opted for extravagant lyricism.

'I'm in love.'

'Well put.'

'Look. I was a playful girl, not exactly a playgirl, but, ah, reluctant to envisage consequences. Hector, just as afraid as I was, transported me to...'

'Vich? Afraid?'

'Yes'.

Ric, to my utter amazement, hushed:

> On aime d'abord par hasard.
> Par jeu, par curiosité,
> Pour avoir dans un regard
> Lu des possibitités...

The fact and figure, the calculating and scheming Ric reciting Paul Géraldy, my favourite poet?

'Women in love tend to become hostages of an absence. Careful, Al. Hector's an expert at being absent.'

This I resented. Since when posing as a sage? Any of his business? Then, a nasty afterthought: 'Is it *about* business?' My third afterthought: 'How unfair of me!'

I was on the verge of tears. Back on with the sunglasses. Pulling out the notebook I never part with and where I scribble my most unspeakable thoughts (the kitschy ones, mainly), I read aloud:

'Can anyone explain, in retrospect, why, in the midst of silent or deafening crowds, witnessing the death of a star or the rising of a curtain, why, amongst tossed dice, a single, random combination becomes a winning joker?'

'Ha!' smiled poker-playing Ric, nodding off.

The pilot's voice, urging us to fasten our seatbelts, made Ric recover his wits with a vengeance.

'Cut the crap, Al. The man will never live up to your

expectations. He'll be nothing more than another episode more in your serial-infatuation saga...'

I'd have jumped at his throat had I not been nailed to the spot.

'Wrong! Hector's attracted me in some foggy way for ... a long time, let's say. Then the fog lifted. When he declared that he was, er, I ... how should I say...?'

'... in love, you *decided* to love in return? As Amador *determined* to love Florida?'

'Ric?! You can't possibly have read Stendhal!'

'Not Stendhal. Washington Irving. The Alhambra something-or-other. A tale.'

'Since when do you...?'

'Since Leonor.'

What had happened to the cold-fish Ricardo I had mummified?

To change the subject.

'Did you know Ced was getting married?'

'Had no idea', he replied, visibly hurt.

'D'you know to whom?'

'Not the faintest.'

'D'you understand why he didn't tell...?'

'No.'

Even though I had resolved not to drift onto the subject of Nush, I did.

'Look, Al. I have been taking care of our friend for years. You heard it from her: buying her paintings, transferring money to her horrendous mother, making her believe that things were fine because if they were not – I'd just make sure they were, you get my drift.'

'What about Ced? Didn't he help?'

The ensuing silence sounded hostile.

'I've kept a letter Cedric wrote to Nush after he sent her a big cheque for the best wheelchair money can buy. Shall I read it to you?'

My intuition told me that he had been waiting for this opportunity for a while. Be it as it may, he hastened to retrieve a crumpled envelope.

My darling Nush. I could not sleep all night, got terribly drunk. I felt like a child. The image of you dancing or bouncing around, driving like an ace and behaving like an ass haunts me. You've always represented temper and passion. You injected pace in our rather sedate life and I loved it. You need a brotherly figure. I need a platonic companion. Actually, I'm immature myself. As you might know, even my father calls me a Peter Pan.

Ric paused, grinned, said 'I'll spare you the rambling on.' He tore up the sheets.

'Have you noticed the numbers of I's in this piece of prose? Men like that don't get married. Someone who won't grow up and boasts about it is an emotional cripple.'

'How can you say such things about your oldest friend, someone who's always supported you?'

'It suited him, didn't it? Peter Pans are experts at making others feel in charge or in debt, and women, motherly. Meanwhile, they're busy with more important things: themselves! Peter Pans get away with it by virtue of being endearing. But basically they capitalise on the need to be needed. Feeling indispensable, not only do they feel entitled to be demanding but also expect their demands to be met without delay. One hell of a psychological swindle!'

Ineffable sadness overcame me.

'You exaggerate. Ced, in his heart of hearts, is the best person ever.'

'We've established that, haven't we? You, Nush and other

needy ladies might have come in quite handy with his set-up, but as he writes in no uncertain terms, commitment is for adults. Not for him. And he's getting married!'

Had Ric met too many fakes and frauds over the years? Could he still see a credit card without starting to sniff? One way or the other: why – *why* such resentment? Cedric had never interfered with Ricardo's ambitions. There had been no women-rivalries. Ced was unaware that his friend had slept with his mother – and, should he have been, I doubt it would have perturbed his own sleep.

So? So:

> Where ignorance is bliss
> 'tis folly to be wise.

33

A FUNERAL, A WEDDING

Later.
Sorry.
Forgot something important.

34

WHATEVER HAPPENED TO BABE BANES?

B abe? What Babe?
An agile operator, that's what Iris was.

Seen too much, too young, for her own good? As far as men were concerned, she had realised early on that a display of awed admiration coated with helplessness does the trick, be it with alpha-men or losers.

Rewinding: Rhodes.

At the whatever-it-was-called restaurant, she meets Cedric. They laugh, talk and discover, perchance, that they both know Dr Amar Khoury. Other than that, they have little in common.

Correction. They're both left-handed. Ced, like his mother; Iris like her father.

A coincidence, shrugs he.

Aha, thinks she. Iris does not believe in coincidences; only in cause and effect. Only the weak believe in luck.

Be it her wearing a 'petite robe noire', the kind of dress that suggests modesty whilst sculpting the figure, or wearing no jewellery other than a titanium Rolex worth more than two gold ones, discretion seems to define beautiful Iris, muses Ced.

Ironic, for Iris has moved on in the shoplifting department.

Make-up, perfumes? The past. The chewing-gum trick isn't yet the classic it later became. She'd walk into Cartier or Bulgari, elegantly casual, pretending to look for a present: her mother's birthday. Her undecidedness and charm causing zealous havoc, the display-desks are soon covered with velvet-lined trays. In the midst of the confusion, Iris snatches a diamond ring or a brooch, uses chewing-gum to stick it under one of the tables, and apologises: better return next day with her mother in tow. She wouldn't want to molest the staff with the complications of an exchange.

Should a member of the sales team notice something was missing (seldom the case) Iris, wearing an outraged but polite look, would put her handbag and coat at their disposal for examination. With a slanted glance at the masculine personnel, she'd suggest a body-search – subsequently marching out, head high.

Shortly thereafter, in other words before authorities were called (the employees still hoping for an oversight), Iris' accomplice would walk in, signet ring much in evidence; sit at the designed desk, curling her chinchilla shawl around; ask to see a bracelet (emeralds only) and, need it be said, remove the valuable from under the desk before rushing off, pretexting an almost forgotten dentist's appointment, her driver having held the Rolls' back door open.

Whereupon the two ladies would meet, have a glass of Cristal and a good laugh. Not to mention sharing the loot.

Did Iris need it? Not in the least. She's become a partner at one of Saatchi & Saatchi's prestigious competitors. They had head-hunted her: rumours were circulating that she'd been the inspiration for slogans such as 'Labour isn't working' (an invitation to 10 Downing Street), 'Look better, see further' (a generous side-kick from an chain of opticians); 'Happiness is the Best Revenge' (ditto from Benson & Hedges).

But back to Rhodes.

Iris and Ced spend three days and nights together. Rather dull to her. An epiphany for him. Though approaching thirty, he's still, sexually speaking a, er, bit of a novice. She introduces him to sensations and pleasures unsuspected. Enough time for him to become hooked and for her, to hatch a strategy.

Another forty-eight hours might dissolve the spell. A newly-minted relationship must be stamped with exactitude – to insure this, nothing like separation. Hence, she organises a telefax to be handed to her and puts on one of her catalogued masks: the forlorn look.

'Must fly back to London, darling. Awful…'

He squeezes her hand with both of his.

'Why?'

'Problems.'

'What kind of?'

Iris shuffles on her chair, her eyes clouded.

'Look, sweetie. I only tell you this because you, *only you* might understand. I've worked in the advertising business for a long time, see? But I'm disenchanted: no dignity, you know? It's all about creating superfluous needs in order to generate frustration in order to sell exactly things that won't, ultimately, make anyone happier and which, and that's the nasty bit, are meant to become obsolete so they'll need to be replaced quickly, meaning…'

'Got it', Ced compassionately retorts. 'Out of a job?'

Iris can't believe the guy's naivety. Were she not pre-programmed for steely self-control, she might indulge in something resembling affection. (Let's not forget Ced's amber eyes nor … yeah. He's a fast learner.)

But no. Iris, as always, is on a mission.

Fiddling with her watch – a universal tic, it seems – she finally *consents* to opening up.

'I want out.'

What? panics the young man: does she mean him … them?

Iris lowers her eyes. The moment of doubt must be stretched.

Never let emotion interfere with ambition. Emotion leads to failure. Forget *temper, temper*! Life's all about '*concentration, concentration*!'

'So?' insists Ced.

'I want to start my own business. Not saying that it's a philanthropic proposition, but again *you*, of all people, might understand.'

The likeness between his lover and his mother unsettles him. The consummate art of listening while delaying answers, the gracious gestures… Ced feels itchy.

'Look', Iris hastens to continue. 'You, I and millions of people are left-handed. Don't you think it's unfair?'

He doesn't but nods, just in case. Her glance – one she's rehearsed to perfection – so focused, so exclusively attentive, makes him feel special. Chosen. He's never felt important. Never wanted to. Now he does.

'Tell me more, beautiful.'

'Please interrupt me if I bore you, all right?'

How adorable, thinks Ced, ordering some Ouzo. (Iris never drinks alcohol, lest it interfere with alacrity. More lucid, a drink or two later, might she have become aware that her heart is atrophied, robbed – intended pun – of the capacity for passion or compassion?)

'So', she sing-songs. 'Why do we say all *right*, by the way? Why not *all left*? Why is *right* synonymous with the law; take *el derecho* in Spanish, *das Recht* in German. Expressions such as *you have the right* or *how right you are* entail entitlement and approval. The word *sinister*: from the left in the Latin! To be gauche! Maladroit. From the French, also meaning *left*. And I'll spare you politics!'

Clever and original, that's was Iris was. For instance: upon hearing, a day before, of the derailing of a train in some tunnel and of bodies so mutilated they could only be identified by the imprints of their teeth, she'd giggled in that sometimes girlish way of hers: 'If they don't know these individuals' identity, how can they possibly know who their dentists are!'

Iris continued on her own track.

'In those countries where everyone still drives on the left, why not create a range of products and facilities tailored to the left-handed? Door or telephone handles. Cutlery. Gardening tools, kitchen utensils or surgical instruments. Ink pens. Guitars. Even clocks! Imagine the hands turning the other way round! The time we'd gain!'

Ced, a captive audience, again laughed.

Guitars reminded him of Aleana and Aleana, of his father. Which is when a luminous idea, or so he thought, occurred to him.

Needless to say – as people say before stating the obvious – Iris had had the same. Having examined Ced's wallet, she knew his surname and, quick to put two and two together, her calculating nature being her first, knew he was the hotel tycoon *and* Leonor's son – the latter having been her former idol, plus her own father's boss. The very one who had forced her to use her right hand as a child. 'Table manners! Can't you see that you'll always kick the person sitting on your left with your elbow? You must change your ways, dear girl.'

Really!

A thwarted left-hander, Iris had become dyslexic. Already an object of mockery because of her weight, it made school even more traumatic.

The Ouzo helping, Ced finally said:

'Look, Iris. Is it a capital injection you need?'

Looking demurely offended, she looked away.

'Don't be shy!' the candid boy protested. 'My father is …
well, quite well-off and I haven't asked him for anything for
many years. But he likes innovative ideas, so long as they amuse
him. Now here's the thing: he's been getting very involved in
'theme-hotels' – art, music, animals, can't remember – in the
States. What if we suggested a 'hotel for the left-handed' in
London? It would allow you to manufacture the objects you
mentioned while allowing me to spend more time … close to
you. What do you think?'

Getting better all the time is what Iris thought, logos dancing in her mind.

'Would you stay a bit longer if I persuaded my father to
come to Rhodes?'

'Don't know if I can…'

'Let me make a phone call. Back in a sec.'

Little did Ced know she had a business proposition all
ready and tied up.

Hector did agree to come, only too happy to see his son
getting interested in hotels, and in love.

He arrived on the island the following evening. A large
martini didn't soothe his discomfort. That Iris woman. Almost
a Leonor clone. A second martini brightened his mood. Allow
the boy his experiences. Redheads weren't necessarily pit bulls.
The association with dogs made him chuckle. Suddenly, comic
exasperation swung into cosmic sorrow without warning. It
often happened to him – as to Aleana.

'Fine', he said. 'On one condition: you must produce
approved designs and architectural projects asap.'

Watching the girl watching her watch, Hector hoped this
would take a long, long time.

35

VANUSHED

Returning from Nantucket, no trace of Nush in the flat. No letter.

But a tape in an envelope.

Nush had recorded her farewell (Well? Fare?)

She sounded somewhat hypnotic but made sense. Off to South America, first on the traces of Frida Kahlo, then, not sure. Couldn't take the gloom anymore. Needed sun and solitude. Needed to stop, not sure what, or in which order. Everything and its converse scared her. When looking at herself, it felt like she were observing two contrasting images in a pair of funhouse mirrors. What did it remind her of? 'My whole life. How can you hide from what never goes away? Not face oneself or the music, but re-invent...' [A long fragment blurred, we'd never know what exactly she meant.]

I could hear Ric thinking: another Peter Pan.

Then: 'Leonor's death was the last straw. Now I'm on my own, kid. Must atomise the strain, the pain, the...' [Then inaudible again. Something like catastrophe, catatonia?] Last thing we managed to hear clearly: she had to fly high and far to avoid freefall. Also, in order to inflict no more bruises. She begged for understanding and apologised.

End of tape.

Bruises? Trouble? An euphemism for murder?

The phone rang. Detective Jonas. Vast amounts of cocaine had been found in Mrs Vich's kitchen. The rubber boots had been ditched near the house. No fingerprints. No concrete suspect.

Who, to my knowledge, took coke – other than Ric? Oh no.

Might any vaguely legal medication keep my wayward imagination from waywardly meandering?

36

FUTURE, A FORETASTE

At long last! Hector calls.
Before even mentioning his ex-and-late wife, he exclaims:

'My treasure! So sorry. Busy preparing a surprise for you!'

Last time I'd heard this was hours after our graduation. Did Hector mean all of us, or only *moi*?

'Where are you?'

'Just landed in Geneva. Been difficult to get hold of for reasons I'll explain. Terrible news about Leo, Lea.'

A polar silence ensued. We both realised at the same moment that he'd been calling me Lea (didn't like Al, wouldn't use Aleana) but that he had also abbreviated Leonor's name to Leo.

'Will you attend the funeral? Next Monday, the 24th?'

'Will *you* be there?'

'Out of respect and friendship, I think I should – unless you'd prefer me not to.'

'…'

'I'm thinking of Ced, you know? Leonor I didn't really…'

'Does he know about us?'

'Don't know.'

While I waited for him to resume, I realised that he had taught me patience. Also absence, as Ric had remarked. Not the kind I'd known as a child: the unpredictable kind. Friends and employees called him The Submarine. Yet when he *was* there, it was so completely, so undividedly, that his eclipses would pale into insignificance. As I said: Hector was the most tender of men. And yes, I had learnt to love. Put another way, to accept dependency.

'This is what we'll do. My son needs us both. But *mon chou*, you *must* make sure Ricardo is nowhere in sight. I happen to know what I'm sure you also do. The *QE2* and all that... Ced might suspect it – my hunch. Might you arrange?'

'Why don't you, Hector? He works for you. Send him to Rome, Istanbul, Jakarta, whatever!'

'No. I don't want to interfere.'

Hey man, I was tempted to scream. Since when do you deny calling the shots? But I worshipped *that* man, and had also learnt to curb my impulses.

'How on earth can anyone but you prevent him from going?'

'Use that imagination of yours! Please...'

'Sure. Get him arrested for coke-possession? Organise a Pretty Woman? Set fire to his flat? Get him kidnapped?'

'Whatever!' I heard Hector smile. 'Thank you my treasure!' He hung up.

Should the warning lights have started blinking there and then? In the midst of his plethora of responsibilities and duties, he had found time to prepare a surprise – for *us alone*, he'd whispered. Shame on me if I couldn't help untangle the tricky situation.

Just then, Ric walked into the door.

'Sit down,' I rather solemnly asked.

'Wash my hands if I may?' he inquired in a tone reminding me to be his guest.

Some sniffing and sneezing later, a bottle of white wine uncorked, he reappeared, looking perky.

'So? Want to propose?' he teased.

'No. To pack.'

'Off to Mexico perhaps?'

'No. To that little hotel in Nantucket.'

'You fancy the detective, don't you?' he grinned. 'Could be Mexican by the look of him.'

'Oh please. Even Egyptians couldn't attract me anymore. No. I feel I should help Ced if I can. And wait for Hector. He'll be at the funeral.'

'No funeral. A memorial service following the cremation.'

'How d'you know?' I exclaimed.

'The gardener.'

'You talked to that … gigolo?'

'Indeed. Some mutual tastes.'

Was Ric referring to Leonor, to drugs, to begonias?

'Look here. Al. I'm not going anywhere near that island again. Fed up. With Nantucket, with sleazing around, with being a flunkey – and with the Vich set-up too, for that matter. Yes, he gave me my chance. Yes, he trusted me and YES, I delivered.'

I gasped with relief. Problem solved.

Yet the rabid trait of Ric's personality startled me yet again. Coke is known for making people aggressive. But there was more to it. Here we were, sitting in beautiful surroundings, with many reasons to be optimistic. He, successful and soon to become independent by the sound of it. I, in love and loved in return. Ced, sad but not excessively: his mother had been an intermittent light in his life and her home, no Greek lighthouse. And oh! His forthcoming wedding!

Last Saturday of this month. My tickets were booked from JFK to Heathrow and from there to Nice. Truth be told, I longed to get back to Arles and to my (provisional) life. I missed writing. I longed for silence.

'Will you be at the wedding, Ric?'

'I'm the witness, silly. Now: a stiff one? Medicinal!'

When had alcohol not helped to smoothen things, round the edges, relax high-strung nerves? When had alcohol not boosted confidence, helped to fall asleep or to get into third gear after waking up in neutral? When had it not given us the illusion of feeling unloaded, batteries recharged, fears over-swept? Coke, alcohol, what was the difference? A burst of adrenalin followed by an indifference.

But there it was, the legal way to numb distress and doubts. Tasting good too, let's not face it too closely.

Ric, on my suggestion, called AmarK.

'Coming to the wedding?' the latter asked. No preambles.

'How'd you know?'

'Cedric sent us an invitation.'

'Really? Well, neither Aleana nor I received any such thing.'

After a brief pause, the doc exclaimed he had to rrrrrun.

Another sweltering evening in New York. Everything felt oppressive. As was Hector's absence.

Unbeknownst to me, he was at this very moment closing his suitcase. He'd fly from Geneva to New York via London – intent on avoiding a meeting with his son's fiancée.

Hard as he had tried, he couldn't stand Iris. Her steward-ess voice exasperated him. Behind the smooth surface, he detected high-octane ruthlessness. She had refused to come to Leonor's funeral on the grounds that wedding preparations required her presence. Bollocks. Everything was ready. Again on her insistence, the ceremony would be intimate, as she put it; intimacy not something in her chords, Hector's sensitivity suggested. He knew that kind of woman. Wealthy men usu-ally do.

The Left-Hand-Hotel & Accessories project had been

completed more briskly than he'd have thought possible. Iris was undeniably efficient, disciplined, and hard-working; in that sense, a spurring influence on hitherto indolent Cedric. And yet, and yet ... there was something dodgy, or was it sly, about her. Having preferred solitude to seduction all his life (to the point he, Hector, had sometimes wondered whether his son wasn't point-blank asexual), Cedric wasn't immune to manipulation. *Au contraire.*

As bad luck would have it (or was it the goddam press), she had learnt of Hector's presence in London. Velvety as ever, she had offered to take him to the airport.

On the way back from Heathrow, where she had dropped her future father-in-law (far more fascinating than his son), Iris turned up the volume on the car radio, wiggling to Michael Jackson's 'Billie Jean'. Alone at last!

The man had insisted on a prenuptial agreement; she had gracefully complied. So far, so good: she had enough money of her own not to worry, but would, henceforth, have enough to not even think about it – the very definition of wealth. The main added value, however: marrying a Vich was bound to endow her with a respectability Iris could only have dreamt of, once upon a time. Not to mention final revenge on Leonor, the haughty bitch breeder.

Would father and son realise that faithful Banes-the-Butler was her old man? Maybe, maybe not. One way or the other, she didn't care. Cedric was besotted, and she in control.

Afterwards? Consolidate the situation by having a child? Kids are life-insurance ... but so very fattening before becoming tiresome. Fuck the father? No-no-no-go, she laughed, turning the volume up ever louder. Well: once in the saddle, she might find some idle prince, get pregnant, divorce and then, who knows... A Maharajah?

Everything's possible, provided you don't miss a beat.

PART FOUR

37

ONE FREAK FUNERAL...

Leonor's will was concise: cremation; a simple memorial service in the garden followed by a small reception under the music-pavilion built on the Marienbad spa model. Generous provisions were made for the cook, the gardener and of course, the dogs. All else: Ced's.

The music – no surprise there.

Having failed to find an address-book, Ced had inserted an obituary in the local paper and the *New York Times* with the relevant information regarding her burial.

An intestinal flu kept me bedridden. The day's events were recounted by Hector very late at night, his stomach aching.

He's picked up at the miniature airport by Detective Jonas – whose mien betrays his disappointment at my absence.

An autopsy having been declared redundant – so argued the Mayor, a golf-tournament on his mind – Leonor's body has been cremated the previous day, Ced not disinclined to get the unpleasant procedure over and done with.

It's noon in Leonor's garden. The sun shines as furiously as the barking of dogs locked up in their kennels.

A none too impressive amount of people gather near the pavilion. Butlers (with the exception of Banes, in London we know why) present the guests with Dom Perignon or whisky-sours: Leonor's favourite drinks. The Mayor is growing quite red in the face. His greedy eyes observe the sumptuous buffet being laid out.

Hector, intrigued by a well-groomed, handsome man, approaches him.

Ced gestures to the guests, please be quiet.

The urn containing his mother's remains is to be buried under her favourite poplar tree (murmur of approval) next to the urn containing the ashes of Garfield, her favourite dog – in order for the latter to watch over her in the Yonder-Beyond (some take out their handkerchief, not so much to dry tears as to muffle irrepressible laughter).

The elegant man Hector had noticed produces a shovel and starts digging two holes. The urns inserted, flowers strewn on top, he readjusts his silk tie, wipes his forehead with the same, and strides towards a drink tray, impassive as a sphinx. The whole ceremony has lasted less than twenty minutes.

Hector addresses the ... undertaker?

'Good morning, if I may say so. I'm Mrs Vich's ex-husband. And who are you, might I ask?'

'The plant-whisperer.'

'Well. You look...'

'Camouflage,' Robbie amiably smiles.

Seldom baffled, easily bored, Hector's curiosity is titillated.

'How long have you been the, er, gardener, if I might prosaically say so, on these ... premises?'

'Various years. Don't ask me how many: I never count. I studied graphology, you see, before redirecting my interest to Dzongka.'

'*Pardon?*'

'The native language of Bhutan. Just in case, see?'

'Who wouldn't?'

They sip more champagne, fine-tuning the wavelength.

'But why exercise your, er, talents on Nantucket?'

'Because I'm afraid of heights,' Robbie explains with pains-
taking patience. 'No offence meant'.

'None taken', replies Hector.

'And you? Why a hotelier?'

'I love giraffes.'

'Of course.'

This coded conversation is interrupted by the crimson
Mayor, who clinks a glass with a knife and smashes it.

Dear friends and foreigners, it is my unfortunate prerogative to
render homage to a pillar of our community. A major supporter
of our canine silent, when not barking, very much respected
minority. Not to mention [a hiccup causes a tipsy pause] her
influence on young men who, without her, might have slithered
into homosexuality, the plague of our times, even though the
pharmaceutical lobby transforms the traumas of Vietnam into
the perspectives of a new Ibiza, thus … where was I? Yes: our
esteemed Leonor, an inspiration! Also to the vegetation' [he
adds, contemplating century-old pine trees in hazy awe]. 'Who
now doubts that classical music makes plants grow?

This said, the rest incomprehensible, the Mayor collapses with
the smirk of one having complied with his duty and confident that his performance will warrant re-election. Hasn't he
avoided new political correctness, on the lines of *chemically
inconvenienced* for junkies, *wildlife management* for fishing
abuses, *developmentally challenged* for loonies or *custody suites*
for jails? Official accountants on the take, the maths will add
up, he concludes, the logic of it all escaping him, but as his
Teutonic grandfather used to translate, 'with time comes bicy-
cle' (from the German: *mit Zeit kommt Rad*).

Hector is now harpooned by the cook and her spinster
sister.

'Oh Mister, Oh Mister!' they chant, evoking a parody of the Andrews Sisters, immemorial years ago. 'So glad to meet you at long last!' they now mimic in parrot-fashion.

Hector would gladly reunite with the bizarre gardener, but the man seems lost in combat.

'We just loooooooved your ex-wife!'

'Delighted to hear it.'

'So motherly to us!'

'I couldn't have expressed it better,' echoes the other. 'In fact, we overcame the tragedy of barrenness thanks to her.'

'Oh?' ripostes Hector, eying the lush vegetation.

'Yes. Not being able to have children.'

'Really? So sorry'.

Who were all those nutters? Performing a furtive entrechat, he manages to remove himself: a small leap for a man, a big one for me, he grunts. Just when he thinks nothing more aggravating can happen, it does.

A group of neighbours, or so everyone calls each other on the small island, closes in on him like octopuses.

'Have you noticed that the dogs' collars have been replaced by black ribbons?' marvels one of them, wearing a hat more suited to a drag queen than to the Queen Mother.

'Such a recluse, our adorable Leonor. Pity! How we would have loved to see more of her,' another chimes in.

'As our teenage kids would have', grunts her husband. 'Especially Jr'.

'She was chaaaarming with children,' hastens to add a man bearing a strong resemblance to the Mayor. 'No charity she wouldn't contribute to… Not even for the poor kids of Monaco. Who'd have thought such a dedicated lady would commit suicide?'

Robbie-the-Buddhist-gardener, whom Hector hadn't seen standing nearby, declaims:

'We're the slaves of our freedom! Death's a release.'

As a result, the small group scampers.

'Thanks. Nice line. May I plagiarise it when explaining why I can't stop smoking or won't go jogging?'

Now it is Ced who pulls at Hector's sleeve.

'Shall we ... escape?'

'Good thinking. The Mayor's in charge, right?'

'Of the *light brigand*, most certainly.'

They find the detective in the kitchen, watching a soccer match on TV. What was the matter with the ventilation fan? Sounded like a rattling train. Or the Bhutan radio, pirated? Jonas practically begs Vich to leave with them.

Once in the car, all sigh with relief.

'Some memorial service! Another two hours before take-off. Why not go to that place Aleana raved about?'

The traditional restaurant in question had been sold, meaning it will most probably become a sandwich-joint, a sports shop or a piercing & tattoo parlour.

For the time being, mercifully, it's still the traditional place with its old-fashioned bar. A beer, at long last! Detective Jonas heaves with relief.

Ced asks his father:

'Have you told Ric about...?'

'No. I promised, remember?'

'Neither about the Left-Hand Vich Hotel?'

'Do I have to speak in Mandarin?'

'Has Al?'

'Of course not. She's a tomb.'

How filthy tactless could the one percenters get? No communist, Dollar forbid, Jonas nevertheless feels throttled. The thought of pulling Hector Vich aside and distilling some subtle information first invades then deserts his mind.

What the hell. Let those parasites dig their own ... grave, he chuckles, looking forward to a barbecue with his wife Jeannie and their sons, Johann and Jeronimo: some parents need not display fantasy, he proudly explains.

The reason why Hector had stomach cramps when narrating the events? Like most gifted raconteurs, he was prone to ornate recollections with exaggeration. His mangling of names compounded the fun. We rolled on the bed and, one thing leading to the other...

To make love while shaking with laughter is a vibrant kick. I recommend it.

38

... AND A WEIRD WEDDING

London. On the Friday before Ced's wedding.

AmarK had invited us for dinner. His wife with the meowing voice wasn't around: her bridge evening. Nor was I: beauty sleep.

They reminisced about Kenya. Hector announced that he was building a lodge-hotel on Lamu as a present and surprise for Aleana – me.

This called for a Chateau la Lagune '67 to be opened.

Ric on one of his bathroom expeditions, the doc asked, not without irony:

'Does he know that Ced's marrying Iris Banes tomorrow?'

'No clue'.

Was any of them aware that Ric had had an affair with the toxic girl, the doc wondered?

'Nor does he know that the reception will take place at the new Left-Hand Vich!' smiled Ced. 'Iris thought it might be a flattering surprise since it was Ric who introduced the theme-hotel concept!'

Ric returned from his lengthy leave of absence, a small fortune down his nose, the rest of the evening was spent with inconsequential small talk. After jovial back-slapping in a cigar-smoke haze, they parted swearing eternal allegiance, masculine solidarity, and so on.

Marriages in town halls are rarely romantic and the Marylebone one, no exception. But dramatic: yes. Iris, clad in a snow-white dress with a hip-low slit at its back, on the arm of Banes-the-butler-who-didn't-do-it, glided in, a crown of white lilies on her head: lilies! Virginity in the language of flowers! Why not daisies, the symbol of innocence, while she was at it?

Even Hector, whose sense of humour was serpentine, was not amused.

The large assembly in attendance? It was composed of the kind of socialites who turn a buffet into rush-hour Tokyo; of journalists keen on a scoop, and of, by and large, people who had been told, in no roundabout ways, they'd only be welcome to the opening of the new Vich Hotel if making an appearance at the town hall.

Blinding flashes harassed us from the latter to the former.

Ric and Iris exchanged glances. Was his heinous – or was I once more imagining things? Hers, all silk and velvet.

'What a happy coincidence!' she fluted in that voice of hers.

Hypocrisy! From the Greek *hupokrinesthai*: *hupo*, play a part and pretend + *krinein*, decide and judge.

Ric and Ced also exchanged glances.

The latter didn't understand the former's hostile one. What was the matter? Yes, Iris rather looked like his late mother but then ... was it a crime? Or might it be that he and his bride had conceived and completed a theme-hotel without involving him? No big deal. There was no patent protecting an idea which, after all, didn't require a PhD in astrophysics.

Ced felt a twinge of sadness. Never had he intended to antagonise his school-friend. On the contrary: he had remained in the background, encouraged Ric's endeavours and proven loyal in every which way. Plus: he had not a clue regarding the Formentor episode.

AmarK strolled towards him.

'All well?'

'I am, dear Doc. But is Ric? Behaves strangely…'

'Probably vexed not to be the centre of attention, that's all. Remember: what kills us is not the disease; what kills us, dear boy, are the remedies!'

'I'm now a husband!' boasted Ced. 'Stop calling me Boy!'

'Right, husband. Piece of advice, may I?'

'Not even a crumb!'

Uh-oh, thought AmarK. Not such a fool after all. He'd suspected as much.

At this point Hector bowed to his now daughter-in-law.

'My son being shy and modest, he suggested I'd say a few words. Knowing you, better sit down,' he added icily.

'Thank you Hec,' she beamed, teeth grinding, 'but no thanks.'

How dare she? She did. Standing up, she declaimed:

'Hi all! What an occasion! Isn't marriage as much as an opening to the future as throwing ajar the doors of a new hotel? History on the make!'

The applause was tepid. Not only because of her pitching voice, but also because divorce had become the norm rather than the exception; women were the new super rich. Marriage no longer a cause for rejoicing, as many male attendees mused.

'My beloved husband is left-handed – as was his mother – and as was Beethoven, the *true* love of her life!'

(Here, she threw Hector a darting look.)

'Are we a minority? Yes. Everyday conveniences have been designed by and for the right-handed, from cheque-books to golf clubs.'

Undeterred that the more subtle minds didn't laugh at her double entendre, she proceeded:

'Society is divided into clubs – meant to cement a sense of belonging among likewise conservative thinking or inclined individuals. Well: we lefties are *also* inclined westward, if you see what I mean…'

Yawning swept like a draft.

'Right – sorry. Joking. Now consider this, dear guests: other than left-handed Beethoven, Paganini, Cole Porter or Jimmy Hendrix, so is Paul McCartney. Other than Tiberius or Bismarck, so were Billy-the-Kid and Jack-the-Ripper. Goethe, Nietzsche, Freud! Boxers, fencers, car-racers? The examples are galore.'

After a gesture indicating demure fatalism (and pride): 'So am I.'

Still no trace of the anticipated feedback. Her conclusion: drinks were missing. Imperiously, she gestured to the waiters who, trained to appear left-handed, started rushing around with precariously balanced trays.

Ced and I exchanged glances; both distraught. Was he aware of my forebodings? However erratic the ticking of minds such as mine, even the proverbial broken watch sooner or later gets it right.

AmarK joined us in some remote corner.

'Congratulations! The concept of this hotel is revolutionary. Not in planetary terms, when *re-volution* ultimately entails returning to square one. Let's not confuse the left-wing with the left-hands! Or the magnetic north with sentimental gravitation,' he twinkled.

'Don't the Arabs write from right to left?' I said, merely to say something.

'Quite. But let's leave them and terrorism aside for a moment. Nor dwell on the fact that one's past is usually perceived on the left, the future on the right… The spiritual Doppler effect, if you will.'

Had the doc gulped down a refreshment too many?

After a pause and a warm (or was it a warning) wink to Ced: 'Long live the newly-weds! Good luck to the new hotel!'

Followed by Ricardo, Iris ran to the powder-room.

What happened there? A 'it would be nice, wouldn't it' quickie? They certainly looked flushed upon returning.

'A word, if I may,' Ced said, finally stepping onto the podium (yet reaching for Iris's hand as if to ask permission).

'You've all seen the lobby, and some of you, the suites. I would now like to present the dining-room. My very discreet contribution.'

Called Da Vinci, the place was – astounding!

Hung with mirrors facing each other, lined with a calligraphy only readable when reflected by its vis-à-vis, they had been realised with outstanding craftsmanship: Leonardo had been ambidextrous. He could sketch, paint and write with both hands. In between the panels, photographic negatives.

A dolled-up lady ventured: 'What about the author of *Alice in Wonderland*, also a mathematician may I point out? Didn't he write backwards too?'

'Left you are!' Ced exclaimed. 'Incidentally, Lewis was plagued with a stutter, like many left-handers and notorious writers. Take…'

On the verge of epilepsy, Ric rushed toward the revolving door. Its mechanism, predictably clockwise, meant he hit the glass head-on. His none-too-gentlemanly swearing made Hector laugh and me, lean my head on his shoulder.

39

PARENTHESIS – ACCELERATION

Benita, without whom the world would seem as strange as Paris without the Tower of Pisa, came to visit, messing up my writing rhythm. Her thermometer aspect startled me: had she overdone the healthy lifestyle?

Having read what I've written so far, she insisted that in an age of dwindling attention spans, better put my skates on. 'Deadlines race backwards,' gluglu…

Hence, I skip three years.

So: as we know, Ced and Iris were married.

This, plus the new Vich Hotel has exacerbated Ric and Ced's latent, long-time tension.

Another Christmas on Lamu.

Both impatient loners, age difference notwithstanding, we had discovered tenderness. Sounds banal? No. An epiphany when you've been deprived of it. The flip side: fear of loss. Such was mine that I'd wake up at night to make sure he was breathing. Life without Hector had turned into a thought too ghastly to contemplate.

Sensing surrender, he became proprietary. Began to talk about long-term projects; insisted I use eyeliner; wear dresses, high-heel shoes – and, aouch, buy a new guitar. Now if there's something I'm attached to, it's my old, very old, guitar.

Having ignited passion, I panicked.

As happens in such constellations, another man comes into the picture. Though not called Madjid, he could have been Persian as looks go. Aggravating circumstance: a writer. More ominous still: working on a manuscript called *Love Only Lasts Three Years*.

I call Benita. Need to talk to someone I can trust. Ask whether she's awake. 'NO!'

I call Ced. Busy.

Hector had ambled to the tiny Catholic Church in Lamu town. To inquire about weddings?

I go for a walk on the not-so-deserted beach – as Frederik sits on a rock, scribbling away, a joint dangling from his lips. Though the stuff sickens me, I inhale a puff or two.

'Read some of it if you wish.'

Resisting curiosity, I wave away the pages Fred hands me. With a shrug, he reads them out loud:

'It's beginning to be known that I'm alone. An omnisexual bachelor my age in Paris is as rare as a beggar in Gstaad. In any case, life's programmed on a repeat mode. (I like to compare myself to machines because machines are easy to repair.) Love is the only pre-programmed misfortune we ask more of.'

I ask: 'Does love last three years?'

He answers with compassion:

'Three years? A bit too grandiose an idea! Actually, who cares how long love lasts? You must find the person you can envisage getting bored with. Then, dying of boredom won't come as a blow.'

Tossing his scribbled sheets of paper aside, he leans back and ad-libs: 'Only the most pessimistic people fall violently in love, because it's good for what they have... Over the last three days I have, Aleana. But in three years? I'll stop shaving before going to bed (having long ago ceased to share a toothbrush). It's mathematical.'

'Does passion start and finish in a bathroom?' I giggle, albeit mirthlessly.

What about Hector? Had he failed to decipher the 'Please Do Not Disturb' sign?

Meanwhile.

Nush's still adrift, wherever.

The redhead's no longer interested in a husband who reminds her of her father. She treats both with mellifluous contempt. Now accepted by the socialites she despises, she dresses in Chanel but no longer wears jewellery. The display of money – her utmost interest in life – is vulgar, Iris hints in the presence of aristocrats hung with ancestral gems under the seven carat league. Cedric hopes for her to become pregnant.

Get fat again?

On the pretext of his most unusual blood group, AB-, together with hers, O+, she pays some doctor to certify that any baby would be bound to suffer a genetic malformation. He proposes all manner of trials, treatments, tricks. The answer remains no.

Ced can no longer suspend disbelief.

Who does he turn to? To Ricardo, his best friend. Exasperated, Ric calls me. At loss, I call Benita.

(Short rewind. Benita's allergic to Iris: a fraud and a fake, she had already sentenced at the Formentor Hotel.)

But her fantasy is as loopy as mine. What does it come up with? To involve the deeply hurt Banes... Buy modelling clay... Later on, at the Left-Handed-Hotel, pretend, say, hypothermia... Iris' father would offer his jacket, and I remove the master-key, press it into the paste, *et voilà* the perfect copy...

Whereupon, we'd steal all sorts of things all over the place, hide them in Iris' office in order to open Ced's eyes to her kleptomaniac past...

Scheme discarded. No way would I risk putting beloved Benita into a jam.

40

LAMU, FREDERIK AND BENITA

No Homeric hero, Hector retreats.
 Have I not written, time ago: 'Little did we know, back then, that I would, one day, injure his'?
 Well, back then was now. And his was a hurt heart.
 Frederik thinks: chessboard cleared. He catalogues me as another pseudo-hard-to-get-conquest. Aiming at the wrong tower, he takes his swanking time. All over the place, full of solicitude one moment, cranky the next.
 He was damn attractive. Wow-white teeth. Mocha skin. Hazel eyes. He reminded me of Nerval's poem,

Je suis le Ténébreux, le Veuf, l'Inconsolé
Le Prince d'Aquitaine à la Tour abolie:
Ma seule Etoile est morte, – et mon luth constellé
Porte le Soleil noir de la Mélancolie.

Girls surely fell for him like skittles.
 Had it not been for a vainglorious hue in his eyes, might I have – for longer than three weeks? Don't think so. His bone-dry humour was too tinged with unsparing disdain.
 That said: I'm a good player too. But *waydamoment*: even though exuding wired discipline at times, utter helplessness at others, I'm no calculating vixen. Hand on heart. Yes, I've been called *une allumeuse* (a cock-teaser) but no! No! Seduction

comes easy. Quite often, unexpectedly. My turquoise eyes help. More importantly: I don't worry about the future. Men like that.

Benita's call interrupted my musings.

Might she join me in Lamu?

When she agreed I was aflame with happiness.

The three days until her arrival stretched like tasteless chewing-gum.

No sooner by my side, I started pouring out my heart in, I admit, a maudlin fashion.

'It hit me was that I'm no good at love. Hitme. Boom. Even sex doesn't beguile me beyond a tepid measure. A curse in disguise?'

Benita was quick to mock.

'Anatomizing yoorself?'

'Only rigoletting!'

How delicious to be reunited with – the sister I never had.

I banged on about the beauty of soul-mating, bla, the complex subtleties of the very … blabala, friends representing unshakable foundations…

'What an authentic bore you've become!' gurgled Benita.

'I know, and not truthful. Ashamed to admit I miss Hector beyond words. In his presence, things seem magically uncomplicated. He has a knack for untying knots in the most Gordian of situations. Randomness amuses him. Consequences are not upmost in both our minds. We are much alike.'

Did I mention we were swimming?

Probably not. We were drunk and might have been deadly so, had Frédérik not come to our rescue.

Benita took a hazy look at the guy and disliked him instantly.

A whole lot of coffee later, I sobered up. Not selfish for a change, my next move required swiftness. One did not keep *the* Lamu notary waiting.

Apart from the paintings stashed in some Swiss vault, Benita owned nothing on this planet. The house in Lamu I was building would belong to her in case of my demise. She loved the island.

Back at the Peponi, I squinted twice: Benita and Fred, most improbably but unmistakably, had bonded. Big way! He was wearing a gabardine over his bathing trunks, claiming to be Clouseau, and she an improvised banana-belt, wiggling her hips Josephine Baker-ishly.

I fetched my guitar. We started singing 'L'Eté Indien', provoking cheerful derision.

Finally we showered and changed.

Frederik, whose shine to Benita positively scintillated, had organised a dinner laid out on the beach in between two huge fires embalming the air. Mangrove wood does. The jasmine thrown over made the scent dizzying.

To see my dearest friend happy; to feel the sand under my legs; to eat fresh crabs watching the stars... Wow. (Haven't used the word for ages!)

Benita is a very well read person. This, combined with a sense of humour as twisted as Frederik's was wicked, led to a conversation I thoroughly enjoyed.

After a banal exchange about the love for books, paper, its smell, texture, possibilities for annotations and mistreatment; having agreed that reading allows one to live in parallel worlds (and when writing, to invent them); having compared the majesty of the mental image to the prefabricated ones on screen, Benita inquired:

'What's your first criterion when buying a book?'

'The author's photograph on the cover.'

'Aha?' she frowned. 'Title a detail?'

'In most cases.'

'*Completement* nonsense!' she retorted.

'Not at all. Then the author's biography. If he's dead, good, especially if he committed suicide. The younger, the better. And then, of course...'

'Debauchery? Drugs? Delinquency?'

'Definitely helps,' Frederik chuckled. 'Also: the first twenty pages must make you want to underline at least three sentences.'

'Three?'

'Yes. Three. Three is *the* number. Don't know why.'

Benita jumped up. In full regalia, meaning a crumpled dress and ill-matching earrings, she glided into the sea.

'Why so silent?' Frederik asked me, not caring a fig.

'Just thinking of, perhaps, writing a book myself. No bestseller, for sure, being neither debauched, drugged or delinquent. Based on the seven so-called deadly sins. They seldom kill, but OK. Merely saying that the number seven is as meaningful to me as the number three to you...'

Benita came undulating back. 'What about the fatidic number 40? About 280 freaking years in dog count!'

'Forty's a magic number!' Frederik exclaimed.

The man had understood that Benita's age was a cause of distress to her.

'Associated with redemption. Saul, David and Solomon reigned for forty years. Moses is forty when God calls him and thereafter goes into meditation for forty days on Mount Sinai. Jesus is first seen in the Temple forty days after his birth. He preaches for forty months, rises from the dead after forty hours before spending the forty days preceding Ascension with his disciples.'

'Nice try', snapped Benita. 'Zewish, by any chance?'

This exchange was going places. Not necessarily pleasant ones.

'Buddha and Mohammed started preaching age forty,' I casually remarked. 'In most African tribes, funerals last forty nights. Take the Bambaras; their initiation rites require offering forty hair-streaks, forty horses and as many goats, or the Amerindians.'

In the absence of anyone begging me to shut up (probably not listening) I rambled on.

'Louis XI imposes the King's quarantine, during which no revenge was permitted. It is again on the basis of the supposed virtues of that number that Venice declares a forty-day isolation in 1484 to keep the Black Death at bay. On a lighter note, darlings, Ali Baba's forty thieves!'

'What about the CAC 40?' interjected Frederik. 'Another stock-market exposed to tumult. Ah! The vagaries of human behaviour and our perennial failure to learn from history! The only novelty is acceleration overtaking reason.'

'What's that to do with anything?' I laughed.

Deep down, Frederik was kind. His deviance from the subject had restored Benita's good mood: she much preferred being compared to financial tsunamis than to Biblical mummies.

'Where were we?' she cajoled. 'Yes. We've ticked off the author photograph; his biography; his capacity to make you want to underline three sentences.'

'Right. My next criterion, no longer for buying but for not tossing the book into the bin: exasperation!'

'Exasperation?'

'Yes. Emotional responses must be violent. Either you exclaim, how beautiful, how moving, how unforgettable! Or else you go *quelle horreur*, how obnoxious, how futile, how ... in short, exasperating. Whether you want to kiss or kill the writer, he has avoided the worst of fates: indifference. If violent enough, your reaction will make you sit down and write him a letter.'

Benita smirked, unconvinced.

Frederik smirked appreciatively, and resumed.

'Especially if it's a pretty woman! Then infatuation enhances the fascination. My last point: a book must be shorter than 250 pages. Printed in big characters. We sometimes want to read by candlelight.'

We?

Benita and I gave up listening. Frederik, on the subject of love, was as tiresome as atheists who constantly talk about religion.

41

A LOGICAL MESS

Iris had harpooned some elder Duke whom she fascinated by virtue of her lack thereof.

Benita stayed on Lamu, thrilled to supervise the progress on my house. At the risk of being tedious, I simply *must* describe it – so thrilled was I: walls and floors made of coral stone or rag joined together by lime plaster. Vaulted spaces. Shaded courtyards. Square-cut beams, called *banas*, painted with the most colourful pigments. In the *vidaka*s (the niches), ancient olive presses, coconut graters, porcelain jugs, wooden drums covered with goatskin, ivory blow-horn. Carved mahogany or bamboo doors, elaborately executed by Hindu craftsmen. All of it a harmonious mix of cultures: Swahili, Arab and Asian. Through the interaction of traders and pirates, even Chinese antiques had found their way to the island.

Nush, shortly married (under pressure from her father?) and divorced soon thereafter (under her mother's?) had seemed so weary when I'd met her earlier in Paris that I had, notwithstanding reluctance, commissioned her to paint *trompe-l'oeil* motifs on the windows.

'Why not on mirrors?'

'I do not like mirrors, except to reflect light and amplify space. My novel *Mirrors Lie* is explicit enough in this respect. Are you too busy talking to read?'

Everything and everybody were getting on my nerves.

In between it all, I had also gone to visit Ced on Symi.

Having realised he'd been a stepping-stone and trampled upon he felt – *jinxed,* his word.

From Greece, I'd flown to London. Ric no happy man either. Fed up with hotels. More alarmingly, with whom he had become. A slut and slot machine, his words.

When I thought things couldn't get sadder, a massive shock hit me: Hector was diagnosed with late-stage kidney cancer. A radical man, he decided to have one of them removed. 'Cassius Clay won his most important boxing matches with a single kidney!'

I flew to Geneva at once.

Yes, my short-lived attraction towards Frederik had hurt him. Not deeply, though. He and I knew we'd always be magnetically drawn to each other.

How to describe our peculiar bond, relationship, affinity? We shared the same inclination and passion for logical incoherence. We understood and cultivated the language of the unspoken. Also, we shared the need to be touched and the desire to caress. We loved waking up next to each other. He kept comparing me to a feminine version of Marlon Brando – physically, that is – whilst I compared him to nobody: a compliment. But mainly, and returning to the beginning: incongruity was the tightrope on which we danced with grace and levity. Below, no nets: only life.

Ours was an Amouritié (telescoping – friendloveship?).

He once asked, almost shyly, for a blow-job as a relief from pain. Glad to oblige, I took his cock into my mouth and … blew, blew, blew. He screamed with laughter – not pleasure, clearly.

'*Mon Chou*', I said, half-choking, 'you know I'm very precise with language! The expression blow-job is one of the most ridiculous ever.'

'Haha. Just as well you're not in politics – the second-oldest profession, but one that bears a gross similarity with the first! You'd be no good at either!'

'At least I won't get pregnant!'

'Everybody in favour of abortion has already been born.'

His condition having improved, we returned to Lamu.

It's Christmas 1992 – another birthday for me.

Apart from the Peponi crowd, the usual suspects had gathered for the double-occasion: adored Benita; Ric, Ced, even Frederik – and Nush.

Big party in the Vich-Lodge-Hotel. With a theme. Hector and I also shared a passion for jazz and more particularly, for Miles Davis who had died some months earlier. To describe his genius? The difference between him and Chet Baker or Dizzy Gillespie? Impossible. But his outfits were legendary and the island's originals revelled in emulating the mix of Brooks Brothers with African dashikis worn with bow-ties, brocade frock coats or pyjamas, Nehru collars and shades as big as scuba divers' masks. Davis, addicted, on and off, to self-destructive substances, would self-mockingly remark that cool applied as much to his personal as to his music genre. Well! It took us days to recover.

Long story and all that: on New Year's Eve, my lovely house went up in flames. Amid the fireworks, no one noticed the place on fire.

The Somalis? A Civil War had broken out in 1991 and the country seethed with tensions that would, a few years later, lead to the bombing of US embassies in Kenya and Tanzania.

The locals (irritated by my debonair spending)?

Or.

Nush had vanished. So had Hector.

On amber-red sands, Benita hugged me with all her heart's strength.

'Ultimately, people *always* resent you for knowing them too well.'

Subtle (she did not ask about Hector's whereabouts) and maladroit (no contradiction), Benita tried to alleviate my pain by painting a satirical picture of Lamu's worst-case future. The Lodge would be renamed:

Residences Sea and Sun
Sun & Sea Apartments
For the Rich only

All over the place, she continued, kites and bikes, by now equipped with thumping engines. The noise! A bunch of Scandinavians, scarlet in spite of factor 50 creams, trail prams, fluorescent buoys and mini-fridges. Techno-music is blasting from New Age bars. Cross-dressed waiters and movie-moguls speak Volapük. Polluted for obvious reasons, the sea is full of drunk fish. Half-empty bottles float around. Satellite dishes mushroom on the dunes.

'But enough bad joking, *chérie.*'

I sniffed inconsolably, thinking, where in this charred earth is he? Why not with me?

Hector is striding along the seashore. Alone. He doesn't notice the donkeys or sneeze. Nor does he reminisce about his first time on the island with Vilma and her jingly voice – or was it her bracelets?

No. He could picture Aleana at Ric's bedside after the motorcycle incident. Her arriving at Peponi's while the boys were volunteering (not quite) with The Flying Doctors. In New York, suddenly grown-up (not really). Fast-forward to recent times – is it already years? Aleana's mania for tooth-brushing, then eating chocolate as she loathes the taste of menthol. Her frantic looking-up words in dictionaries. Her melodious laughter ignited, like outbursts of rage, by trivialities. No. That's unfair. Only injustice really caused her to fly off the handle. Her sitting for hours in front of a pond, expecting the improbable turtle to emerge. Angelically patient or else, mercurial. Her ruthless sincerity followed by sincere remorse at having hurt someone's feelings. Insecure and arrogant; impulsive and level-headed; all of it at the same time. Then: her exasperating habit of leaving half-smoked cigarettes lying in ashtrays, or her reading-glasses in some cupboard. Or her aggravating insistence on never throwing withering flowers away. Her brownish lipstick.

I must not die. I must fight that goddamn cancer. I...

42

DERANGED YOUNG MEN

Ric left: something, perhaps redheaded, requiring undivided attention.

Hector left: chemotherapy.

Again, he had waved away my desire to accompany him. Non negotiable. 'Wounded animals go into hiding,' he smiled.

I lost my sleep and my appetite. Became a jerky zombie. I even contemplated joining Ced in Tibet. His next destination, Lhasa.

His inclination towards Buddhism furthered by latest disappointments, he'd soon be on his way. The valley on the Kyichu river bank was all the more legendary for the Drepung monastery being one of the Dalai Lama's refuges.

'Wake up!' Benita and Frederik teased in unison. 'You? Cultivating awareness, equanimity and wisdom on some holy path amongst silent monks? Please! At an altitude of 12,000 feet? No booze? No guitar?'

I looked at Ced. He looked remote. Obviously not too keen to be accompanied by spoilt and jittery me.

Frederik's recently published first novel, *Memoirs of a Deranged Young Man*, had provoked outrage, meaning acclaim. He insisted I come back to Paris: he'd introduce me to the 'glitterlitterati' and help me overcome my blues.

Now looking at Benita, who merely shrugged, I didn't know what to think anymore.

She and I went for a walk on the beach, in the opposite direction from the still-smouldering ashes of my old home.

'Don't worry about me, *ma chérie*. Fred is Fred. His heart leaps. His mind drifts. The present's a rehearsal. To him, *La vraie vie est ailleurs*. In some Neverland, I suppose...'

'But you two were so well ... assorted!'

'Assorted, like in *accessoire*?' she laughed. 'Aleana, the man will never love three years. Not even three weeks. He's on an eternal honeymoon with himself.'

Remembering her high spirits and admiring her gracious silhouette (she had lost don't know how many stones) I was terrified about making a faux-pas on shifty sands.

'Why not give another three ... pennies for his ... feelings?'

'*Toss* vould be a better vord!' she smiled.

How could I forget that *The Dice Man* was Benita's cult-book?

It's about a New York psychiatrist who begins to question the presumed scientific claims of his *trade*. A disbelief which leads him to experiments involving sheer chance: the tossing of dice now determines his every decision and behaviour-pattern. His more gullible patients (the majority) embrace the procedure; it's an antidote to tormenting responsibility – also called free will. Things, of course, get out of mind. What starts like a game morphs into a hell in which you must confront demons. In other words, yourself.

Whatever happened to the author, Luke Rhinehart?

Benita had no idea. I'd look it up.

The sun was setting. Again.

'Not sad, Benita?'

She laughed. Girlishly.

'At my fossil age? Ecstasy? Anger? What for? But Al, what's the matter? You're normally too self-centred to ask questions and too discreet to provoke them?'

Aouch.

'Don't forget: I had fuuuun! Listen Al: it's quite simple in

the end. Even at the beginning. No lover doesn't sense, intu-
itively, why his dream will crack. There's always *that* moment
when one knows, just recognises – be it due to an imperceptible nuance in the voice or an ever-so-slightly refrained gesture
– the cardinal nexus in an architecture, the epicentre in a
relationship, where the Whole is bound to implode. A second
later, a millimetre further, nothing would have changed. But
at this unique breaking-point, a fracture becomes terminal,
irremediable, un-mendable.

It hit me hard.

Lying side by side, the moon now rising, she fluted:

'Let's play at Etruscan graves.'

'No. The Etruscans had no written language. Always
annoyed me. Let's play at Orpheus and Eurydice instead. I
rescue you from the dead. A miracle. Puzzled and elated, I
keep playing the lyre. The condition was clear, the instruction
simple: I must not look back, not turn around, for behind you
is eternal darkness, to which you will return should I disobey.
Yet I do. And lose you forever. Why?'

'Might you be stupid?'

'Or you, blind?'

'It might all boil down to a sense of the absurd, also called
humour, see? Of course you do, *mon amour*! Of curse!'

Frederik returned to Paris to bask in celebrity.

I left to seek companionship with my gypsy friends.

Benita stayed on Lamu, adamant, notwithstanding her flippant prophecies and my protests, to save or restore whatever
could be in the damaged house. Good thing Ric had insisted
on negotiating the insurance policy.

On the plane from Nairobi to Paris, the classical middle-seat
situation: it being vacant, my neighbour and I share it. All I

wanted was to tilt my head against the window, repress tears, and sleep.

Why does space in between passengers almost inevitably lead to rapprochement instead of distance, Dog knows.

The dishevelled Spaniard, from hair to moustache, bore one of these innocent smiles that discourages rudeness.

'I respectfully beg you to forgive my curiosity, a complicit cousin of distraction, but may I ask for the honour of your name?'

I did. His: Clementino.

'Doña Aleana, *encantadísimo*. Kindly do not disapprove of the preciseness I pay to trivial matters.'

Whereupon he opened a comic-book. Fantômas! Rapt in concentration, only dinner being served made him clap it shut.

'Reminds me of my childhood!' I could not help remarking. 'Though reckless, I liked Fantômas for being a master of disguise…'

'Ah! A trifle Houdini-like, true? On no pretext would I wish to become personal, but my dream is to be a ghost-writer. *El problema*: no one tells me life story. Is it I talk too much?'

The guy was beginning to amuse me.

'Do not flagellate yourself, esteemed Don Clementino. Write yours under the name of Mary Ann Evans.'

'Your indulgent pardon?'

'George Eliot's real name. In other words, her pen-name.'

Most confused, as had been my intention, he chewed thoughtfully for a pleasantly silent moment. Then:

'Excellent! I used to work as a transvestite!'

'Anonymously, I presume?'

'*Claro*. "Security is the fiercest enemy of mortals", if you permit me to quote Macbeth, III/5,' he humbly added.

Don't ask me why, but I told him about my lovely house on

Lamu having burnt down.

'No Woman No Cry' Don Clementino parodied in vintage Bob Marley fashion at the top of his voice, off-tune. Passengers, some incensed, some bemused, turned around.

Tears were trickling down my cheeks: from hilarity.

Sweet Don Clementino misinterpreted.

'No cause for tragic thoughts,' he consoled with emphatic courtesy. 'Though your sadness has a cause, *melas + kholé* only add up to black bile. Nothing ambrosia cannot cure. May I have your aristocratic permission to entreat for the best wine aboard to be presented?'

At this point, I needed to go to the loo.

Having laughed my throat out and fixed my smudged mascara, I returned.

'Do you play the guitar, honourable Clementino?'

'Yes'.

A laconic answer: the erudite lunatic was finally falling asleep.

I took out my yellow pad. Game-playing with Benita on the beach at Lamu had fuelled my book idea. Why on earth – or rather, a step away from returning to its surface – does Orpheus turn around? Could I link the hypothetical answer to the seven deadly sins?

I started scribbling.

Hi man! Eurydice's first death was tough luck; yet mercifully, snake venom acts like a bullet. Now however! Disillusion doesn't merely kill – it's an amputation. Your bouncing upon the scene made her feel incandescent and fragile, timid yet petulant in her hope that an After-Life could happen back home. She trusted your guidance and your resolve.

One has pictured you exulting with joy, too impetuous to resist the impulse to reach out to the woman you saved at much risk and peril. One has depicted you playing the symbolic lyre, starry-eyed in the midst of a sub-telluric haze. Love exonerates all. Or does it? I have my doubts, man.

Take your motivation. Could this undertaking be more of an ego-trip than a rescue operation? Do you need Eurydice more than you worship her? More primitively, it could be that you abhor a vacuum. No. That somehow doesn't fit. We want you be a hero!

Might you, after all, be an impostor who succeeded in fooling us – the kids, the composers, the poets, the film directors – into condoning your volte-face with heart-breaking lyricism? But then again...

To hell (or Hades, haha) with it. Various glasses of Chateau something or other precipitated me into the arms of Morpheus (hahaha).

I'll skip the horrendous journey to Avignon (taxi strike, train delays, torrential rain – in short, shitty Paris).

There I found hotel rooms, much too exhausted to rent a car and make my way to the small *bastide* rented time ago near Arles – *our* way, as it were: I had invited Don Clementino. He had executed a complicated reverence in acquiescence.

Better than Prozac? Impossible! In addition, Vitamin Y. On closer inspection, the man with the timeworn manners was rather young.

The narrow streets of shuttered houses, art galleries, café terraces bathing in the light that so fascinated Van Gogh *et al*; and then, Arles' Roman amphitheatre, made him goggle in sheer wonderment. A gift rarely intact passed a certain stage or age, right? He remained in a semi-trance all the way to my limestone house near the vast delta of the Rhône valley, bordering the Camargue, southwest of Arles. Only when we stopped to let men riding white horses flanking a dozen bulls pass by did the Spaniard recover the use of language.

'May I request the pleasure of your company for a frugal lunch?'

He could. I was ravenous. We stopped at some restaurant which looked simple but turned out to be a gastronomic treat. I was about to slip away to settle the bill when he pulled out a credit card. A Centurion Amex!

'Doña Aleana, would you allow...'

Not the last surprise the *hidalgo* had in store.

43

ZEN?

'My head's screwed on my shoulders and my feet to the ground,' Ric once riposted to Ced, who'd dared to suggest his friend was too speedy to be precise. Quite. Ric did nothing without a purpose and utmost precision.

What, then, was his motive in booking two places on a train moving at a reptilian speed? In Japan, of all places? A country where he would have to navigate an invisible code of etiquette, point at plastic models of dishes to order a meal, at a loss amongst ciphers and ageless faces?

His motives were twofold.

Another redhead mistress. She had raved about curving hills and bays, local delicacies, the charm of the derelict, and so on. 'Not to mention that the window coverings are paper screens etched with *kumiko*-style latticework!'

Let her chirp about jasmine, dragonflies and whatnot, thinks Ricardo. Let her marvel at rice fields and seaweed farms near silky water. What he was interested in were the scientific and technical aspects of the bloody trip and the 20 million pounds spent to delay arrival in an age of chronic rush.

Feeling betrayed by Hector, another stunt was on the agenda. A train-hotel? Across the US?

The 14-suite train was named *The Seven Stars of Kyushu* – and Kyushu was Japan's third largest island, a major producer of car parts and semiconductors. And Japan was still better than Chernobyl. Well ... Kyushu's internationally known name is Nagasaki. About 80,000 killed instantly in one terrifying flash, August 1945. The volcano Aso, its crater one of the world's largest (128 km in circumference), also interested a man drawn to everything XXL.

A propos redheads: a battery of lawyers had drawn up a stringent contract entrusting Iris, whom neither Ric nor Ced trusted half an inch, with the management of the thriving Left-Hand Hotel.

Exasperated by both his mistress and the Japanese, Ric returned to New York – then to Nantucket, his ever generous school-friend having given him a key. Some sharp thinking and fitness-recovery to be done.

These were the nineties – the age of ageing...

Forgetting for a moment about the Wonderbra, super-productions such as the movie *Titanic*, electric punk-rock, rave movements or Tibetan Freedom Concerts alternating with the bimboish Spice Girls – the most commercially successful group since the Beatles – the world was changing.

Did Ricardo care about fertility-drugs, cloning, HAART therapy reducing mortality from AIDS, black holes confirmed, a first landing on Mars? The break-up of Yugoslavia or the USSR? The Iraqi, Congo, Chechen or Somalian wars? Whether Yeltsin and Clinton exchanged hookers? No.

One sociological phenomenon mobilised his full attention: solitude. One hell of a potential market, he mused, masturbating.

There were by now more pets than human beings. About 370 million of them, mostly cats and dogs, compared to about 290 million human beings. As a consequence, the pet industry was worth 30 or so billion US dollars a year. Conclusion: selling food to animals could be more lucrative than selling it to people where, in any case, niches were rare.

This Ric exposed to Ced. The latter had returned from Tibet, none the wiser other than awareness that a life of contemplation and meditation, without challenges or champagne, was bloody boring. Pale and weak, watching his old friend running, swimming and whatevering, details censored, enhanced his despondency.

Would joining the rat-race restore his confidence? Reconcile his diverging identities?

What exactly was on Ric's mind?

Drinks and fags at hand, he explained. Crisply.

'The animal food market will become more ferocious than it already is. The time to jump in is *now*. Like with most commercial innovations, the premise is simple: medically sophisticated pet-care will soon be the rage.'

Ced wasn't exactly fascinated. However, Ric had arithmetic arguments: people marrying later, if at all. The divorce rates. Old people getting older, exponentially raising the number of widowers. Gays out of the cupboard but living in some such. *Bref*, single people in suburban homes (cities having become too expensive) desperate for a devoted and dependent presence. One that would neither leave nor die, if it could be helped. It could.

The health craze and obsession with diets was bound to extend to the meowing, barking or chirping friends of the lonesome. The so-called mature societies became more childish by the minute. Pets were their new dolls, tin-soldiers, substitute kids. Yes, the most sought-after companions of humans were no longer human.

'How sad,' sighed Ced.

'Yeah,' shrugged Ric. 'Even alarming. Yet my friend, you know what alarm calls entail: a quick reaction.'

Ced went for a stroll in the garden.

With Robbie-the-gardener's complicity, and inspired by his nightmare visit to Kyoto, Ricardo had prepared a surprise: half of the grounds were now a Zen garden. No more lawn; instead, a stylised arrangement of rocks, moss, well-pruned trees and bushes on gravel raked in such a way as to represent ripples in the water. 'A dry landscape is an aid to meditation about the true meaning of life,' Robbie had explained, accompanied by cryptic gestures.

Ced? Stunned and appalled. His mother's cherished flowers? Gone.

Robbie had been strolling in tow. On this occasion, he wore a bandana and cufflinks together with his gardening attire. All the more incongruous for someone who looked like he'd reached puberty that very morning in Rimini.

Sad to observe the reaction of his new boss, the poor guy, in a puerile attempt at consolation, recited verses from the Upanishads. The hoped-for euphoria not kicking in, he switched to the Groundwork of the Metaphysic of Morals. (When this was related to me, in between giggles, I fathomed Don Clementino and Robbie to be spiritual kins.) The latter let his efforts lapse. If the rich weren't happy, who was?

A number of Aw! Boo! Yay! and Oms! later, Cedric went to his bedroom – the one Leonor had so painstakingly decorated in a nautical style to please him. He missed her. He missed his father. He missed Iris. He missed Aleana. He missed the insouciance of childhood. And ... Buddhist breathing exercises notwithstanding, he felt invaded by a deep, gnawing, cancerous rage. How dare he? How dare Ric violate his space and memories?

After a while, he recovered a semblance of serenity. Why refute the rectitude of his friend's intentions? To work with him, though?

On the other hand, why not? He was like a brother. One

who had touched a raw nerve: solitude. And if solitude could be alleviated, be it in such roundabout ways as to prolong the lives of lonely people's non-biological families, where was the harm? Also, it would be homage to Leonor. 'A spot of work' as the Brits would say, wasn't a bad thing either.

Whatever money could be derived from it didn't concern Ced. He needed little to be happy.

He could afford not to care, Ric ruminated. The revamping of that fucking garden had been meant to be a present. But what's a gift to someone who can buy it all? Not a nice thing to point out? Realism isn't always magic.

Meanwhile, he needed Cedric. He'd be the communicator in this new venture, someone who could relate and connect with people, especially the sad and destitute. In addition, the Vich name might help. The theme hotels (his, no one else's idea) had endowed it with a romantic aura.

44

WHO WOULD HAVE THOUGHT THAT?

'Doña Aleana. Do you know this not ... most polite man?'

'Absolutely, DC.'

A month had gone by since we had arrived at that *bastide* I had grown even fonder of since Clementino had planted lemon-trees, gardenias, whatnot. On a bike, he would explore the region all day long, returning with the tastiest vegetables. I was in charge of the meat and the occasional fish.

Fed up with the Don Clementino business, I now called him DC. Formal as he was, it took him some time to get used to. On the other hand, he didn't mind being associated with the great Washington. Another *Generalissimo*!

In the evening, after some exquisite dinner he'd cook, we would often play chess. Mostly though, we'd join my gypsy friends and play the guitar, dancing now frenetically, now languidly. He was a natural talent. Made me feel like a beginner (music-wise). Other than that, our relationship had continued to be courteous, to put it mildly.

Only on Friday evenings would I insist on watching television. My Bernard Pivot Night. Pivot was the Larry King or David Frost of literature on French TV. *Apostrophes*, insolent and instructive, was a cult program.

That particular night, he was interviewing Frederik who, not surprisingly, presented himself in the worst of lights. With phoney auto-repulsion, he declared he had nothing to say.

'A streetcar without desire? A cat without a tin-roof? Might you explain why Tennessee Williams is your revered reference while you castigate Hemingway and Scott Fitzgerald?'

'Easy. I live in the Ritz. The latter two just drank in the bar.'

'I see,' answered Pivot.

Liar.

'I do of course not, *estimada anfitriona*, wish to ruffle feathers, nonetheless…'

'I know Frederik quite well. He was in Kenya at Christmas when my house…'

'But Doña Aleana, do you notice his à-la-von-Stroheim stiffness? Is it not typical of terminal alcoholism or desperation? Hysteria? Feminine hyper-sensitivity, perhaps?'

'No. He's multisexual all right.'

'Oh.'

Whenever a tactful retreat from conversation was called for, he would puff on the hookah-pipe he had acquired no idea where. This had inspired my idea of sucking baby's dummies in order to quit smoking. Less fattening than lollipops, but then of course, neither would have done the trick: an addict remains an addict. The positive flip-side: I talked less.

Pivot's interview seemed to mesmerise my Spanish pal.

'Tenne-SEE was visionary.'

'Care to elaborate?' shrugged Pivot.

'What for? Almost nobody understands darkness. One wears sunglasses after dusk and masks after dawn. Living fast is incompatible with longevity.'

'Not with immortality, if I may venture. Would you not, perchance, strive to become one of those *poètes maudits* with a grave in the illustrious Montparnasse cemetery?'

Frederik threw him the sort of provocative glance which invites complicity.

'Let's resume and finish. Is your book an *autofiction*?'

'Mr Pivot. I'm a good writer. Meaning, a hypocrite and an impostor. Am I sentimental? No love, no novel. Of course it's vaguely biographical. And by the way, I hate cats. Soft fur and scratching claws. Enough women around.'

Whereupon Frederik stood up and left.

The following morning, I was surprised to see DC in the kitchen. At elevenish, he was usually gone.

'Listen to your *contestador*, Doña A. Cognac first?'

Even he had finally abbreviated my name. But cognac before breakfast?

The answering machine was blinking furiously. It reminded me of something not too pleasant.

I pushed a CD into the whatever-it's-called. KC & The Sunshine Band? Michael Jackson? Anyway, something that would cushion any shock ahead.

Benita. In tears.

Hector. Angry.

Ced. Would I invest in a promising venture?

Ric. Would I please not?

Don Clementino had obviously listened to all of that.

'All your friends complicated hedonists?'

Having fetched the best bottle of wine in the cellar and drunken half of it, I became aggressive.

'How dare you listen to my messages?'

'I'm a spy,' he retorted, puffing out his chest.

'You don't say!'

'But I do. It all started with my father. A shoe-polisher in Nairobi. Currency used to be smuggled out of the country in the soles of shoes. He was granted diplomatic status. As his son, I was taught Oxbridge with an American slant, just in case, as well as Russian plus Ukrainian slang – which superpower would gain the upper foot back then, if you will excuse the image, most honoured Doña Aleana, was uncertain. Follow me?'

No point in answering.

'To convert the subject: might I humbly suggest calling your friend Benita first?'

'Exactly what I intended to do. Would to be ever so kind to f, f, and f … off?'

'Most obliged. A frolicking day I wish to you too.'

Off he went. Truth be told, I wish he'd stayed.

I ignored Ced and Ric's calls. Let them sort out whatever it was.

I returned Hector's: the 'procedures', as he called them, had been successful. The cancer seemed in remission. Might he stay on my houseboat in Paris, in order to 'hide'? Would I join him, if possible? The answer to both was yes. Happily!

Benita: fed up with Lamu. My house was beyond repair. How to reproduce the unique? *Impossible, chérie.* I told her to come to Arles and keep Don Clementino company while I was gone. (Though suspecting their kinship would be made in heaven, I did not anticipate they'd get married months later.)

The night before my departure to Paris and Benita's arrival, Don Clementino and I joined our friends. They had adopted the Spaniard wholeheartedly. Not only because of his guitar skills or his off-tune voice – no. It was his good-nature and good-will that seduced each and every one who met him. The guy was a sweetheart, *punto*.

We spent the entire night dancing. A happy night.

He told his story. So implausible, it was believable.

I was dozing off when one of them told us that three left-handed guitarists in the group played on instruments strung for right-handers, hence upside-down. Wow!

This brought me back to earth. In other words, to the past.

45

DAVID & GOLIATH

'Your father asked me to marry him. Can't make up my mind ... what do you think?'

'I thought you'd never ask!' Ced chuckled. 'Or should I say, I thought *he'd* never ask!'

Ced fiddled with his watch. Atavism.

'Look, Al. The longer that we postpone things, the harder it becomes to accomplish them, right? Take letters: guilt at not having written them compounds the delay – thus the guilt – until you convince yourself that, being no longer expected, they're no longer important. I used to divide A3 pages into neat columns, determined to respect the plan and sequence and to tick off every obligation as days went by. Wishful ticking. I'd cram the whole lot into the last twenty-four hours.'

I pointed out that *pro* means for; *crastinus,* tomorrow.

'Most procrastinators are extremely busy,' I went on, as I tediously do when on the subject of semantics. 'Busy with lots of irrelevant things which provide a pretext not to do what really matters. Cleaning a house or walking the dog requires neither effort nor creativity. Routine is reassuring. But accepting a marriage proposal?'

We were yet again sitting on the terrace of the Café de Flore, Boulevard St Germain.

'Oh well,' Ced shrugged, arching his left eyebrow.

'Another trait common to those who keep delaying things, though not precisely applying to you [wink], is an unassailable optimism. Believing time to be so elastic and plentiful that losing it makes no difference, urgency is alien.'

I let ice cubes clink against my glass, averting his glance.

'Familiar with the problem?'

He groaned.

'Guess so. Aren't we all? We've become so used to instantaneous problem-solving that we tend to dismiss ... whatever the word for discipline is nowadays.'

More wine was called for.

'Instant gratification is one hell of a motivation. Perfectionism, nothing but its inverted extreme,' said some guy who had overheard us, then decided to interrupt.

I recognised nasty Ken's voice. Ric and he had been pals in London. Totally unwelcome, he slumped on a chair, bent on dominating the conversation.

'If the ratio between postponement and realisation is balanced, so is one's life. Like with most bottom lines, balance is the golden standard.'

His business had been gold-mining. But his heart was ashen.

'Get lost!' I bristled.

He did indeed remove himself, but lost and gone forever? Parasites won't do one the favour. Sure enough, he returned some ten minutes later.

'Where's that blue-eyed clone of yours?'

Ced cringed.

'Worry not! Though Goliath's a giant, it's weak David who wins, remember?'

Oh Dog.

Ken took a breath. I held mine, lest I strangled the a-hole. Creepiness notwithstanding, Ken was deviously clever, hence (?) amusing.

'As I was saying,' he snorted. 'David achieves a miraculous and implausible victory in the face of ogre-like Goliath. It's all about tactics as opposed to strategy, as so often is the case. Read the *Art of War* by some Chinese chap or other. Astuteness as opposed to strength. Dexterity as opposed to might. A stone thrown at the right angle – especially with a sling – is more efficient than a javelin thrown in blind rage. Not forgetting that Goliath suffered from acromegaly, get my drift?'

(Why do we identify *understanding* with *drifting*?)

Finally and mercifully bored by the sound of his own voice, Kenneth hailed a taxi. Good riddance.

As I was about to hail one too, Ced stopped me.

'A propos marriage. I'm going to get married again. She's a dog-trainer. Works for films and for the NGOs – you know, dogs taught to rescue victims of natural disasters, wars, etc. No beauty but Al, what a good heart! She's ... how do I put it? Tranquil. What's more: whenever she offers me things, little things, she's the one thanking me for the joy I show. Believe that?'

I could. Benita and Clementino were the same.

'Quite a change from your ex!'

'You can say that again. But also from working with Ric. I *did* get involved in the PET-HEALTH venture. After a slow start, it took off in a big way. I was on TV, I was in the sub-urbs, in the homes of grannies or single mothers, in superstar's mansions, you name it. Then came the branding and all that. Guess what: Ric resented me for the success. He felt, don't know ... second fiddle? Do you know what he accused me of?'

I had a foggy idea.

'Of being nothing but a follower, as opposed to an entre-preneur, a maverick, a shaker and mover. In other words, not to be Him. Moreover, he called me a crushing bore.'

Thing is that Ced, with all his qualities, was no firecracker.

We remained silent for a while. Restful.

It allowed me to think. Generally speaking, murder motives

boil down to jealousy, money, vengeance, competition – but what about boredom? How many crime stories have mentioned boredom as the prime impulse for removing someone from their cosmic radar? Might I build this idea into my Orpheus stories? What if the guy, having had quite a ball as a bachelor, suddenly thinks that, transgressing the interdict, Eurydice will be washed back into non-existence? He'll then be able to enjoy a second youth? Not a bad deal.

'What's her name?'

Ced, used to my haphazard mind, answered:

'Teodora'.

'How Byzantine!'

'Expected you to say so… But uncomplicated.'

Just as well. Because apart from being no scintillating joker, Ced, like many over-gifted people, was extremely distracted and accident-prone. He was one of these geniuses who don't know what foot to put first when crossing the road. Whatever foot it would be, the undone laces would cause him to trip. No matter how many small disasters he'd accumulated over the years, none had seriously injured him (physically speaking, that is).

Luck, good or bad, is contagious.

I decided, there and then, to marry Hector.

It was September 15th, 1998, by the way.

Time doesn't fly. It merely waits.

46

SIMPLICITY, A PAUSE & A DRINK

It's complicated to be simple. Neither in art nor in life does it come naturally.

Rereading what I've written so far, I'm plagued by doubt. Are the characters likeable? More importantly, intriguing?

I've read too much.

Two of my literary cult figures found it was twice the work trimming a book than writing it. Stefan Zweig is one; Somerset Maugham the other.

Somerset Maugham practised as a doctor for years. 'I must have witnessed pretty well every emotion of which men are capable [...] What has struck me is their lack of consistency [...] and I am more inclined to expect them to do ill than to do good. This is the price one has to pay for having a sense of humour.'

In my view, the latter is precisely what SM singularly lacks. 'I can never forget myself' he admits. All through *The Summing Up* (published in 1938), Maugham emphasises clarity over style – be it at the risk of dryness.

'Kings, dictators, commercial magnates are from our point of view unsatisfactory. [...] The ordinary is the writer's richer field. Its unexpectedness, its singularity, its infinite variety afford unending material.'

A matter of opinion. Let's imagine that people likely to meet their destiny on the very road they took to avoid it are the stuff of novels. Maugham's and Zweig's credo: stick to the point and whenever you can, cut. If you let your reader's interest wander, it's most unlikely you can recapture his attention later on. Also: readers are swayed by emotion rather than by reasoning. But okay. If writing well were enough to be successful, it would be known.

Is there enough action in this text book? Can't remember who said that if someone walks through the door, you have a situation; but if he climbs in through the window, you have a story.

In mine, no plane-hijacking, no car-chases, no Moneypenny in disguise, sorry. But also, no dawn breaking twice in a day, like in Stendhal's *Le Rouge et le Noir*. That said, people will die. Prematurely, that is. Worry not.

47

BITTER MOON

Hector and I did indeed get married. A marriage of complicity. Two loners whose strongest bond was the same sense of the absurd.

I'll skip the ceremony in Nyon's town hall – just us, Ced and Benita. No fuss, no scandal, nothing to report other than the certificate and a rubber ring that, when pressed upon, started emitting fluorescent flashes. Anticipating some such, I'd bought a Japanese copper statuette stamped with purple dragons. To the Mayor, who was eyeing me with appreciation, he slipped: 'Who wants to marry a woman old enough to be one's wife?'

Of course, we had a joyous and liquid dinner after that, but Hector was awfully pale. Chemotherapy, though less frequent, did take its toll.

Our honeymoon, so to speak, was spent in bed – doing what's easy to imagine but mostly, watching *nanars* on VHS.

Nanars? An untranslatable French word coined by the brilliant critic François Forestier, referring to films neither bad nor good: way beyond kitsch. Barmy. They shift the limits of involuntary comic towards sublime bad taste.

Take *Hudson Hawk*. It starts with Da Vinci, continues in the Vatican and if logic ruled the world, would have ended in the bin. But it's a jewel for *nanar*-lovers. Produced, written and starred in by Bruce, need one dwell on the artistic level? Hudson H, an ace among thieves, is released from *Sin*-Sing (subtle) only to discover that his favourite restaurant now serves pizzas with cheap sheep cheese. Out of the blue appears one of the dead-brained Stallone brothers (Frank), who spits: 'Don't tell me you want to sell petunias!' No one has ever hinted at anything of the sort. His intelligence insulted, Bruce decides to steal a 'shit-horse' (sculpted by Da Vinci). James Coburn, a CIA mercenary, catches him in flagrante. Willis: 'I'm tired of not understanding anything.'

Another example:

Mahler, by cult director Ken Russell. Gustav Mahler (the Adagietto and all that) is in a bad mood. 'I was the music, hence the rock, thus the rock was me. Everything is anything, vice-versa and conversely.' *Donnerwetter!* Take it easy on the absinthe, man! He suddenly abjures his Jewishness to please Cosima (Wagner, ach so). She's dressed in a sado-masochistic outfit while riding a gramophone (phallic, see?).

But nothing could top *Cleopatra* to trigger Hector's mirth. La Taylor needs pasty make-up. During the filming, she was plagued with meningitis. (Possibly because Egypt had been reproduced in Hollywood, air-conditioning and stuff; unless it was because of her new lover Richard Burton's acne?) There are lots of Romans around, wearing tutus. Cleopatra, wrapped in metres of synthetic curtains, provokes an epileptic attack (it's Rex Harrison by now, go figure). All this triggers off the burning of the great Library of Alexandria. Mark Antony appears in a palace resembling Ludwig II of Bavaria's worst nightmare. Pyramids now erected in Cinecitta. Three consecutive directors throw in the towel. One of the most expensive flops in film history.

Respecting an implicit pact, Hector and I would never talk about his disease. We spent three months in or around Geneva, on the shores of Lac Leman, full of picturesque enclaves.

The countdown had started. Were we so intensely happy because of it? And yet ... I sometimes felt like a sentinel, circling a fortress under insidious attack.

Other than the lousy movies, our cascading laughs and the exquisite lunches, something happened: Hector revealed a homo-eroticism requiring multiple, omnipresent mirrors – mirrors! The very objects that traumatised me.

Playing along, I complied. Unwillingly at first, but then... Isn't perversity an acquired taste by the very token it forces one to overcome reluctance? While Hector contemplated his image with keen fascination, I became dizzy, observing my multiple identities de-multiplied on neutral surfaces.

Then he died. Just didn't wake up one morning.

Ric, Ced and I lost the man who had represented a backbone in our lives. The three of us now orphans might have welded us closer together. Might.

48

MONEY, AN OPIATE?

Hector's death made me discover the seismic significance of the word *devastated*. Ced's emotion compounded mine. In the face of death, one painfully rewinds time, visioning lost opportunities. Questions not asked. Postcards not written. Comfort not given. To have ignored, albeit unconsciously, another's pain. Worst of all: gratitude not expressed. All of it, suffusing.

Ced's casual speech about procrastinating boomeranged. Nagged by self-reproach, he flagellated himself – all the more because of the avalanche of telegrams, flowers and letters which poured in non-stop. We had not known how many employees he had helped financially, medically or emotionally. Other than gentle and generous, Hector had been a discreet man.

Not so Iris. The malicious, by now 'tabloid Duchess' (her affair with flamboyant Sheikh Gubondayed made headlines) sent a curt note on a card heavily embossed with some elaborate coat of arms.

Teodora, definitely a sweetheart, decided a de-dramatizing evening was needed.

Where do you go in Geneva to have a fantastic dinner and some fun? The Griffin's. Half-nightclub (old-school, in the double sense, since it was our hangout back in Rosey days), half-restaurant, it still remained *the* meeting place. Playing footsie under the table, they cooed:

Ced: 'How divine!'

Teodora: 'You're the divine one!'

Ced: 'Do you prefer white or red?'

Teodora: 'Salmon.'

Ced: 'Amazing! So do I!'

Salmon wine? Rosé. No. Roses. Some cryptic codes.

Teodora: 'I shall be sent to Morocco soon to train an Idefix-look-alike in an Asterix and Obelix adaptation of...'

Ced: 'Always adored the dog!'

Galvanising.

Seeing them dance, however, and should the rhythm of body-language tell all, a numerous family was a far-away possibility.

Hector's will, read a few days later but written when he was diagnosed with cancer two years earlier, was simple.

Cremation. An intimate memorial service. No requiem, nothing classical. Only 'J'aurais voulu être un artiste' by Claude Dubois and 'What's New Pussycat?' – presumably as a wink to me: Romy Schneider had starred in the film, another *nanar* according to Hector, who had repeatedly insisted the actress and I had an identical voice.

Other than that:

To Ricardo Moralli, speedy, time-obsessed Ric, his collection of wrist-watches (Audemars Piguet, Jaeger Lecoultre, Vacheron, Patek Philippes – you name it – all but Cartier which, Hector contended, were for hairdressers).

To me, the Lamu Lodge Hotel plus – couldn't believe it! – the *bastide* near Arles. He had bought it without a whisper.

To Ced, everything else. Everything else being the dozen or so Vich hotels, including the 'Theme-Hotels' in the US. Two provisos, though: Ric was to remain the manager. Iris, not even allowed to use a telephone.

He had also bequeathed a generous amount of cash to his faithful staff, all of them listed by name, nicknames included.

Nor had he forgotten Robbie the 'Buddhist gardener' to whom he had taken an amused shine.

Ric was obscenely incensed. That was it? One hell of a fool's bargain!

Watching his reaction, just as well I had donned sunglasses. Had he forgotten that Ced's father had lifted him up by the stirrups back when the teacher's son had nothing but balls, ambition and complexes? What would have become of Ric without Hector?

Meant to be a private affair, it grew into a big one. As I said, Hector had been esteemed, respected and very, very much liked. Even Dr AmarK had flown over for the memorial. It being impossible to describe my sorrow, why try? Suffice it to say that it took me by surprise: never ever had I felt anything remotely like it.

I had to stay in Geneva various, endless weeks. Everything reminded me of Hector. His absence engulfed me. I lost my marks and much weight. I was a walking, open wound. My body and soul ached like after a fall into some precipice. Hector and I had not even been given the chance to dwell in the hope, the most tenacious folly of the heart, that love would be forever and that our life together would stretch along winding, unending paths.

Couldn't wait to seek refuge on Lamu, where we had shared so many precious moments. But – alone in my paradise lost? Benita and Clementino were travelling all over Africa, where orphans were galore and famished for protection: they had decided to adopt a child.

I called Frederik. He was entertaining, insane and self-sufficient. Perfect combination.

'Cool', he said.

Good, I thought.

Strangely enough, I experienced new effervescence when writing. However staccato my sleep, the sentences I'd been raking my brain for at dusk seemed to be waiting at dawn. Bubbling out. All that was needed was to transcribe.

Orpheus and Eurydice stories, intertwined with the seven deadly sins, were flowing. Either a glutton, or a sex-maniac, or slothful … the man changes his mind at the eleventh hour, either too hungry, horny or lazy to muster the patience or discipline to abide by the strictures laid down by Hades (the King of The Beyond). Hence he turns around. The twist: what if it were Eurydice who didn't fancy the future back on earth? What if she teases and provokes him into making his mythical *volte-face*?

Fred, to whom I read some of my text aloud (a must in order to ascertain its fluidity) was quick to snicker:

'Don't we all? Haven't you, Aleana?'

'What?'

'Adopted attitudes bound to precipitate a void, accelerate the denouement; in short, *fuir le bonheur avant qu'il ne nous abandonne*. Without realising it, one opts for the unhappiness one knows – the unknown, however idyllic it may seem, per-ceived as a danger-zone.'

'Cowardice?'

'Whatever. Point being that you and I have always cringed at the mere mention of the words *settling down*.'

Why had I called him? I sunk into dark silence. The wrong man at the wrong place. Fred's cynicism wore me out. I was dead tired anyway. Mourning? Writing non-stop and skipping meals? Point is that I fainted.

Diagnosis? All of it. But also: pregnancy. This, the doctor summoned by Fred, declared with enthusiasm.

Dog All-Freaking-Mighty.

'Now, Milady, you are two.'

As usual when under shock, I stumbled to the bar where Fred reacted in the most unexpected way: ecstatically.

'Why the gloom? What's the problem?'

'Other than that the kid's father is dead and I'm devoid of even the slightest iota of maternal instinct?'

Fred, for a change, shut up. For a short while, that is. Then:

'Look, Al. Many children don't even know who their father is... Besides: haven't you told me that Benita and that weird husband of hers want to adopt! Well! Bingo! They'll surely be delighted to take care of Junior or Junioress — and you, delighted to know the little one to be in loving, if loony, hands.'

Taken aback, I watched him gulping down yet another whisky.

'The bonus?' Fred resumed, visibly pleased with his master-plan. 'You'll be able to see the creature whenever you want. Only occasionally, that is.'

Crazy as it sounded and indeed was, why not? It made sense.

So much so that I managed to join Benita (by now we had cellular phones, even if they were still the size of walkie-talkies).

Simplification being our favourite concept, Benita was over the moon. 'Wonderfoooool' she kept repeating.

As weeks went by, an invasion of spleen sort of paralysed me. It grew proportionally to my stomach. I'd sit for hours at the green baize card table on which I usually wrote, watching the snotty French waitress roam around with disdainful non-chalance. Knowing Peponi's clientele, she wouldn't last long, as Henry VIII might have said. As for me: unable to move a finger.

How would Hector have reacted to all of that? Oh. Hector!

Unable to drink or smoke, I stopped writing. Instead, I walked and swam and walked again. The Peponi crowd kept telling me how glowing I looked. Really? I had removed all mirrors from the Lodge-Hotel.

Whereupon I burnt what I had written. Bah. The ratio of dreaming to scribbling was about one hour to five minutes. Conclusion: time for serious stuff. I applied to magazines such as the *New Yorker* and the *Spectator* as a freelance reporter.

One day, I received a letter from Ced. He was ignorant of the fact that his old school-friend, now widowed stepmother, was expecting a ... half-sibling. Dr AmarK had persuaded the *boys* to do a detox in Lugano. Ric needed to stop the coke; Ced, to start eating healthily again. Bottom line, they were off to Switzerland and would afterwards drive down the Italian coast: affected by Hector's death, Ric wanted to kneel by his own father's grave.

Hmm.

49

DOMINO EFFECT

Benita (who'd rushed back to Lamu) and I amble to the modern, Saudi-funded hospital, for a routine check-up.

Having remained pretty thin and as ever inattentive to my body, I almost collapse upon learning I'm expecting twins. No inkling had preceded the shock.

As I'm four months pregnant by now, the ultrasound suggests a boy and a girl.

On the way back to Peponi's, I'm seized by convulsions. Half-laughing, half-sobbing.

Benita holds my hand, guzzling on an Evian bottle. Water? Benita?

'*Chérie*', she murmurs, 'this is one *good* omen!'

'Is that what you call a *double* pregnancy?'

At this point and typically for equatorial latitudes, it started pouring without warning. Like a glass curtain or ... shivered I, shredded mirrors. I also started shaking and sweating.

'Am I going mad?'

'Look, Al. The idea that some variant of insanity is inextricable from one's self is new, but not all that new. It doesn't entail that we have learnt to acquire pentagrams against its encroachments...'

'Stop talking like Don Clementino! Make it simple. *Insanity is an appropriate response to reality* will do.'

Back at the safe haven of Peponi's bar: 'Are you aware that Hector wanted a child with you? Not really for his sake. Thought that what you'd most missed was a family. He believed it might allow your provisional selves to crystallise into a definitive identity.'

Had I not drunken some Chardonnay, I would have sent her packing, in the most literal sense. But as can't-remember-who said in can't-remember-what *nanar*: 'Alcohol is not the answer, it's the question. YES is the answer.'

Hence I retorted, please Benita, no melo, and ordered more wine. Let the twins get giddy in my womb.

'Al. I've known you for years. You've always been the one who declares that a party's over, to panic at the prospect of remaining alone amongst the debris, the music fainting, make-up running. Time to drop masks. Time to overcome fears.'

Benita wrapped her chubby arms around my bony shoulders.

A welcome diversion materialised in the form and shape of mischievously candid Don Clementino. On the flight from Nairobi to Paris, he'd been the only one not to travel dressed in pyjamas as seems to be the new norm nowadays; now, he looked as if coming out of the Grand Hotel on the Lido, wearing what looked like a bathing suit from the twenties.

'*Querida*, what an unmitigated joy! Joy is the...'

'DC!' I wailed. 'Spare me pearls of wisdom. Just had my share!'

'Wisdom, Doña Aleana, is the art of renunciation, would you not concur?'

I would not – but what kingdom or horse would I not have given for silence. Silence...

'He encapsulates the truth,' teased Benita.

We hardly spoke or saw each other until the night when I screamed in such agony that I awoke most hotel guests. Who but Benita would have organised my precipitate transportation, on a donkey-cart, to the hospital? Who first held the twins wheeled into my room?

Too exhausted to react, I nonetheless noticed that she examined them with the bland interest she'd have shown ballerinas in a shop.

Upon emerging from my comatose state I, the non-maternal mother, felt a pang. The two miniature babies lay side by side in a cot, not even covered by a sheet. All of a sudden, I was overwhelmed by protectiveness.

Ugly, as all newborns are, they were Hector's. And mine, like it or not.

The words of one of my countless nannies weighted on my mind: 'Beware of the harm we innocently inflict. We're just prompters in plays written by or for another, the meaning of which escapes us.' Come to think of it, she sounded like Don Clementino.

Then it hit me – hitme like a fist: I'd NEVER inflict the lack of love, or love by proxy, with which my parents had damned me.

Ced would help, I decided. Even though he was unaware of having been a twin himself, some instinct might kick in. If not, I'd awaken it.

50

SOME GODMOTHER

Pinkie and Punky (not my choice of nicknames, you might imagine) could, age five, speak fluent Swahili, Spanish and English (not Don Clementino's quixotic version thereof!). He was forbidden from teaching anything but the guitar and flamenco. The twins excelled at both. Good manners he also infused with bravado.

Allow me to say that the kids were adorable.

Other than their eye colour, mine, they were Hector's chiselled replica, ink-black hair and all. The resulting physique was stunning.

Having renounced restoring or rebuilding my house, we transformed the Vich-Lounge into a private house. To hell with hotels. It'd seen enough, and so had Cedric who, as I had hoped, became emotionally involved. Other than visiting on a regular basis, he'd send containers of books and games. For we had created a kindergarten (space was plentiful) to which small children of all backgrounds swarmed with glee.

Most teachers were volunteers refusing to be paid.

'Learn by playing' was our motto. It involved craftsmanship, music, poetry… To advance creativity was essential. Even – or especially – as regard to language. My modest contribution was to instil a passion for Scrabble: in five-year-olds, you may well ask? Yes. If you present words as puzzles, it's easy to generate enthusiasm.

Pinkie and Punky (Benita would put blusher on the girl's

cheeks and spike the boy's hair with gel, poor devils) were given the most precious of presents. The one my parents never bought. Love. Apart from, or above all: they doted on each other.

Character-wise, they did not resemble each other. Leonie, Pinkie's real name, took after her father. Facetious, restless, generous and a compulsive liar. A comedian. Leopold showed a tendency for mood-swings. Taciturn one moment, elated the next, he read all he could get his hands on. When I saw him devour the Fantômas comics sent by Ced, I burst into laughter. Atavism, here we go again!

Both had a wicked, but not a vicious, sense of humour. An *astounding* thing they also shared: synaesthesia. Etymology, Greek. What it means is that sounds are associated with colours. It applies for music as it applies for words. What it would entail for the future? No idea. To visualise acoustics should prove no handicap. But is it a gift? What is a neurological phenomenon in the first place? Or virtual reality, for that matter? To the twins, it was perceived as fun.

Summing up.

The first five years of their lives: happiness and freedom. They could swim and walk around without impediment: no cars, no sharks (the coral reef). As for the locals, they had accepted us to the extent of fierce protectiveness.

Leonie and Leopold called me Mamalana.

They called Ced Pampa. The half-brother bit they couldn't, or wouldn't understand, in spite of the blatant resemblance.

I too came and went. On and off, I spent about five months on Lamu.

Inspired by my friend Hubert Nyssen's Arles-based Actes Sud, I founded a small publishing company named Espoir (Hope). First novels only. So small that its office fitted on my Parisian houseboat.

I also re-met a Turkish man I'd had a major crush on as a schoolgirl. Life is a palimpsest... Unlike Hector, he was unfailingly reliable. Like Hector, he was generous, gentle and handsome. In the exotic way I'd always been drawn to. Intelligent, very. Polyglot, like me. A married workaholic, our encounters were as sporadic as they were intense.

In love? 'Nyes.' What I discovered was a feeling hitherto unknown to me: jealousy. May I confess the pain was rather delectable? Be it as it may, I felt alive again.

Shortly before the twins' sixth birthday, Benita, Don Clementino, Ced and I sat down. We agreed they should attend a proper school. We decided upon Arles. Paris would be too much of a culture shock: the noise, the crowds, the pollution, the violence. Too chilling a world for small children.

'Aleana really loves them,' I overheard Benita say.

'Yes', Clementino dreamily replied, 'but more like a godmother than a mother.'

'What's *that* supposed to mean?'

Pause. Hesitation. Sigh.

'A trifle aloof. Somewhat distant...'

'How dare you? She's so sweet and caring!'

More of the above.

'Yes *queridísima*. But, if I may surmise and express, in a semi-detached fashion...'

I walked away.

Wasn't my affection tangible? (Why do I employ the word affection?)

Would Pinkie and Punky fit into a totally new environment? Effortlessly, I trusted, the capacity for adaptation defining intelligence. Distraught by their sadness at leaving their piece of paradise, I would try to inculcate a philosophy of sorts with that image I so revered: '*Birds don't sing because they're happy – they're happy because they sing.* Never forget to sing, my darlings!'

Would I, later on, send them to Le Rosey? An expanded Rosey (there were about a hundred students more by now); a Rosey without Mr Johan, our severe but soft-hearted Colonel and revered schoolmaster? In a sheltered world, yes, but surrounded by kids from dysfunctional families, when not other harrowing circumstances?

On the other hand, education in an international context meant friends for life, all over the world.

Time would tell.

The most reassuring certitude being that Leonie and Leopold would never, ever be alone. They adored each other. For all to see, they already protected one another in every which way.

Certitude! How dare I, of all people, use the term?

51

THE IMPOSSIBLE TAKES
LONGER

A new millennium.
My return to Geneva on January 1st, 2000.

Bubble-bath; Sancerre; Cole Porter; the telegram.

What had Evelyne, on New Year's Eve, said? Something like, 'Don't try to predict the past.' Well. Had I been prescient, I'd have gibed, 'Better prevent it!'

No hoarder – far from it – I have, however, kept a box the size of a dozen wine bottles throughout the years – do note my measurements.

In it, my vintage ink pens, the Guerlain perfume Hector had given me once upon a long time, very few legal documents ... and letters. Including the ones I had written to Hector, almost daily, since his demise.

Life never begins again: it's a palimpsest, as probably said before. About to toss the telegram into the box, an envelope sprung to sight.

Addressed to Hector in Ced's handwriting, I had never opened it. Now...

What scares some but seduces others, is her capacity for indifference. It stupefies. Suggests she is watching her existence like a ... playground? A mine-field? Some laboratory for the arcane? Whether plagued with moral indecision or very resolute indeed, she mesmerises, so much is certain. No wonder we love her.

Thus was I described by Cedric. The letter was undated.

Sounded almost like an obituary, though it wasn't I who had passed away. Another bottle of Sancerre later I did, however, pass out.

Yet as Churchill pointed out to Lady Astor ('tomorrow I'll be sober but you, still ugly') my mind was machete-sharp upon waking. Sharply aware that, as the same Churchill had once remarked, people are 'riddles wrapped in a mystery inside an enigma'. (That he was talking about the Russians back then is beside the point: it's universal.)

Ignorance boils down to a lack of curiosity. And curious I always had been. No sleuth, agreed, but still: there was something rotten about it all. Ric's death didn't sound plausible.

He had competed in the Mille Miglia with old-timers and raced in Australia's Formula 1 – to cite but two instances. In other words: an excellent driver.

After the detox episode, it was hard to imagine him drugged or drunk out of his brain. An accident? On deserted December roads?

The 'boys' had rented some old Alfa Romeo, no Testarossa, happy to slither down the coast from Portofino to Amalfi, allowing for gastronomic and cultural interludes. (Destination, as aforementioned, Mr Moralli's tomb in Nocelle.)

The provenance of the unsigned telegram narrowed the field of research. Speaking Italian helped.

It took me two days to locate the hospital and various semi-pornographic conversations, sprinkled with promises of bribes, before they faxed me the report.

Intriguing, to put it wildly.

Ricardo, severely injured in the crash, had hovered between life and death. Sharing the same unusual AB- blood, only superficially bruised. Ced had offered his for an urgent transfusion.

Ric died instantly.

On January 10th, 2000, I jumped into my own car – direction Positano. Obviously, I needed stop-overs. And when upset, I need to write. The other day, I retrieved a crumpled paper from back then.

> *Caprices denoués demain*
> *Quand l'aurore nous abandonne,*
> *Qui peut dénoncer la maldonne,*
> *Et par quelles coupables mains?*

I met weird people. I attract them. Slovenly Hungarians with mirror-sunglasses presented me with caviar – stolen, they boasted. An anorexic teenager played a Mongolian flute: 'Paul Anka in Thai'. Whilst she was creaking away, a postman sold Bibles. A crimson-skinned couple ranting about consumerism, about flaunting wealth with shameless abandon; about the ubiquitous rising price of vegetables; depravity; conspiracies; washing machines etc. handed me their card. Eaton Square, London. Surname: Westminster.

The revelation of no longer being loved ulcerates. The awareness of no longer loving mutilates. My Turkish lover had left me. My sense of orientation became somewhat addled.

As I moved south, my sense of purpose kept ebbing. Discrepancy between movement and intent widened by the hour. What was I looking for?

Insomnia enhanced my emotional fatigue. Tired during the

day, awake all night, my mind spiralled into bleak zones. For instance: recalling New York in the seventies, it wasn't lunches with Mapplethorpe and his muse Patti Smith, nor Nush's exaltation, nor Battery Park at dawn nor Hector's kisses nor Eggs Benedict that surfaced: it was the squalor, the broken windows, those unbearably shrill police sirens.

That my car's radio was stolen didn't help. Silence, treasured silence, has become unbearable.

Finally, the Positano Hospital. One of those places where you do *not* want to use the loo. Where you arrive with one infection and leave with MRSA.

But I needed to assuage my doubts. Just couldn't believe the official version of the story – if a story there was.

And, by Dog, there was.

Money, my cloak and dagger, accelerated the 'investigation'. Perchance (more likely, per negligence) they had kept a sample of the blood Ced had given in order to save his friend.

I had it analysed, looking over the technician's shoulder all the while. No umbrage taken – he was rather cute, but *basta* with drifting. The blood was poisoned. Lethal toxins undeniably present. Which? It would have required sending the blood sample to Rome, then probably to NASA, considering Italian efficiency.

In actual fact, who cared? What was the difference? Nothing is poison. All is poison. Depends on the doses. In life like in blood…

Cedric's soft-spot? Over-salting everything.

Thus, therefore and hence… Exactly.

There are many slow-working, untraceable drugs, easily slipped into food or drink. Arsenic: a classic. Dimethylmercury? No side effects. Even selenium or iocane powder: easily dissolved, they're odourless and tasteless. Not to mention polonium-210, a favourite amongst the Russian Mafia.

Such substances are not tested for in standard autopsies.

In Positano, of all places?

Ric had been cremated – last thing Ced organised before disappearing.

The one thing that mattered – to me – was: had he even been aware of his blood being irremediably contaminated? Probably not. He must have thought Ric had succumbed to the consequences of his injuries, the transfusion performed too late.

Now.

Now my imagination started tip-toeing, side-stepping, tap-dancing – some or all of it. Anything to prevent it from racing: if conclusions were to be reached, they had to be approached in a rational – *not* in a rushed – way.

I chartered a small day-boat. No contact lenses.

If hoping not to think, wishful thinking: who ever manages?

The following two hours of lulling waves felt so endless they would, I mused, have sufficed for people to conceive offspring, kill lions, or debate existentialism with sardonic nonchalance. My alas unstoppable fantasy surfed.

So: after Hector's demise, Ced becomes Ric's boss. Right?

The boss is a dreamer; Ric, the achiever. It's always been this way. Justice?

Should Cedric die, to whom would he bequeath his fortune, other than his forever faithful alter-ego? Ric concludes – he knew nothing about the twins.

Let's now say…

… that Ric had tried to kill Ced but, the aleatory kicking in, died as a consequence of the latter's well-intentioned blood-donation;

... that Ced, his blood still contaminated, was agonising somewhere. Unless his body absorbed, rejected, neutralised, oh Dog, I'm no expert, the poison Ric had slowly but regularly been feeding him?

Another possibility: Cedric, no fool, might have anticipated that I'd discover what he already suspected. High treason with criminal intent!

How to find him?

He was not in Nantucket. He had checked into none of the Vich-Hotels. The lighthouse on Symi? In January? Didn't believe so. Sun is what he must have longed for. More than a Buddhist, he was a Zoroastrian – or was it a zoetrope, as Hector would have shrugged? (Adding: whatever God may be, he'll forgive us – it's his job!)

Then another possibility HITME.

However convoluted the thinking that this one required, not altogether crazy.

After extensive research, he had deliberately poisoned himself.

He had, according to Benita's inkling, turned homosexual. (Hence his vagueness about his life and whereabouts.)

He had provoked the car-crash near Positano.

Knowing full well what a blood-transfusion would entail, he knew that Ric would die.

Taking advantage of events, he dissolved into thin air. At long last.

He'd booked the longest flights available, like Paris to Dallas then to Sydney (altogether thirty hours). Unless it was to the Orkney Islands (via London) to Papa Westray (a two-minute flight, the shortest in existence). Then, why not, on to Zanzibar or Mandalay? Where Nush was waiting for him?

Just kidding.

slmmihc @ hotmail . com